TIE THE KNOT IN
GOOD HOPE

CINDY KIRK

WAVERLY
HOUSE

ISBN: 9780990716655

CONTENTS

CHAPTER ONE

Lindsay Lohmeier was having difficulty finding her happy place. Normally, the interior of the Muddy Boots café made her smile. She loved the cobalt-blue splashes of rain, er, paint, on the white walls and adored the mural of a happy girl in a bright red raincoat kicking up water.

Though her lunch hadn't yet had a chance to settle, Lindsay knew the words lodged in her throat would choke her if she didn't get them out.

"I did it." Nerves had her speaking more loudly than she'd intended. "I quit."

Lindsay's friends, who'd been arguing about something to do with the upcoming Harvest Festival, paused the debate to focus on her.

Eliza Kendrick and Ami Cross sat directly across from her in a booth that overlooked Good Hope's Main Street. They'd scored a primo spot by the window because Muddy Boots was owned by Ami and her husband.

"*What* are you quitting?" Eliza's gray eyes narrowed. She was a beautiful woman with shiny dark hair cut in a stylish bob and lips of bright red. "You better not say the Cherries, because no one leaves the Women's Events League. Not under my watch."

The frostiness that invaded the voice of the Cherries' executive director made Lindsay smile. Many on the Door County peninsula were intimidated by the woman's forceful personality. But she and Eliza had been friends for as far back as she could remember.

"I sense a story here." Ami rested her arms on the Formica tabletop, green eyes dancing with curiosity. Her blond and brown sun-streaked hair gleamed in the glow of the fluorescent lights.

Eliza glanced at her phone's display and checked the time. "Don't keep us in suspense, Lin."

"I believe"—Ami shot Eliza a warning glance—"what Eliza is trying to say is we know Shirley is a stickler about your lunch breaks."

"You have something to tell us." Eliza pointed a long, elegant finger at Lindsay. "Just say it."

Lindsay told herself she should be scared out of her mind by this latest development. But compared to the news the doctor had laid on her this morning, not having an income was the least of her concerns.

"Yesterday…" She paused, not so much for dramatic effect as to still the tremble in her voice. "I quit my job."

Ami's eyes grew wide. "Seriously?"

A slow smile lifted Eliza's red lips. "Well, hallelujah."

"If you're happy"—Ami reached across the table to give Lindsay's hand a squeeze—"we're happy."

Eliza nodded, then cocked her head, her sleek hair falling like a dark curtain against her cheek. "What made you decide to take the plunge?"

Lindsay understood their surprise. She'd worked as a floral designer at the Enchanted Florist for nearly ten years. She'd lived in her apartment for nearly that long. She'd never been one for change.

Looking ahead, she saw a future that held nothing *but* change. Lindsay swallowed against the bile rising in her throat.

"Was it that hideous uniform Shirley insisted you wear?" Eliza chuckled. "Or did you finally get sick of her bullshit and snap?"

Ami turned to Eliza, a smile tugging at the corners of her lips. "Why, Mrs. Kendrick, I don't believe I've ever heard you say bullshit."

"Blame it on my husband." Eliza flashed a sly smile. "Kyle is a bad influence."

Lindsay and Ami looked at each other and burst out laughing. Everyone in Good Hope knew Kyle was the best thing that had ever happened to Eliza.

Eliza knew it, too. Her happiness shone as brightly as the diamond on her finger.

"Shirley never gave you the credit or the freedom to create that you deserved." Eliza studied Lindsay. "I wouldn't have lasted a week. How you lasted ten years is beyond me."

"You're not Lindsay," Ami told Eliza, then refocused on Lindsay. "What made you decide to leave now?" Ami added an encouraging smile to the question.

"Shirley informed me the twins would be taking over my design work." Anger she couldn't quite control licked at the edges of Lindsay's voice.

"Her daughters?" Eliza's brows pulled together in puzzlement. "They're in high school."

"They graduated last May," Lindsay reminded her. "After one class, they are now officially floral designers."

Her friends appeared as stunned as she'd been when Shirley delivered the bombshell. Lindsay had completed a two-year program in floral design, had ten years of experience and had received numerous accolades. The twins' only education was the recent completion of a six-week online course.

One online course, Lindsay thought bitterly, then shoved the anger aside. She would not dwell on the negative. She told herself this change in circumstance was a blessing, the shot in the arm she needed.

"I didn't go to school to ring up sales and schedule deliveries." Lindsay didn't mention Shirley had simpered that *unfortunately* she'd have to cut her salary since her job duties would be changing.

"I wish I could have seen Shirley's face when you quit." Eliza's lips lifted at the thought. "Mark my words, her business will take a nose dive. I only sent Cherries' business her way because you worked there."

Ami nodded. "She's taken advantage of you and your talent for years."

"I let her," Lindsay admitted with an embarrassed smile.

"The job worked for you." Ami's tone had a matter-of-fact-ness, but sympathy filled her eyes. "When it no longer did, you quit."

Lindsay nodded, still embarrassed by the number of years she'd let Shirley trample over her.

"If you need a job while you decide your next step, I can always use help at the bakery." Ami's voice radiated reassurance and told Lindsay she wasn't in this alone.

It was a generous offer, but with Labor Day in the rearview, Good Hope had officially entered the off-season. And Blooms Bake Shop was fully staffed for the winter months.

Eliza, not to be outdone, met Lindsay's gaze. "There's always a place for you at the General Store."

Lindsay's heart swelled with love for these two women who would always have her back. In high school, they'd dubbed them-selves the Three Musketeers. Over the years, they'd weathered many tough times, including a horrific car accident the summer before their senior year.

Ami had been driving, and Lindsay had been seriously injured. Now, the only reminder was a scar across her cheek. What had hurt most was the chasm between Ami and Eliza that had lasted for years, with Ami guilt-ridden and Eliza blaming Ami for Lindsay's injuries.

That was behind them. They were a united front now. For that, Lindsay was immensely grateful. She needed their love and support more than ever. Especially after the news she'd received barely two hours earlier.

"I appreciate the offers, but I've got some savings." Lindsay hoped saying aloud the plan circling in her head would make it real. "I've decided now is the time for me to follow your lead. I'm going into the floral business for myself."

Excitement skittered across the table like the leaves dancing in the outside breeze. Before Lindsay could catch her breath, Eliza offered space in her store and Ami mentioned giving her several commercial refrigeration units.

"I have no need of them," Ami insisted. "We went with all-new when we remodeled the bakery."

Lindsay found herself touched by the offer but unwilling to take advantage. "I'll buy them."

"Absolutely not." Ami lifted her hands, palms out. "The units work, but they're old. You'll be doing me a favor by taking them off my hands."

Lindsay bit her bottom lip. "If you're sure…"

"I'm positive." Ami smiled. "I'm happy I can help."

Eliza glanced around the café, known for its comfort food and warm ambience. "If Muddy Boots had a liquor license, we'd open a bottle of champagne and toast your new business."

"I'm afraid the bottle would be wasted on me." Ami's hand dropped to her abdomen, reminding Lindsay that her friend's second baby was due in February.

"It would be wasted on me as well." Lindsay clasped her fingers together to still their sudden trembling.

"I know you're not a big drinker." Eliza offered an understanding smile. "But this is a special occasion."

"I'm afraid the drinking door is solidly closed for now."

Ami shot her a quizzical glance.

Eliza circled a hand in a get-to-the-point gesture.

Lindsay took a deep breath, then exhaled the words. "I'm pregnant."

OWEN VAUGHN rarely took time for lunch. His business, the Greasy Wrench Automotive Center, kept him too busy. Though he had a great group of employees, it felt as if they were always short a mechanic or two. Which meant, in addition to his administrative duties, Owen helped out in the bays.

Once the workday ended, everyone scattered. Everyone, except him. He had no reason to rush home. There was no one waiting for him there. Not anymore.

"What are you going to have?" Dan Marshall, pastor at First Christian, glanced down at the list of specials for the day. "I came here for a burger, but the Bunza sounds intriguing."

Owen glanced at the description. Cabbage. Beef. Onions. Spices. Wrapped up in some sort of bread pocket. He shook his head. "I'm not a big cabbage fan."

When Owen lifted his gaze from the list of specials, intending to ask Dan why he'd set up this lunch meeting, he saw her.

Lindsay sat at a table by the window with her two closest friends. Though he couldn't see her eyes, the light from the window turned her hair into spun gold. Today, she'd pulled those long strands back from her face with a couple of clips that sparkled in the café's fluorescent lights.

Though it was a workday, instead of the "uniform" her boss—Shirley Albrecht—had implemented last year, Lindsay was dressed casually in jeans, sneakers and a blue cotton sweater. The simple fact that she was eating out for lunch, rather than chowing down a sandwich in the tiny break room at the back of the floral shop, told him she'd taken the day off.

His gaze drank her in. Owen had been stunned last spring when she and Pastor Dan had become engaged right before his eyes. The engagement hadn't lasted long. She and the minister had parted ways shortly after Mindy had—

"I suppose you're wondering why I called." Dan's voice broke through his thoughts.

Realizing his gaze was still focused in Lindsay's direction, Owen pulled it back. "Yes. I—"

A dark-haired young woman who reminded Owen of Lindsay's niece, Dakota, stopped at the table. With pen poised over a pad, she smiled. "Do you gentlemen need more time?"

Owen glanced at Dan. "I'm ready if you are."

Dan waited until the orders were taken and drinks on the table before getting down to business. He leaned forward. "How are you doing?"

With careful precision, Owen lifted the glass of soda to his lips. They both knew Dan wasn't asking about his business. "I'm getting by."

"Have you thought any more about the grief group I—"

"I'm not interested." His voice could have cut glass. Owen set down the glass. "Is that why you asked me to lunch? To push the grief group or play psychologist?"

In the six months since the death of Owen's daughter, Dan had mentioned the grief group on more than one occasion.

"If I thought either would do any good, I would." Dan's chuckle eased the tension. "You've got a hard head, Owen. Any prodding by me would likely be counterproductive."

The tension in Owen's shoulders eased. He reminded himself that Dan was a good guy and his concern genuine.

"Fin Rakes came to see me."

Owen cocked his head. "What does Fin have to do with me?"

A shining light in Mindy's life during the last months of his child's life, Delphinium, known affectionately by everyone in town as Fin, had been like a mother to Mindy. She'd loved his little girl, and that love had been reciprocated.

Swallowing the ball of dread rising in his throat, Owen braced himself. The fact that he was here and Fin had been brought into the conversation practically guaranteed his lunch invitation had something to do with Mindy.

Dear God, he prayed, please don't let it be some sort of memorial service. Owen didn't know if he could survive another one. He was a private person who refused to lose control in front of everyone, so the services were always difficult.

"—Mindy's closet."

Owen realized that while his mind had been embracing worst-case scenarios, the minister had continued to speak. How had he known all of Mindy's clothes were still in her closet? Owen shut the door to her room whenever anyone stopped by.

Besides, how was that any of the minister's business? "What about her closet?"

His voice came out sharper than he'd intended. But, darn it, between Dan bringing up Mindy's death and seeing Lindsay across the dining area, it was almost more than Owen could bear. Lindsay had been a bright light in his life during those dark months after Mindy died.

In the weeks they'd been apart, he'd—

"Fin proposed Mindy's Closet be the name of the project."

Project? Owen frowned, then shot the minister an apologetic look. "I need you to start again at the beginning. I'm not clear on what you're asking."

Dan's gaze shifted to the window where the pretty blonde who'd once been his fiancée sat with her friends. "I may have been distracted and not made myself clear."

They had Lindsay in common, Owen thought. The realization had his spirits sinking even lower.

"Fin approached me with a proposal. She wanted to run it by me before mentioning the possibility to you."

He'd been right. It was another memorial service. Damn it all to hell and back. "She wants to plan some sort of memorial to Mindy."

"Yes. And no."

"Which is it?" Owen lifted a brow at the cryptic response. "Yes? Or no?"

Then, darned if his gaze didn't slide once again to Lindsay. The fact that the three women looked so serious concerned him. Especially Lindsay, whom he'd once teasingly accused of scattering sunshine wherever she went.

The compliment had made her smile.

"No."

Owen jerked his attention back to the minister. "Not a memorial."

"Not in the strict sense of the word." Dan opened his mouth, but paused when the waitress appeared with their burgers and fries.

Once she was out of earshot, Owen picked up a fry. "What does Fin want?"

Dan cleared his throat and straightened in his seat. "While there are several consignment stores in Good Hope, they charge for their merchandise."

The day, Owen thought, just kept getting stranger and stranger. "I don't know anything about clothing sales, Dan. I'm a mechanic."

"Fin wants to start something called Mindy's Closet at the church." Dan paused. "Residents will be asked to donate new and used children's clothing. Once a week, or perhaps more often, we'll open the doors to Mindy's Closet for our neighbors in need."

For a long moment, Owen didn't speak. Couldn't speak. He thought of his daughter's closet at home, filled with dresses and glittery tops, all in various shades of pink. The thought of giving away the last reminders of his precious child brought a jittery feeling to his gut.

"You wouldn't be expected to donate Mindy's clothing. Unless you want to, of course," Dan quickly added, as if he'd read Owen's thoughts. His voice deepened with emotion. "Fin wants to do this for the community as a tribute to Mindy. She and Jeremy were very fond of your little girl."

"Mindy loved Fin." As if of their own volition, Owen's lips turned up. "Being Fin's flower girl and walking down the aisle in her 'princess dress' was..."

Owen's voice trailed off, and his smile disappeared. If the wedding was the best day of Mindy's life, finding his daughter cold and lifeless in her bed the next morning...

"I understand talking about this brings back memories."

Owen sat back in his seat and fought to bring his rioting emotions under control. It had been six months. Losing his daughter hurt just as much now as it had then. Maybe more.

Yesterday, a song triggered the pain. The pop tune blaring from the truck's radio had been one he and Mindy had always sung together at the top of their voices. Owen's fingers had trembled so badly he'd barely been able to switch the channel.

"What is it you want from me, Dan?" Owen shifted his gaze away from the window. His voice sounded hollow, as if he'd spoken in a tin can.

"Your blessing."

Owen jerked his gaze back to the minister.

"I need to know if it's okay with you if we call the project Mindy's Closet." Dan shifted uneasily in his seat. "When it's time for the grand opening, you could come and say a few remarks. Or not. Fin and I don't want to make this uncomfortable for you, Owen. But we'd like to honor Mindy by providing this needed community service in her name."

Glancing down, Owen saw his hands were balled into fists at his sides. His little girl had possessed an infectious smile and a vibrant personality that drew people to her. While some kids hated being the center of attention, Mindy had embraced the spotlight.

"She'd like this." Owen pushed the words past lips that felt frozen. "She'd appreciate the project being named after her, and she'd love the idea of helping those in need."

"Then we have your blessing?"

Owen glanced at the table by the window. Lindsay knew him in a way that no other woman had and would understand his conflicted feelings on this issue.

But the closeness they'd shared after Mindy's death had ended. His life and hers no longer intersected.

For the best, he reminded himself.

"Owen," Dan prompted.

Owen met the minister's gaze. "You have my blessing."

CHAPTER TWO

"You're Pregnant?" Ami's voice rose, but she pulled it down.

Lindsay saw the shock in her eyes. She had no doubt that she'd had the same look in hers when the doctor had told her she wasn't sick, but pregnant.

Eliza simply gazed, unblinking, those almond-shaped gray eyes giving nothing away.

Lindsay's heart beat like butterfly wings in her throat, and she suddenly felt lightheaded. To steady herself, she took a breath and forced herself to look around the café. Anything was better than seeing the shock and questions in her friends' eyes.

It was a mistake. While Dan talked, Owen stared. At her.

The odd look in his eyes had her heart shifting into overdrive. She'd spoken in a whisper, barely loud enough for the two women sitting across from her to hear. As she wasn't facing Owen, he couldn't have read her lips. No, she reassured herself, he hadn't heard. She was being paranoid.

"Lindsay." Eliza's voice held an urgency.

Lindsay returned her attention to her friends. A tightness filled her chest.

She. Would. Not. Cry.

Not here, surrounded by so many people who knew her, knew her mother.

Not here, with Owen so close.

Calling on an inner strength she hadn't known she possessed, Lindsay forced a smile. "I've always wanted a child."

But not like this. Not without a husband.

"Are you sure you're pregnant?" Ami asked.

"Sometimes, a missed period is just that." Eliza spoke with false heartiness.

"The doctor confirmed it this morning." Being a wife and mother had always been Lindsay's dream. She couldn't count the times she'd visualized walking down the aisle in a white dress.

In her mind, the ceremony was small. Lindsay didn't like big splashes. But the mystery man at the front of the church was always looking at her with such love that it brought tears to her eyes.

The second part of the dream took place a couple of years later. He was at her side, rejoicing in the news when they learned they were expecting a baby.

Not meant to be, Lindsay thought, squaring her shoulders.

"When are you due?" Ami asked.

"March twenty-seventh."

"We'll have our babies around the same time." Genuine excitement, filled Ami's voice. "It'll be wonderful."

"Lindsay hasn't said whether she's continuing the pregnancy." Eliza's gray eyes never left Lindsay's face. "Or whether she plans to keep the baby."

Seized with a sudden urge to lash out, Lindsay curbed the impulse. None of this was Eliza's fault. Her friend wasn't advocating those options, simply letting her know she had choices.

But she didn't have choices. Not regarding the little one growing inside her. "I want him or her. I know it probably doesn't make sense. Heck, I don't even have a job."

To her horror, Lindsay felt a couple of tears slip down her

cheeks. She brushed them aside with a quick swipe of her fingers and prayed no one else in the café had noticed.

Ami's expression softened, and tears filled her own eyes. "Oh, Lin, I—"

"You both know I never wanted to be a single mother." She didn't want to interrupt her friend, but if Ami started crying, Lindsay knew she wouldn't be able to hold it together.

Too late, Lindsay realized she shouldn't have brought this up in a public venue. She should have thought of an excuse to meet at Hill House, where the Cherries met. Or even trumped up some reason to get together at one of their homes. There, she'd have been assured privacy.

When Eliza opened her mouth, Lindsay continued, not giving her a chance to speak.

"I've seen what that can be like. My sister has had a rough time." Lindsay paused, wondering why she was comparing herself to Cassie. She wasn't at all like her older sister, who had four children by three different men.

"Your sister wasn't even sixteen when she gave birth to Dakota," Ami pointed out. "You're thirty-one. A mature woman with a stable—"

Ami didn't finish the thought. She didn't need to, because Lindsay knew where she'd been headed. Lindsay had a stable job. Now, she didn't.

Would things have been different if Shirley had dropped her bombshell *after* the doctor's visit, rather than *before*?

For the best, Lindsay told herself, but the assurance rang false.

"You're a strong woman." Eliza made the pronouncement, and the look in her eyes dared her to disagree. "When you hold that new life in your arms, you'll realize you've been given an unexpected blessing."

Some of the tightness gripping Lindsay's heart eased at Eliza's confident tone. "You really think so?"

"Darn right I do. And I just realized I'm going to be the odd one out. I won't have a child to bring to the playdates you and Ami are going to arrange." Eliza tapped a perfectly manicured fingernail against the Formica tabletop. "Kyle and I will have to step up our efforts."

Lindsay smiled, not sure if Eliza was joking. But true or not, the thought of playdates with Ami and her children brought a lightness to her heart.

"Have you told Owen?" Despite being voiced in a soft, gentle manner, Ami's question had Lindsay jerking as if she'd been poked with a cattle prod.

Pure reflex had her blurting, "What makes you think it's Owen's baby?"

Eliza chuckled. "Who else? Unless you've been hooking up with the minister."

Lindsay straightened, stiffened.

"Eliza," Ami chided.

The executive director of the Cherries lifted her hands, a not-so-innocent expression on her face. "I assume nothing. You never know what people do behind closed doors."

That the statement held some truth couldn't be denied. Last spring, Lindsay had been engaged to Pastor Dan Marshall. But their relationship had never been a physical one, and once she'd broken off the engagement, she'd seen him only in passing. And, of course, in church.

"It's Owen's baby." Lindsay swallowed past the sudden lump in her throat. "And no, I haven't told him."

"Though neither of you planned this pregnancy, I think he'll be excited." Ami continued to speak in a low tone, as if determined to make sure her voice didn't carry past the confines of their booth. "After Mindy—"

"My child will not be a replacement for Mindy." The vehemence in Lindsay's tone took all of them by surprise.

"I wasn't saying that," Ami hastened to reassure her. "One child can never replace another. I was just—"

When Ami paused, a look of abject misery on her face, Eliza stepped in. "I don't presume to speak for Ami, but I thought the same thing. Owen was a loving, caring father."

"He was." It was all Lindsay wanted to say on the topic. At least for now.

Owen had been a stellar father. When he and his wife had divorced and she'd moved away, he'd been granted full custody. Mindy had been the light of his life. When she was diagnosed with a brain tumor, he'd been at her side.

When the fight had proved futile, he'd done everything he could to make his smart and funny eight-year-old happy.

Her friends were right. He would want to be a father to this baby.

"When he finds out I'm pregnant, he'll ask me to marry him." There wasn't a single doubt in Lindsay's mind that that was how the conversation would go.

Ami and Eliza said nothing for several seconds. Then they both nodded.

Eliza lifted a dark brow. "What will you say?"

"I'll say no."

Surprise lit the depths of Ami's green eyes. "You love him, Lin."

"I do." Lindsay saw no reason to deny the truth. Besides, she'd already confessed the depth of her feelings to her friends when Owen had dumped her six weeks earlier and broken her heart. "But he doesn't love me. He didn't even want to continue to date me."

That had hurt the most. Lindsay understood his heart was tender. He was still grieving for Mindy. But she'd thought they had a connection, hoped in time friendship would turn into love.

She'd been willing to wait.

Though he'd insisted he wanted to remain friends, he'd made it clear he didn't want to continue to date her.

"Maybe he's changed his mind." The doubtful expression on Ami's face told Lindsay her friend didn't believe that any more than she did.

Lindsay shook her head vigorously. When the doctor had given her the news, she'd wanted oh-so-much to travel down a road strewn with hearts and flowers.

Maybe Owen loved her.

Maybe, if he didn't, after they married, he would grow to love her.

Maybe—

Lindsay pressed her lips together and slammed that door shut. She was going to be a mother. She couldn't afford to indulge in foolish dreams.

"What is it you want, Lin?" Eliza's gaze searched hers.

"I want what you have with Kyle. His eyes light up whenever you walk into a room." Lindsay blinked rapidly to clear the tears that had reappeared and turned to Ami. "I want what you have with Beck. He uses any excuse to take your hand in his, to touch you."

The women remained silent for several seconds.

"I don't want someone who's only with me out of obligation. I already know how it feels to be planning a wedding with fake feelings—because I was the one faking it. I want a man who adores me, who can't wait to marry me. And I not only want those things from my future husband, I want to feel the same about him. I want *real* love." Lindsay squared her shoulders. "If I can't have that, I'll go it alone."

"I'M NOT USUALLY a fan of weddings, but this one was nice." Ethan Shaw held out his arm for Lindsay as they left Jeremy and Fin Rakes's large home, where the ceremony uniting Steve Bloom and Lynn Chapin had been held.

"Your sister's wedding was beautiful," Lindsay reminded him. Like this wedding, Eliza's marriage to Kyle last spring had been a small, intimate affair in the parlor of the house that had brought the couple together.

"I enjoyed that one immensely." Ethan, Eliza's younger brother by two years, flashed a grin.

Lindsay couldn't believe she was out on a date a day after discovering she was pregnant. But then, this wasn't really a date. Eliza had set her up with her recently returned-to-Good-Hope single brother nearly three weeks ago. Lindsay hadn't been able to come up with a reason to cancel the plans.

"The best part was when my father saw Eliza's black wedding gown." Ethan chuckled. "The look on my dad's face was priceless."

Lindsay realized with a start that he was still focused on his sister's wedding.

"Eliza looked lovely." Lindsay's tone turned wistful, despite her efforts to control it. "For me, the best part was the look in Kyle's eyes when she walked down the stairs toward him."

"They're happy." Ethan, appearing bored by the topic, glanced at the barn up ahead. "I haven't been to a reception here in several years."

"It's become one of Good Hope's most popular venues." Lindsay's heart swelled when her gaze landed on the flowers arranged in large containers on either side of the entrance. Her designs. One of her last assignments before she and the Enchanted Florist parted ways.

While the barn was often decorated in a rustic or country style, neither of those styles suited Lynn, the bride. Elegant and stylish were two words often used to describe the bank executive. When Lindsay had spoken with both Steve and Lynn about their preferences, the high school teacher with the graying ginger hair and wire-rimmed spectacles had taken his fiancée's hand. All he wanted, he'd told her, was for Lynn to be happy.

The arrangements with a burgundy focus, along with calla lilies and eucalyptus, had made both Lynn and Steve happy. In terms of personalities and sensibilities, the two lifelong residents of Good Hope complemented each other perfectly.

"I bet it seems strange for you." When Ethan inclined his head, she hurriedly added, "Being back in Good Hope."

Eliza's brother had left the township on the Door County peninsula for college and never returned. Most recently, he'd been in a business venture with a friend in Chicago. Lindsay still wasn't certain what had caused him to move back.

"It's a bit strange." He followed her into the barn. "But in a good way."

Instead of a sit-down dinner, there were tables of appetizers and entrees and dessert. All had required floral accents.

This wedding, Lindsay realized with a pang, was truly her swan song for the Enchanted Florist. Her heart rose to her throat, and to her horror, her eyes filled with tears.

Darn hormones.

Lindsay hurriedly blinked back the moisture and forced her attention to the man at her side. With his dark hair, gray eyes and lean frame, Ethan qualified as a real hunk. When you tossed in intelligent, kind and rolling in money, he was every woman's dream man.

Every woman but her.

She wished she hadn't agreed to let Eliza set her up. So much had changed since she'd accepted the offer.

Back then, she'd been concerned what her mother would say if she showed up to the wedding without a date. Her mother had become overly concerned with Lindsay's love life once she hit thirty.

Lindsay had lost count of the number of times her mom had told her that her chances of hooking a "big fish" decreased every month.

As if thinking of the woman had conjured her up, Anita strolled up on three-inch heels.

"Well, isn't this a nice surprise?" Her mother's hazel eyes lit as her gaze slid from her daughter to Ethan, then back to Lindsay. "I didn't realize you and the illustrious Mr. Shaw were dating."

Approval ran through her mother's words, thick as warm honey. Now in her late fifties, Anita could pass for a much-younger woman. Tonight, her trim figure was showcased in a burgundy wrap dress with a left leg slit that showed off her toned legs.

For the late-afternoon event, Anita had pulled her dark hair into a simple chignon, a style that drew attention to her hazel eyes and high cheekbones.

Lindsay suddenly felt dowdy in her blue jersey dress and kitten heels.

"Ethan and I aren't dating." Lindsay spoke firmly, keeping her eyes focused on her mother. "We were just talking. We're not together."

When Ethan opened his mouth, she shot him a sharp glance. Lindsay could talk until she was blue in the face about Eliza setting them up simply because they were both at loose ends.

Anita would still see this as a date.

"You look lovely, Mrs. Fishback." Ethan offered her mother a warm smile. Apparently, he'd decided that when in doubt over what to say, best to lead with a compliment. "I'd never guess you have a daughter Lindsay's age."

Lindsay watched her mother blossom like a bud opening to the warmth of the sun. Even during the ceremony, Lindsay had noticed his smile had that effect on women. For some reason, she was immune to his charm.

"Aren't you the sweet one?" Anita slanted a glance at the man at her side. "You both know Sheriff Swarts."

The man in the dark suit with the bolo tie looked every bit of his sixty-five years. Though still handsome, his face was weathered and lined. He was tall with broad shoulders and a mop of gray hair that matched his mustache, so it was easy to see how Leonard Swarts, former sheriff, had earned his Silver Fox title.

Lindsay hid her surprise. She hadn't realized her mother was dating Len. Or perhaps, like she and Ethan, they weren't together. "It's nice to see you, Sheriff Swarts."

"Good to see you both." Len nodded to her, then to Ethan. "These days, it's just Len."

"I have to admit, I still expect to see you driving down Main in a black-and-white," Ethan joked.

Len chuckled. "Those days are in my rearview."

Lindsay caught her mother eyeing Ethan again. It took everything in her to keep a smile on her lips. She knew her mother had been invited to the wedding and reception, but she hadn't been certain she'd make an appearance.

Anita and Steve Bloom had dated for several years. Lindsay knew her mother had been convinced she was in love with the high school teacher. When Steve had broken it off, Anita was devastated.

She'd gone through several men since then, but hadn't been dating anyone in the last month. A fact that had Lindsay wondering about Len. She hoped he and her mother were dating. When I-Need-a-Man, a nickname Anita had been given by Steve's daughters long ago, had a man in her life, she left Lindsay alone.

When Anita was between men, she focused on Lindsay's love life. Lindsay didn't need that additional stressor on her plate.

The band began to play, and Ethan turned politely to her. "Would you care to dance?"

Although Lindsay didn't really feel like dancing, she didn't feel like eating, either. And she *really* didn't feel like making conversation with her mother.

Something told Lindsay she and Ethan shared that goal.

"If you'll excuse us." Ethan smiled and placed his palm against the small of Lindsay's back.

The word *us* and a simple, innocuous touch had Anita beaming.

As she turned away, Lindsay decided it was going to be a long evening.

CHAPTER THREE

Lindsay Breathed a sigh of relief when she and Ethan stepped onto the shiny wooden floor. Since many in the crowd were older, the band, brought in from Chicago, appeared to be sticking to romantic ballads. Or maybe Steve and Lynn wanted their guests to listen to soothing music while perusing the many food options.

Ethan took her hand and placed his other against the small of her back. In seconds, they were gliding across the floor with ease.

It didn't surprise Lindsay that Eliza's brother was an excellent dancer. As a little boy, he'd excelled at everything he attempted.

"You look beautiful tonight." Ethan's voice in her ear was as smooth as his dance steps.

When she turned her head, he was right there.

His dark hair, expertly cut, was long enough to be trendy but short enough for a *Fortune* 500 business meeting. His face was clean-shaven, and his cologne subtle enough not to make her touchy stomach churn.

But it was those deep-gray eyes and sculpted cheekbones that made women swoon. Though Lindsay recognized his appeal, when she looked at him she saw only Eliza's little brother. The one who'd sprayed her full-blast with a Super Soaker on his eighth birthday.

Lindsay forced a bright smile. "I—"

She didn't have a chance to say more when they were bumped from the side.

A frown furrowed Ethan's brow as he turned toward the culprit.

Ruby Rakes smiled brightly at them. "I was hoping we'd have a chance to chat."

Jeremy, Ruby's dance partner, cast a puzzled glance at his grandmother before returning his attention to Lindsay and her partner. "We didn't mean to crash into you like that. We—"

"Oh, Jeremy, it's fine." Ruby, whose champagne-colored hair had been styled in soft curls around her wrinkled face, gave a dismissive wave. "It was more of a tap."

Coming from anyone other than the eccentric matriarch of the Rakes clan, the cavalier comment would have been annoying. But it was impossible to be irritated at the charming older woman with a big heart.

"It's nice to see you again, Mrs. Rakes." Ethan offered the woman a warm smile, showing his manners hadn't been damaged by the collision.

"You, too." Ruby patted his arm, then focused on Lindsay.

Something in the woman's intense blue eyes sent a shiver of unease up Lindsay's spine. The overpowering scent of Chanel No. 5, Ruby's signature scent, had Lindsay's stomach flip-flopping. To keep control, she tried to breathe through her mouth.

"Owen is here."

Lindsay wondered if it was a coincidence that Ethan's hand dropped from her back a second after Ruby's pronouncement. Her smile froze as she struggled with how to respond.

Ruby knew she and Owen hadn't been a couple for weeks. Nothing happened in Good Hope without Ruby and her two friends, Katherine Spencer and Gladys Bertholf, knowing about it.

Jeremy shot Lindsay an apologetic look, then turned to Ethan. "I was going to ask—"

"This is a wedding reception, Jeremy. You and Ethan can talk business another time." Ruby's tone brooked no argument, and she got none from her grandson. Once again, her gaze returned to Lindsay. "You should track Owen down and say hello. He hasn't been to many parties since he lost—"

For a few seconds, Ruby's composure faltered. Then the determined look was back.

"Ethan will understand." Ruby's lips lifted when he nodded. "In fact, there are several young women here who would love to have a handsome young man ask them to dance."

Obviously used to his grandmother's imperialistic manner, the mayor of Good Hope's lips quirked up in an impish gleam. "In case you aren't getting the message, Ethan, that's an order, not a suggestion."

Ethan glanced at Lindsay. Once he received her nod of agreement, he set out across the dance floor.

"What are the three of you doing standing in the middle of the dance floor?" Looking beautiful in a moss-green dress with a lace overlay, Fin took her husband's arm.

Lindsay's heart swelled when Jeremy leaned over to kiss his wife. Another love match.

"I was merely pointing out Lindsay needs to rescue Owen." Ruby's voice softened at the sight of her granddaughter-in-law. It was common knowledge in Good Hope that the two adored each other.

"Owen doesn't need rescuing." Fin's tone made the statement a fact. "He's busy."

"Busy?" Ruby's head swiveled at the same time as Lindsay's.

The older woman's eyes widened. "Oh my."

Lindsay's heart sank at the sight of Owen stepping onto the dance floor with Katie Ruth Crewes's hand on his arm.

The former cheerleader was a vision in pink, the shade complementing her blond prettiness. The three-inch heels in black eel skin flattered her long, toned legs. She couldn't seem to take her eyes off of Owen. While they watched, she tossed her head and laughed.

Lindsay couldn't stand it any longer. "If you'll excuse me, I'm going to grab something to eat."

The last thing Lindsay wanted was food, but she refused to stand there and watch Katie Ruth flirt with the man she loved. If she waited even a second longer to leave, Fin, or God forbid, Ruby, would offer to come with her.

Lindsay needed to get herself under control before engaging in any more polite chitchat. With a fake smile plastered on her lips, she began weaving her way through the dancers.

Once she stepped off the hardwood, Lindsay smiled and responded whenever someone called out a greeting, but she didn't pause to talk. She hoped anyone looking at her would think she was a woman on some kind of mission. Which was true. She needed to find someplace private to regroup.

When she opened the door to the restroom, the laughter and happy conversation in front of the long mirror told her that place wasn't here.

She let the door fall shut and turned, not sure which way to go. It all seemed too much. The happy couples on the dance floor. The romantic music in the air. The joy.

Tears stung the backs of her eyes.

Darn it. She wanted the joy.

Knowing she needed to get away, Lindsay left the barn and stepped into the crisp air of early fall. Though her dress was long-sleeved, the jersey fabric provided little protection against the cool air.

It didn't matter. All that mattered was getting away. The bite in the breeze instantly dried the tears threatening to fall as she wrapped her arms around herself. When she saw a couple of the teachers who taught with Steve at Good Hope High headed toward the entrance, Lindsay slipped around the side of the building and picked up her pace.

At the back of the barn, Lindsay discovered a smaller building. She was pleased to find the door unlocked. Stepping inside, she flipped on the lights.

The well-organized interior held a shiny green tractor with a large mowing deck, a couple of self-propelled lawn mowers and several sizes of snow blowers. The floor beneath her heels was concrete. While the area wasn't fancy, it provided protection against the wind. More important, it afforded her some well-needed privacy.

A faint scent of motor oil hung in the air. Because of the smell, Lindsay cracked the door, allowing the sweet scent of evergreen to enter the building.

Lindsay wasn't sure how long she stood there. She decided that when she got home, she'd sit down and come up with a strategy for telling Owen about the baby. She also needed to take a hard look at her finances and see where she could make cuts until her new business took off.

The sound of the door creaking open had her realizing her brief respite had come to an end.

It was time she went back inside, anyway. She would find Ethan, tell him she had a headache and wanted to go home. It wasn't fair to make him leave the party, but he could return to the festivities once he dropped her off.

Feeling good about her plan, Lindsay took a step, then skidded to a stop. Her breath catching had nothing to do with the blast of cold air and everything to do with the man standing in front of her, a scowl on his face.

"Owen. What are you doing here?"

~

EVEN BEFORE KATIE RUTH CREWES asked him to dance, Owen had decided coming to the reception had been a mistake.

The wedding had been difficult enough. He had no doubt Lynn and Steve would be happy together. Anyone watching the two could see they were deeply in love. Then again, that's probably how he and Tessa had looked on their wedding day.

The difference was, they'd been young. Tessa had just turned nineteen. He'd been twenty. They'd been away from home for the first time, and the fact they were both from Good Hope had been the glue binding them together.

His parents had adored Tessa, and he'd basked in their approval. He sure hadn't felt much of it growing up.

While it would be easy to blame his melancholy on the fact his marriage had failed spectacularly, he knew that wasn't all of it. Weddings brought back memories of his daughter, his beloved Mindy, walking down the aisle in Fin and Jeremy's wedding, tossing pink rose petals willy-nilly.

Mindy had been so happy, the brain tumor that would take her life pushed to the back of their consciousness for that one day. Emotions, always lurking just below the surface, now gripped his throat in a choke hold.

Still, Owen kept dancing until the song ended, letting Katie Ruth carry the bulk of the conversation. He managed to thank her, then fled outside for much-needed fresh air.

He'd lost track of Lindsay, which was for the best. The sight of Ethan Shaw with his hands on her had brought forward a primitive emotion he didn't want to dissect.

Whatever he and Lindsay had once shared was over, and how he felt when he saw her now didn't matter. The door offered an escape hatch, and he took it.

He'd never been a party guy, but going home to an empty house filled with memories held little appeal. He could change his clothes and head to the Greasy Wrench, but his head wasn't in the right place.

No, he would grab some fresh air, then head back into the reception for a few hours and pretend to have fun.

The breeze had picked up, so he headed around the side of the barn so he'd be out of the wind. The door to a maintenance shed was open.

Owen frowned. Someone had obviously forgotten to secure the latch. Though there was little crime in Good Hope, it was still smart to lock up pricy equipment. Not only that, whoever it was had left the light on. Owen had stepped inside, intending to remedy the oversights, when he saw her.

He inhaled sharply.

"What are you doing out here?" Owen wasn't sure why he sounded so cross. Maybe it was because the thin dress she wore was no match for the temperature outside.

Her arms wrapped around her body as if she tried to hug whatever warmth her body generated. He saw her shiver under his watchful gaze.

Without stopping to think, he pulled the door shut behind him, blocking the breeze. Whipping off his suit jacket, he held it out to her. "Put this on."

His tone brooked no argument.

She slipped on the coat without protest, which told him she was even colder than he'd thought.

At one time, not so long ago, Owen would have wrapped his arms around her, pulling her close to add his warmth to that of the suit jacket. He'd given up that right when he walked away from her nearly two months ago.

For the best, he reminded himself. He wasn't the one to give her what she needed. What she *deserved*.

She didn't speak, just stared at him with startled blue eyes. Eyes devoid of even the slightest hint of happiness. It reminded him of what was reflected back at him every morning when he looked in the mirror.

What reason did Lindsay have to feel that way? Had Ethan...?

The thought of the wealthy scion of one of the most prominent Good Hope families hurting Lindsay had Owen clenching his hands into fists. "What did he do?"

The question came out as a low growl and appeared to nudge Lindsay from her stupor.

A look of startled surprise crossed Lindsay's face. Her eyes widened. "Who?"

"Ethan Shaw." Owen spat the name.

"He-he didn't do anything," Lindsay stammered.

"Then why are you out here in a machine shed all alone, instead of in there?" Owen jerked a thumb in the direction of the barn.

She started to speak, then lifted her chin, her expression carefully composed. "I could ask you the same thing."

One heartbeat passed. Then two.

Owen sighed heavily. "You're right. It's not my business."

Lindsay turned then, her hair falling forward to obscure her face from view. She trailed a finger along the shiny surface of the Kubota lawn tractor.

Owen's mouth went dry. He remembered how it felt when she'd slid that finger up the inside of his—

"We need to talk." She whirled back, and something in her eyes had a sick feeling taking up residence in the pit of his stomach.

"Okay." He watched warily as she began to pace. Not far, just a few steps away and then a few steps back. It was an odd kind of dance.

Come close.

Walk away.

It was a game he and Lindsay had played for years. Until his defenses had been down and they'd gotten together for those few months after Mindy's death.

"I went to the doctor yesterday."

Owen's blood turned to ice. Was she sick? Was that why she looked so pale lately? Was that what she'd been telling her friends yesterday?

There had been little laughter in the booth. All three women had looked so serious.

Owen thought of that time when the doctor had told him and Tessa why their daughter had been waking with severe headaches.

With his heart beating wildly, Owen took a step toward her and asked in a gentler tone, "Are you okay?"

Lindsay chewed on her lower lip, as if trying to decide how much to confide.

He moved closer, so near he could see the specks of gold in the blue depths of her eyes and smell the subtle scent of her perfume. "Tell me."

Though he'd vowed to never touch her again after the night they parted ways, he took her hand in his and found it ice-cold. When she didn't pull back, he began to warm the soft, delicate flesh between his hands. "You can tell me anything."

Without warning, she shivered. A full-body shake that had the alarm bells in his head clanging even more loudly.

Owen enfolded her in his arms, pulling her tight against him in a gesture intended to comfort. She was his friend, he reminded himself. The fact that they were no longer dating didn't change the fact that he cared for her, would always care for her.

Holding her this way felt so right. For a second, her head rested against his chest, just under his chin. He remembered how it had once been with them. Owen stroked her back, murmuring soothing words. After several long seconds, her trembling eased.

Though he told himself it was for the best, he felt bereft when she pulled back.

"Sorry." Lindsay offered a wan smile. "I've been a little emotional lately."

"Will you tell me what's going on?"

Still, she hesitated.

"I'll tell you." Her gaze took on a distant look. "Just not tonight."

The alarm bells that had stilled began to clang again.

"I'd say now is as good a time as any." Owen gestured with one hand. "We're alone and unlikely to be disturbed."

"I don't know." Indecision blanketed her face as she turned away from him.

Owen reached out and grasped her arm. "Please."

He wanted to help her. To be there for her. As her friend, he told himself, but the intense worry that gripped him told Owen what he felt for this woman went beyond simple friendship.

"Tell me," he urged.

With a resigned sigh, she turned and met his gaze. "I'm pregnant."

CHAPTER FOUR

Lindsay wasn't sure which of them was more surprised by the admission.

This wasn't the way she'd planned to tell him, but when he'd pointed out they were alone and would be undisturbed, she'd seized the opportunity.

Squaring her shoulders, Lindsay waited for him to say something.

A second passed.

Then two.

Owen raked a hand through his hair, leaving his sandy-brown strands disheveled. She'd always liked the way he looked at the end of the day, with his hair tousled and a slight scruff on his chin.

In the months they'd been a couple, she'd loved seeing his hazel eyes, rimmed with thick lashes any woman would envy, warm with a smile whenever he saw her.

There was no sign of a smile now. Not in his eyes. Not on his lips.

"Are you sure?" His voice came out as rusty as an ungreased hinge. He cleared his throat. "Or do you just suspect?"

"I did a pregnancy test." The fact she could keep her tone

matter-of-fact encouraged Lindsay to continue. "When it was positive, I went to the doctor."

Almost of their own volition, her lips curved into a smile. Hearing the tiny beating heart had been a miraculous event.

"I'm due in late March." As Owen only continued to stare, Lindsay licked her suddenly dry lips. "I got pregnant in July."

Something flickered behind Owen's eyes. He had to be thinking back to the big Fourth of July celebration. That night, the fireworks hadn't been confined to the waters over Green Bay.

She'd had a sinus infection. Because the doctor had warned of the decreased efficacy of low-dose birth control pills while on antibiotics, they'd used a condom each time they made love.

Except that night.

They'd barely made it into his house before they were tearing off each other's clothes. Despite the urgency, their lovemaking that night had seemed to hold an extra sweetness.

It had been as if they'd both known that some kind of change was coming and wanted to hold on to the happiness of the moment with both hands.

Not long after that night, he'd abruptly ended their relationship.

When the silence lengthened, Lindsay broke it. "I thought you deserved to know."

If Owen had thought he'd latched the door behind him, a sharp gust of wind proved him wrong, flinging it open with a bang.

They both jumped at the sound, then stared, incredulous, as Ethan stepped inside.

He for a long moment. His curious expression gave no indication that he found anything odd about finding his "date" in a machine shed with another man.

"I wondered where you'd gone." Ethan glanced from her to Owen. "Am I interrupting something?"

Lindsay slipped past Owen. "No."

"Yes," Owen asserted. "Lin, we need to—"

Lindsay doubted her smile reached her eyes. But, heck, the fact that she managed to curve her lips at all was a major accomplishment. "Another time."

Ethan lifted his hands. "Seriously, if I'm interrupting something—"

"You're not." Lindsay shot Ethan a reassuring smile.

When she turned toward the door, Owen latched on to her arm. "Don't go."

His voice held a steely edge, but the lost look in his eyes told her he was more upset than he was letting on.

"Owen—"

"Dude." Ethan stepped forward, his jaw set in a hard line. "Release her arm."

Owen hesitated, then dropped his hand.

"It's okay." Lindsay spoke directly to Owen. "We *will* talk later."

When she left the building, Ethan was at her side. Her baby's father remained behind, his gaze boring into her back.

LINDSAY DISCOVERED Ethan had come looking for her at Ami's request. Her friend's father and new stepmother wanted to extend their compliments and appreciation for the floral arrangements.

"You somehow managed to give me exactly what I wanted when I wasn't sure what that was." Lynn gave a little laugh. Her long, elegant fingers fluttered in the air. The strings of white lights overhead sent sparks of color reflecting off the diamond on her left hand.

She looked, Lindsay thought, the way every bride should look on her wedding day—incredibly happy and so very much in love.

Lynn's silvery-blond curls were interspersed with several glittery pins. Her ice-blue silk dress flattered her porcelain prettiness.

Her new husband had eschewed his favorite khakis and cardigans for dark pants and a silver shirt that matched his wire-rimmed eyeglasses. The adoring look he shot his new wife brought an ache to Lindsay's heart.

"Thank you for everything you did to make our wedding special." Steve's gaze lingered on Lindsay, and concern filled his eyes. A high school teacher for thirty-plus years, and the father of four grown daughters, the man had good instincts.

Lindsay didn't worry about him asking her questions in front of everyone. After her father died, Steve had made it clear that, while he wouldn't intrude, his door was always open to her and Cassie. But this problem was one she had to handle alone.

Without thinking, Lindsay found herself stepping forward and placing her arms around him. "I'm so happy for you."

His hug held on for an extra second as he whispered in her ear, "I'm here for you."

Lindsay had a smile firmly fixed on her face when she stepped back. She stumbled and was surprised to feel Ethan's hands on her arms steadying her.

Lindsay had no illusions Ethan was so mesmerized by her that he couldn't bear to leave her side. No, it wasn't male interest she saw in those assessing gray eyes, it was curiosity.

Like his sister, Ethan liked having the answers. Right now, he had only questions.

"The flowers were fabulous, Lindsay." Fin swept up to the foursome, hands outstretched. Since her return to Good Hope and marriage to the town's mayor, Fin's sharp edges—developed during a decade in LA—had softened. She took Lindsay's hands and met her gaze. "Ami told me you're going into business for yourself. Congratulations!"

Her husband stepped up then, and Fin released her hold to loop her arm through his. She continued before Lindsay had a chance to respond. "We'll send plenty of Good Hope business her way. Right, Jeremy?"

As an elected official, there were undoubtedly rules Jeremy

had to follow. Lindsay could see him searching for a politically correct response when Fin let out a shriek.

"Owen, over here!" Fin motioned to him.

Lindsay's heart dropped.

Ethan stiffened.

Lindsay had wrongly assumed Owen wouldn't be returning to the reception. Of course, she'd also assumed telling him she was pregnant in a machine shed was a good idea.

Owen broke stride. He hesitated for only a second before changing course and crossing to them.

"Congratulations again," he said to Lynn and Steve. His smile was fixed as he nodded to the rest of the group. "Have you seen Gladys? I'm giving her a ride home."

At Lynn's puzzled glance, Owen added, "Her son couldn't make it, so I offered to be her chauffer this evening. She doesn't like driving at night."

Lindsay doubted she herself would like driving at night if she was ninety-seven.

Fin's brows drew together. "She could have come with us and Grandma Ruby. I wonder why Ruby didn't mention Gladys needed a ride."

"Maybe Gladys thought she'd be putting us out." Jeremy tucked a lock of his wife's hair behind her ear, a gesture that managed to be both sweet and sensual. "Since Ruby is spending the night."

Fin's frown deepened. "Why ask Owen? Why didn't she catch a ride with Katherine?"

"I have no idea." Owen shoved his hands into his pockets, looking decidedly uncomfortable.

Lindsay shot Fin a sharp glance that clearly said, *Back off.* Owen was doing the older woman a favor. He didn't need to be interrogated.

Either Fin didn't get the message, or she wanted to solve the mystery. For that, she needed facts.

"When did she ask you?" Fin asked.

"Today." Owen shrugged. "She called about her son's Cadillac. We're working on it while he recovers from knee surgery. She asked if I was coming to the wedding. When she found out I, ah, I didn't have a date, she asked if I'd bring her."

Lynn placed a hand on his arm. "That was so nice of you."

The tips of Owen's ears turned red, the way they always did when he was embarrassed. She knew him so well. Or she *thought* she'd known him. Her smile faded.

Owen inclined his head. "You called me over. Was there something you needed?"

Fin nodded. "I spoke with Dan, and he said you're okay with the Mindy's Closet plans."

Hands still in his pockets, Owen slowly nodded. "Thank you for thinking of my little girl."

Emotion thickened his voice, and Lindsay's heart went out to him. She knew how difficult it was for him to speak about his daughter.

"Mindy's Closet?" Ethan stepped into the conversation, inadvertently coming to Owen's rescue.

Lindsay listened intently to Fin's enthusiastic description of the program and how it would work. By the time she finished, Ethan wasn't the only one impressed.

"If you need volunteers to help staff it," Lindsay told Fin, "please let me know."

"We'll definitely be calling on you." Fin's gaze shifted over Lindsay's shoulder, and she frowned. "What do you think those three are cooking up?"

Lindsay turned and saw Katherine, Gladys and Ruby seated at one of the round linen-clad tables. A pad of paper lay on the table before Katherine, who appeared to be taking notes.

"Knowing Katherine and her cohorts"—Ethan's eyes twinkled—"they're up to only one thing—no good."

~

I'm glad we decided to do this." Gladys, former community theater star, tapped a long, red nail against the table while she sipped her gin and tonic. "One can only play so many games of dominoes."

Though she was the oldest in the group and close to the century mark, Gladys showed no signs of slowing down. She'd given up stage performances last year, exchanging acting for directing one play a year while remaining active in the Cherries.

Her dark hair held a vibrant swath of silver, what her granddaughter referred to as her skunk stripe, and her long, thin face was remarkably unlined for someone her age.

"I never thought I'd find a new career at this stage in my life." Katherine, a young ninety, adjusted the jeweled bifocals on the end of her nose. Her salt-and-pepper hair was pulled back in her trademark chignon. "I must admit I never considered becoming a matchmaker. Not until Gladys brought it up."

"Gladys could sell a blind man on a car." Ruby, the baby of the group at eightysomething, shot Gladys a wink. A petite firecracker, Ruby refused to let any gray, including a stylish skunk stripe, anywhere near her head.

Once she'd passed fifty, Ruby had gone the champagne route, a color close to her former blond and one that flattered her peaches-and-cream complexion.

"Here's who I have on the list so far." Katherine, who rivaled Gladys as the most business-oriented of the three, glanced down. "Lindsay Lohmeier. Katie Ruth Crewes. Greer Chapin. Cassie Lohmeier."

"Four is a good start." Gladys took another gulp of gin, then glanced across the ballroom. She lowered her voice a half decibel. "Lindsay and Owen make a nice-looking couple."

"That's what you said about her and the pastor." Ruby's lips quirked up in an impish smile. "We all know how that turned out."

"They made a nice-looking couple." Gladys waved a dismissive hand. The way she saw it, no matchmaker hit it out of the ballpark every time. Besides, it wasn't as if she and her friends had matched the two. "They were ill-suited. Both in interests and sensibility. Owen is a perfect fit."

"He broke it off." Katherine's eyes went dark. "It's been weeks since they've been together."

"He's still interested." Ruby sighed, and her eyes grew misty. "See how he keeps slanting little looks in her direction?"

Gladys decided Ruby was right. "Do either of you know what broke them up?"

The two women looked at each other and shook their heads.

Katherine doodled absently on the page below the names she'd written.

"You need to find out." Gladys decided it best to turn this reconnaissance work over to her friends.

The pencil stilled between Katherine's fingers. "Why us?"

Gladys rolled her eyes, an action perfected back in her twenties. "Do I need to spell it out for you?"

"Yes," Katherine said, and Ruby nodded. "You do."

Gladys had hoped Katherine would demand an explanation. There was nothing she liked more than commanding center stage with all eyes on her. Playing to her strengths, Gladys lowered her voice to a conspiratorial whisper and cast a pointed glance at Katherine.

"Your cousin Eliza is one of Lindsay's closest friends." Gladys paused to let that sink in before continuing. "You see Eliza and Kyle all the time. You're in the perfect position to pump them for information about what happened between Lindsay and Owen."

Gladys shifted her gaze to Ruby, who was eyeing the chocolate truffle on her plate. "Go ahead and eat it. You only live once."

When Ruby continued to merely gaze longingly at the truffle, Gladys picked it up and shoved it into her friend's hand. "That heart doctor of yours isn't God. Cutting down on fats and sweets isn't an edict from on high. Eat the damn thing."

"If you insist." Ruby popped the truffle into her mouth.

"Fin knows everything that goes on in this town, and she and her sisters are close. Ami is also close to Lindsay, so use that to your advantage. And don't forget Marigold. Go in for a trim. Hairdressers know nearly everything that goes on in a community. Don't count out Primrose. All the Bloom sisters spend a lot of time with Lindsay."

Ruby dabbed the last of the chocolate from her lips with the tips of a napkin. "Basically, you want me to shake down the entire Bloom family."

"You're practically family. And if you keep in mind you're doing this to bring happiness to a young woman we all love, it'll make the prying more palatable."

"What about you, Gladys?" Katherine's tone turned teasing. "How will you be aiding the effort?"

"Have you forgotten?" Gladys lifted a brow. Her smile stopped just short of a smirk. "Owen is giving me a ride home."

CHAPTER FIVE

"I appreciate the ride." Gladys forced a cheerful tone as Owen's pickup bounced down the lane to the highway. She couldn't recall the last time she'd experienced such a *lively* ride.

Then again, her Caddy's suspension was difficult to beat.

"I was happy to help." Owen sank back into silence for a few seconds, then must have decided that conversation was part of giving her a lift home. "Did you enjoy the reception?"

Gladys hadn't been born yesterday. She immediately saw through the ploy. Owen hoped to get her talking to divert attention off of him. Normally, Gladys liked to talk, especially about herself. But tonight, she was a woman on a mission.

This wonderful opportunity had nearly been lost. When Eliza had strolled up and told her she could ride home with her, as if it was a fait accompli, Gladys had been forced to rally.

Falling back on lessons learned over nine decades, she'd simply said, "No. Thank you. But, no."

The mistake most people made when declining an invitation was to blather on and on, making excuses. Excuses that often gave the other person's arguments traction.

Gladys considered the startled look that crossed Eliza's face a victory of sorts. Anyone in Good Hope could tell you that not many told Eliza Kendrick no.

"I had a remarkably lovely time." Gladys waved a hand in the air, admiring the way the truck cab's dim light caught the glitter in her red nail polish. "What about you?"

Though the expression on his face didn't change, at least not from the side, Owen shifted behind the wheel. "I've never been much for social events."

"I saw you dancing with Katie Ruth." Though Gladys was ninety-nine percent convinced Lindsay was the one for Owen, that wasn't who he'd squired around the dance floor. "Are you sweet on her?"

Owen's gaze jerked from the road to her. "What?"

"Katie Ruth is a lovely girl, and she's available." Gladys adopted a look of innocence. "You did ask her to dance."

"She asked me." He returned his attention to the dark ribbon of road and pressed on the accelerator.

Though the roadway was dry and he was still under the speed limit, if he continued zooming down the highway at this speed, she'd be home long before she had a chance to properly question him.

Gladys put a hand to her throat, a classic sign of distress in the theater world. "Would you please slow down?"

"I'm not even going the speed limit."

"Please."

At the tremor in her voice, Owen slanted a glance in her direction. "Why?"

"Speed scares me." She'd always been good at injecting fear into her voice, and she knew her matching facial expression was Academy Award level.

"You urged me to go over the limit on the way to the wedding." Though his tone was skeptical, he lightened the pressure on the accelerator.

Gladys smiled inwardly, then brought a hand to her chest and feigned confusion. "Did I?"

Of course she had. They'd been running late. She hadn't been able to decide which scarf to wear with her dress, and he'd been poke-assing his way down the highway like they were in a parade.

A fly buzzed by her face, and Gladys swatted at it. "Back to Katie Ruth."

"I'm not interested in her."

Gladys started to relax, then he continued. "I'm not interested in dating anyone right now."

Words to make an ordinary matchmaker quake in her high heels. It was a good thing, Gladys thought, that she'd never been *ordinary*.

"Why is that, Owen?" Gladys tapped a finger against her lips and studied him. She ignored the fly that bounced back to her, like one of those paddle balls on a string. "You're a young man with a thriving business. You even have a house. Why don't you want a sweetheart?"

He expelled a breath. "It's...complicated. It would take too long to explain."

Gladys settled back against the soft leather. "I'm not going anywhere."

They were driving the highway between Rakes Farm and Good Hope. Night had descended, and clouds obscured the light of the moon. The only illumination in the truck's cab came from the dashboard lights.

It was as if they were in a cocoon of sorts where secrets, long held close to the heart, could be spoken into the darkness. While she needed information to help him find his true love, Gladys would not break any confidences he might share with her tonight.

"You know I was married before." Owen's thick, workman hands tapped a rhythm against the steering wheel. "You know how that ended."

The fly landed on the dash and didn't move, as if awaiting her response.

"Some unions are simply not meant to be." Gladys had seen her share of unhappy marriages. It had gotten so she could sit in the church pew and predict which couples were headed toward bliss. And which were headed toward divorce.

While she hadn't been at Owen and Tessa Slattery's wedding, when she heard the two had married, she'd shaken her head. "I never thought you and Tess were well-suited."

The tapping on the steering wheel stopped. "I wasn't aware you were acquainted with Tessa."

"Oh, my dear boy, yes. Well acquainted. Years ago, we had a director at the community theater who strongly believed in encouraging youth to get involved with theater." Gladys's lips tipped up. She had fond memories of the man. "Unlike many programs, there was no charge to the boys and girls who wished to participate. Tessa was involved for three or four years."

Owen frowned. "Are you saying my ex-wife used to do theater?"

"If I'm recalling correctly, she was with us was from sixth through ninth grade."

"That doesn't sound like her." The tapping began again.

It was an annoying sound. The fly must have agreed, because it lifted off from the dash. Gladys inclined her head. "Tessa never mentioned her stint in the theater to you?"

"No. And I don't remember ever seeing her in any of the productions." Owen's tone rang heavy with disbelief.

"She preferred backstage activities to performing." Gladys's lips curved as she remembered. "She did a little of everything, finally settling on helping with the costumes. She was a hard worker."

"She's always worked hard for what she wanted." Puzzlement blanketed Owen's face. "Her being involved in theater doesn't make sense."

Gladys arched a brow. Though, because of the dim light, the subtlety of the gesture was probably lost on him. "Really?"

"You think it makes sense?" Owen huffed. "Tessa was all about getting ahead. Why would she waste her time with theater stuff?"

Gladys's hand came down hard on the dash, surprising both the fly and Owen. "The theater is a great training ground for many careers. And you seem to be forgetting that your ex-wife came from one of the poorest—and arguably craziest—families in Good Hope."

When Tessa had refused her offer of money for clothes, Gladys had found a way around the girl's pride. She'd begun paying Tessa for "helping" her with her lines.

Of course, Gladys hadn't needed help. Her memory was near photographic. The girl hadn't known that. "Young Tessa didn't have many friends. Being around the theater gave her not only a family but a place to be rather than the hovel she called home."

"I never knew her parents." Owen's eyes remained focused on the road. "She told me they left town a step ahead of the bill collectors her senior year."

"You didn't know her back then?"

Owen shook his head. "We didn't connect until junior college."

"She wasn't in your social circle in high school."

"I didn't have a social circle," Owen scoffed. "I was a gearhead, more interested in cars than in high school."

"You played football," Gladys pointed out. "You had friends. A decent car. A respectable family."

The fly swooped at Owen. His palm connected with it in midair.

"Why are we talking about Tessa?" Owen didn't bother to hide his irritation. "She's got nothing to do with me."

"What happened between you and Lindsay?"

Owen stiffened, but said nothing.

Between that and the way a muscle clenched in his jaw—a classic sign of irritation—Gladys had a feeling he wouldn't be offering to drive her again anytime soon.

"Based on what I heard, you and Tessa broke apart because of her ambition." Gladys didn't wait for him to answer. "That couldn't have been the case with Lindsay."

The silence didn't worry Gladys. She was a master at manipulating the conversational tool to her advantage. When several long seconds passed and the lights of Good Hope came into view, Gladys switched tactics.

Though goading the beast with outrageous comments wasn't her preference, time had become a factor.

"You have drive and ambition. It takes that kind of push to build a successful business." Gladys injected a note of boredom into her tone. "Lindsay is a nice enough girl, but she's always been someone satisfied with the status quo. Spending time with someone like her had to be frustrating."

Owen's fingers tightened around the steering wheel, his grip so tight his knuckles whitened. "Lindsay is a wonderful woman."

"But boring."

"She isn't boring." Owen shouted the words, then stopped and visibly reined in his anger. "I don't know what you think you're doing, but I'm not going to sit here and listen to you bad-mouth Lin."

"Fair enough." The intensity of his reaction told Gladys what she'd wanted to know. While she wasn't sure what had caused them to break apart, it was obvious Owen cared for the woman. "Did you hear she quit her job at the Enchanted Florist?"

His jaw jutted up. "She wouldn't do that."

Not quite calling her a liar, but coming darn close.

"She did." Gladys kept her tone light. "It appears our Lindsay is looking to make a change."

Owen slanted a sharp glance in her direction. "What kind of change?"

Gladys lifted a shoulder, wanting his mind to travel down a couple of uncomfortable roads before she shared.

"Is she moving?"

"You mean away from Good Hope?" Gladys felt a momentary

pinch of disappointment when Owen wheeled the truck into her driveway. Until she realized it was for the best.

She'd discovered what she needed to know. Granted, Owen hadn't revealed any deep, dark secrets. That was okay. She now knew he still held a torch for Lindsay. That's all Gladys needed to move forward.

Owen shut off the engine and shifted in his seat to face her. "Does Lindsay plan to move out of Good Hope?"

Gladys smiled and opened her door. "You'll have to ask her."

As she and the fly—which apparently had been down but not out—made their grand exit, Gladys experienced a surge of excitement. Matchmaking was far more fun than she'd anticipated.

～

SUNDAY MORNING FOUND Lindsay at First Christian, seated in a pew beside two teenage girls who were conversing with each other via text. She didn't mind. It was better than sitting beside someone who wanted to talk.

The last time she was here, Etta Hawley—a former teacher— had grilled her about her breakup with Pastor Dan. She knew the woman had a kind heart and hadn't meant anything by the inquisition, but Lindsay had left church with her stomach churning.

It had been easier to stay away. Seeing Dan every week was too difficult. Not because she loved him and regretted calling off their wedding, but because she regretted accepting his proposal in the first place.

When he'd gotten down on one knee in the midst of friends and family and unexpectedly popped the question, she'd been struck speechless. At that moment, she'd known how a deer felt when caught in the glow of headlights.

Though she didn't love him, she liked and respected the minister. In the end, she'd realized Dan deserved better than a woman who not only didn't love him, but who didn't even want to be a minister's wife.

"Today, we're going to talk about personal responsibility."

Dan's words cut through her thoughts and forced her attention back to the sermon.

"Studies show we're happier when we take responsibility for our actions." Dan's gaze swept the congregation. "But all around us, we see people who don't do that. Making excuses for bad behavior isn't just something others do, we do it, too."

Lindsay shifted uneasily on the pew that suddenly seemed too hard.

"How many times have you taken on a victim mentality? Something goes wrong at your job, and the first thing you say is, 'It's not my fault.' Sometimes you cast blame on someone else, even though you bear some of the responsibility. Or maybe you're in high school. You receive a failing grade on a paper. What's the first thing you do?"

The girls on Lindsay's right stilled. For the first time since the sermon began, she sensed the teens were listening.

She was listening, too.

"You blame the teacher. He or she should have given you more information about what they wanted, or they graded you too harshly on grammar or content."

The girls slunk low in their seats.

"It isn't simply embracing the victim mentality that gets you in trouble, it's that feeling of entitlement. You *deserve* that raise. You *deserve* to be promoted."

Lindsay thought of Shirley Allbright. Looking back, it had been obvious for months that she'd wanted her daughters more involved in the business. The signs had all been there, but Lindsay had refused to see what was coming.

Yet, she'd put all the blame on Shirley.

"God is watching you, rooting for you." Dan's voice, deep with conviction, filled the sanctuary. "He wants you to rise to the occasion, to handle whatever responsibly life throws at you. Sometimes, things happen we don't foresee. Sometimes, our choices put us in difficult situations."

Her hand stole to her abdomen, where a tiny life grew inside her. She and Owen had thought only of sating their physical desires. They were both old enough to know no birth control was one hundred percent effective.

"The media would have us believe that you need to be concerned only about yourself when you make a decision." Dan's gaze searched the crowd. He smiled slightly. "Many of you are probably thinking it's nobody's business how you live your life."

The girl next to her poked her friend.

"You think it doesn't matter because it doesn't affect anyone but you." He stood behind the pulpit, a tall man with dark hair and piercing hazel eyes. "You're wrong. Every decision we make affects someone else."

Lindsay had seen firsthand how her sister's pregnancies and poor choices had affected the family. She'd tried not to think about how *her* being a single parent would affect her mom and sister. How it would affect Owen.

Guilt swelled and threatened to swamp her.

Lindsay couldn't listen anymore. She pulled her eyes from Dan. Glancing around, she instead focused on seeing which friends were in attendance.

Near the front, she spotted Eliza, Kyle, and Katherine in the family pew. Ami and Beck were several rows behind them on the same side. Their baby, Sarah Rose—who these days seemed more toddler than baby—stood in the pew, alertly gazing back over the congregation.

Ami's firstborn was a pretty child, with Beck's dark hair and her mother's green eyes. Lindsay found herself wondering what her child would look like. Blond hair like hers? Or Owen's sandy brown? Blue eyes? Or hazel? Perhaps this child would resemble neither of them.

Her gaze drifted to her left, and she spotted the other three Bloom sisters and their husbands. While Ruby sat with Fin and Jeremy, Gladys sat alone on the aisle, which told Lindsay that her son, Frank, must still be recovering from knee surgery.

Gladys caught her eye and gave her a wink.

Lindsay smiled back, the silly gesture lightening her mood. As the pastor continued to speak, Lindsay's eyes continued to wander.

Until they landed on Owen.

She inhaled so sharply the girl next to her gave her a curious glance. Then, apparently deciding she wasn't going to fall over dead or do anything else interesting, the teen returned her attention to her phone.

Lindsay couldn't pull her gaze away from Owen.

The look in his eyes told her that, while she might have gotten away with not discussing pregnancy implications last night, time had effectively run out.

CHAPTER SIX

While Lindsay acknowledged that while she and Owen needed to talk, a church wasn't the place for such a discussion. Tomorrow would be better.

A part of her wondered if she was simply trying to put it off. She already knew what would happen during the conversation. Owen would propose. He was responsible to a fault. Just hearing him utter the words would be a knife to the heart.

Instead of joyously flinging herself into his arms for a passionate kiss to seal their proposed union, she would have to tell him no.

Pulling her gaze away, Lindsay focused on the service. She stood when the congregation stood, sat when everyone around her sat. Sang words to hymns while on autopilot. All the while conscious of Owen's searing gaze on her.

As the service drew to a close, Lindsay was ready to implement her exit strategy. Being on the aisle and at the back was a definite advantage this morning. Especially with Owen farther up and stuck in the middle of his row.

If she wouldn't look like a crazed jackrabbit, she'd sprint out the door now. Purse strap already over her shoulder, Lindsay bolted for the exit on the last note of the final hymn. The large doors that opened to the front steps were in sight when a woman stepped directly in front of her.

"I was wondering if you had a minute to chat?" Gladys, dressed in a caftan of eye-popping orange and purple, flashed a broad smile.

"Now isn't really a good time." Lindsay stepped to the side, intending to go around the woman.

Obviously anticipating the movement, Gladys moved and once again blocked her path.

"Is there ever a bad time for honest dialogue?" Gladys's pale blue eyes pinned Lindsay. "Putting things off is a coward's way of dealing with a situation."

What was the woman talking about? The only thing Gladys might possibly need to speak with her about had to do with the booths Lindsay was overseeing for the upcoming Harvest Festival.

"Gladys." Owen appeared, slightly out of breath, at Gladys's side. "Hello, Lindsay."

The older woman's gaze shifted between the two, and she cackled. "Oh, I'm interrupting. I forgot you young folks head over to Muddy Boots after Sunday services. Don't let me keep you."

When the woman turned to leave, Lindsay grabbed Gladys's sleeve. "You said there was something we needed to discuss. You made it sound urgent."

"Our discussion can wait." Gladys patted her hand. "I wouldn't want to get between you and Owen."

Then the woman was gone, weaving her way through the crowd.

Owen took Lindsay's arm, a pleasant smile on his face but steel in his fingertips.

"Owen, I know you're upset—"

"Upset?" His voice remained low and for her ears only, but anger ran like a molten thread through the word. "You lay what you laid on me last night, then walk away. Right now, you were headed for the exit, obviously hoping to avoid me. How is that fair, Lindsay?"

Lindsay accepted time had run out. Whether she was emotionally ready or not, they would discuss the pregnancy.

"I don't want to go to Muddy Boots with the others." Lindsay spoke quickly when she saw her friends approaching.

"I don't, either."

"Hey, you two." Ami's gaze slid curiously from Owen to her.

Lindsay ignored the question in Ami's eyes.

"Are you guys coming to Muddy Boots?" Marigold, Ami's youngest sister, rushed up, her blond hair a riot of curls around her shoulders.

Her husband, Cade, who'd been elected sheriff after Len Swarts's retirement, was at her side. The couple, young and in love, had been trying to get pregnant almost since they'd said *I do*. For some reason, having a child had so far eluded them.

Yet, the single time Lindsay had sex without maximum protection, she found herself pregnant.

"Since it's such a beautiful day, Lindsay and I decided to skip breakfast and take a walk." Owen took her hand, his tone conversational. "We'll catch up with you later."

Eliza's gaze zeroed in on Lindsay's hand gripped tightly in Owen's. As she and her husband had just strolled up, she'd missed most of what Owen had said. The fire in her eyes said if Lindsay needed a champion, Eliza was ready to fight the battle.

But Owen was right. Lindsay owed him this time. She met Eliza's gaze. "I'm looking forward to a walk."

Plastering a smile on her lips, she turned to Owen. "Ready?"

Only when they'd turned the corner of the block and were out of sight, did Lindsay pull back her hand. It was difficult to think straight when he was touching her.

Lindsay thought of all the times she'd chastised her sister for letting feelings cloud her good sense. For the first time, she understood how easily that could happen.

In so many ways, Lindsay would love to go along with whatever Owen suggested, especially if he proposed. Her love hadn't waned in the weeks they'd been apart.

But she refused to be like Cassie, begging for a man's love, settling for whatever crumbs he deigned to give her. Logic, not emotion, would guide her decisions and actions.

Her son or daughter deserved better than life with a father who felt trapped in a marriage he didn't want. She deserved better than a life with a man who didn't love her.

All around her, the leaves were taking on the brilliant colors of fall. Some trees, those ahead of the seasonal curve, had not only changed, but were already dropping their leaves.

When Lindsay had been a child, she'd loved the sights and smells of fall. She especially loved the crunch of leaves beneath her boots. Would her child one day find wonder in such simple joys?

"I didn't mean to lay all that on you last night." Lindsay finally broke the silence. "It wasn't the right time or place."

"It wasn't your secret to keep." Owen's tone was matter-of-fact, but a muscle jumped in his jaw. "I imagine this happened July Fourth. Things got a little wild and crazy that night."

Just for a second, his lips quirked upward as if he was recalling their unbridled passion.

"That fits with my due date." Though the air was calm and the day unseasonably warm, it was still September in northern Wisconsin. Lindsay wished her jacket was warmer.

"You said late March. When exactly is the baby due?"

"March twenty-seventh."

Owen gave a jerky nod, then stopped to open a gilded black wrought-iron gate.

He motioned to her, and Lindsay stepped inside the perfectly manicured downtown park. The bushes, sculpted by expert gardening hands into the shapes of mythical creatures, usually made her smile.

Today, she simply moved to the bench by the bush in the shape of a dragon. She sat, fingering the smooth, green leaves, and waited.

Taking a seat beside her, Owen's gaze searched her face. "Finding out you're pregnant had to be a shock."

His tone remained reasonable. Lindsay allowed herself to hope this wouldn't be as difficult as she'd imagined.

She decided to start at the beginning. "When I missed my period in July, I told myself it was simply due to the stress I was under at the time."

His brows pulled together in puzzlement. "Why were you stressed?"

"You and I had just cut ties, and Shirley was acting weird." Lindsay shrugged. "I told myself that once things settled down, my system would get back to normal."

"It didn't."

"No." Lindsay let go of the branch she'd been toying with and realized she'd plucked off all the leaves. "When I missed another month, I began to be concerned."

"You took a pregnancy test," he offered when the silence lengthened.

Lindsay gave a little laugh. "That's probably what I should have done. Instead, I kept my head in the sand a little while longer."

She remembered the exact moment it hit her she might be pregnant. The flower shop had been crazy busy, and Shirley's daughters had been bickering. She'd tried to block out their squabbling by focusing on a centerpiece she was putting together for a baby shower.

Out of the blue, a chill had swept over her. She hadn't been consciously thinking about her situation, but it had struck her then that pregnancy was a real possibility.

"When did you finally decide to do the test?" Owen's voice remained calm.

She jerked her gaze to him, reassured by his placid expression.

Why had she worried he'd initially explode when he heard the news? Probably because that was what Bernie Fishback, her mother's second husband, would have done. While Bernie was a nice enough guy, he was easily riled. When he was riled, he yelled. And he—

"Lindsay?"

"I made an appointment with my doctor. I wanted a definitive answer. I knew over-the-counter tests aren't always accurate, but—"

"But..." he prompted.

"I couldn't wait." Lindsay chewed on her bottom lip. "I wanted to be prepared, so I took the test last Friday, right before my appointment."

"It was positive."

"The word 'pregnant' leapt out at me." She tried a smile, but it wobbled, so she gave up on the attempt. "The doctor confirmed it."

His hazel eyes were as serious as she'd ever seen them, his expression guarded. "I'm sorry you had to go to that visit alone."

Not, I wish I'd been there to share the moment.

Pregnancy confirmations were usually an exciting time, one followed by joyous celebrations with friends and family. Lindsay thought of Marigold and her husband, Cade. If Marigold had been the one who'd gotten pregnant, Cade would have been with her at that first appointment.

She pictured the two grinning at each other as their baby's heartbeat filled the room. As much as Lindsay felt sorry for herself, she felt sorrier for her baby.

Every child deserved the joy.

She clenched her hands into fists to still the tremors. "I'll text you updates after each appointment. Once the baby is born, we can discuss visitation."

"This is my baby, too, Lin." His steady gaze never left hers. "Texting and visitation won't cut it."

❦

OWEN WASN'T SURPRISED at the swarm of emotion that flooded Lindsay's eyes. She was a warm, passionate woman who wore her heart on her sleeve.

He couldn't believe he hadn't seen this coming. Or that he hadn't given a thought to the fact that there could be consequences to not using a condom that night.

"It isn't necessary for us to decide anything right now." Lindsay's voice cut through his thoughts.

"It is necessary. From this moment forward, I want to share in every aspect of my child's life." His voice cracked, then broke. Owen cleared his throat. "The only logical solution is for us to marry."

Lindsay snapped off a branch of the bush next to her. He watched as her fingers began breaking it into tiny sections. She kept her gaze averted and shook her head.

"You told me you'd never be a single mother." He recalled the conversation vividly. The subject of her sister had come up one evening. Lindsay had been adamant that she would never go down that path.

Her lips twisted in a humorless smile. "Sometimes, life takes us in a direction we wouldn't choose to go."

"This pregnancy may not have been planned"—Owen chose his words carefully—"but that doesn't mean you have to do this alone. I want to be a father to our child. You don't want to be a single mother. Marriage makes sense."

Lindsay cocked her head. "You're telling me that, in order to have the child fully in your life, you're willing to have me as your wife?"

In one way, he was awed—and excited—about the new life he and Lindsay had created. At the same time, he found himself wanting to run ninety miles an hour in the opposite direction. He wouldn't. He took responsibility for his actions. "Being married to you wouldn't be horrible."

She flinched as if he'd slapped her.

"Sorry. That came out wrong." He lifted his hands. "You and I get along. We can have a good marriage."

The branch in Lindsay's hands snapped. "How?"

"How what?"

"How can we have a good marriage, Owen? You don't love me. You broke up with me. You didn't even want to continue to date. Now you want to marry me? Live under the same roof? Raise a child together?" She shook her head. "Not happening."

Owen fought to hide his surprise. He'd thought he'd made a good case for the two of them marrying, but he might have been too blunt. "I like you, Lindsay. We have fun together."

When her eyes flashed, he realized that instead of digging himself out, the hole had just gotten a whole lot deeper.

Damn it all to hell.

Owen raked a hand through his hair. Nothing was coming out right. He'd never been a smooth talker, but Lindsay had told him she liked that he spoke the truth without a lot of fluff.

"Liking each other and having fun together is nice when you're dating. It's not enough for a marriage."

When she paused, he jumped in. "What about a baby? Isn't that enough?"

The look of sadness that skittered across her face had him wanting to pull her close and comfort her. He knew the tough exterior she was showing him right now wasn't natural.

He wished he knew why she was being so stubborn.

Just when he'd given up on her responding, she spoke. "No. A baby isn't enough of a reason."

His hands clenched. "Is it Ethan?"

Her head swiveled. "Ethan?"

"Will you continue to date him?" Owen spoke haltingly.

"I won't be seeing him again."

Owen nodded, experiencing a surge of relief.

"I think a baby is a pretty good reason for marrying," he repeated.

"I disagree."

Owen fought an urge to press the issue. The determined glint in her eyes said the effort would be pointless. Worse yet, an argument might only succeed in putting more distance between them at a time when they needed to be drawing closer.

"Are you moving out of town?"

"What makes you ask that?"

He noticed she hadn't answered his question. "You quit your job."

"I'm going into business for myself." Her hand floated aimlessly in the air. "It was time."

"Are you starting this business in Good Hope?"

"Yes."

Owen let out the breath he hadn't realized he was holding. "Okay."

"Okay?"

"We'll table the marriage discussion for now." Owen met her gaze. "But I will be a part of this pregnancy."

Lindsay hesitated. "I suppose if you want, you can come to my doctor's appointments with me."

She tossed the invitation out there as if it was nothing, when in fact he knew it was a huge concession.

"I have an ultrasound scheduled for tomorrow," she added.

Mondays were busy at the garage, and with one man still recovering from shoulder surgery, they were already short-handed. "I'll be there. What time?"

"Four thirty." She rattled off the doctor's name and the office address. "If you can't get away, just text me."

"I'll be there." His gaze never left hers. If he had to go back and work until midnight, he wasn't going to miss this appointment. "Count on it."

CHAPTER SEVEN

The meetings of the Women's Events League, the group commonly referred to as the Cherries, were always on a Monday. Lindsay's conversation with Owen yesterday had left her feeling out of sorts. She'd have skipped the meeting, but she was the point person on the booths that would be set up in the town square for the Harvest Festival.

Lindsay opened the gate leading up to Hill House, then quickened her step. To say Eliza didn't like members arriving late would be an understatement.

Now that she didn't have a job, there was no reason Lindsay couldn't be on time. Other than dread.

Her mother would be attending today's meeting. So far, Lindsay had managed to dodge her texts and e-mails, all of which centered around Ethan Shaw.

The heavy wooden door leading into the Victorian home that was now used for civic events was unlocked. Lindsay pushed it open and winced at the loud creak.

Stepping inside, Lindsay pushed it closed, then padded as quietly as she could through the foyer to the front parlor.

As expected, wooden folding chairs were arranged in a semi-circle. Eliza stood at a podium in the front, giving a report.

Lindsay scanned the chairs for an empty one. She'd hoped for something close, one she could slip into without creating too much notice.

"Over here." Gladys's booming voice filled the air as she waved to Lindsay, pointing to a chair next to her on the far side of the room.

Eliza paused and fixed her gray eyes on Lindsay.

The fact that they were friends didn't stop the executive director of the Cherries from giving Lindsay a disapproving glance. "May I remind you the meeting starts promptly at one?"

"Sorry." Lindsay slipped around the back of the chairs to where Gladys sat and took the empty seat next to her.

The older woman winked and gave Lindsay's arm a reassuring squeeze.

Lindsay kept her gaze focused straight ahead.

"You didn't miss anything." Gladys spoke in what could only be described as a stage whisper.

Lindsay didn't shift her attention from Eliza. After arriving late, there was no way she was going to give her friend a reason to come down on her for talking.

"Katie Ruth." Eliza's gaze shifted to the perky blonde. "Please update the membership on what you've learned."

Lindsay studied the pretty blonde with the cornflower-blue eyes. The woman had held a variety of jobs since returning to Good Hope after college. Currently, she served as the youth activity coordinator for the YMCA.

Replacing Eliza at the podium, Katie Ruth flashed her trade-mark smile. "As you know, the Harvest Festival will be early this year. We are incorporating the special homecoming activities planned by the high school into our normal festival events."

"I've said this before, but I'll say it again." Anita's voice rang out in the silent room from the front row. "I'm not in favor of combining the two events."

Unlike her daughter, who'd gone for comfort in black leggings and a leopard-print tunic, Anita looked ready for a Fifth Avenue board meeting in a boxy, gold-tweed suit.

As if conscious that all eyes were on her, Anita smoothed back a wayward lock of hair before turning in her seat. Her gaze swept the room. "I feel that—"

"Anita." The second of preening had given Eliza time to reclaim the podium. The tight set to her mouth showed her displeasure at the interruption. "Please allow Katie Ruth the courtesy of completing her report. Then, if you have a question, raise your hand and you will be acknowledged."

The executive director, stylish in a black cashmere dress, stepped back and gestured for Katie Ruth to continue.

There weren't many people who could put Anita Fishback in her place, but Eliza Kendrick did it without breaking a sweat. The way her mother's lips pressed together told Lindsay she was holding on to control by a thread.

Katie Ruth smiled, and her gaze drifted around the room. "I anticipate the details in my report will answer any of your questions. But, like Eliza said, if I've missed something or not explained it clearly, I'm certainly open to questions."

Eliza glanced at the grandfather clock. "We're behind schedule."

Everyone in the room knew what that statement meant. Katie Ruth needed to speed up her report.

"My contact at the high school confirmed Krew Slattery will return to Good Hope. He *will* be on the field when his jersey is retired." Katie Ruth clapped her hands. "Yay."

Eliza's throat-clearing had the blonde continuing. "The fact that Krew was the NFL's MVP last season will make the parade and the ceremony a huge tourist draw. He's also—"

Katie Rose paused, and Gladys made a drum roll sound that had most everyone in the room smiling, including Eliza. "He's also agreed to direct a one-day football camp while he's here, with the money raised from registration going into the Giving Tree coffers."

The Giving Tree wasn't a charity, but rather a neighbor-helping-neighbor fund with money raised going to help residents who'd fallen on hard times.

As Katie Ruth continued to speak about the homecoming weekend, Lindsay stole a look at her mother. Though her mom gave no indication of inner turmoil—other than maybe a jaw clenched a little too tightly—Lindsay knew the mention of Krew had reminded her of his past with Lindsay's older sister.

Cassie had once been a bookish, straight-A student. She'd also been very close to her father. When Richard Lohmeier died of a heart attack when Cassie was twelve, she'd had difficulty coping. The fact that she and her mother had an oil-and-water relationship had made middle school a difficult time for Cassie.

By the time she'd reached her freshman year in high school, they had a stepfather to deal with as well.

Co-captain of the Good Hope High football team, Krew had been a senior, a good-looking, popular boy from one of the most dysfunctional families in Good Hope. When Cassie had shown up pregnant after a beach party where she'd been seen kissing Krew Slattery, Anita had made the leap that he was the father.

Cassie had admitted kissing him, but denied having sex with him.

That fall, Krew had headed off to Ohio State on a football scholarship. The next spring, Cassie had given birth to Dakota. Though she eventually got her GED, Cassie's downward spiral had begun.

"To say I'm excited would be an understatement." Katie's glee-filled voice broke through Lindsay's thoughts, and she lifted her head just in time to see Katie Ruth sweep the air with one hand.

"This is going to be the best Harvest Festival and homecoming ever."

For a second, Lindsay expected Katie Ruth to pull out a couple of pompons from behind the podium and lead the group in a cheer. The image made her smile.

Applause filled the room.

"Fabulous work, Katie Ruth."

Eliza's words brought two bright spots of color to Katie Ruth's cheeks. The executive director was not one to be effusive with her praise.

Buoyed by her success, Katie Ruth glanced at Anita. "Did I answer your questions, Anita?"

Lindsay's heart froze. She knew Anita's objections didn't have a thing to do with combining the Cherries' events with homecoming.

"You answered them." Anita waved a dismissive hand. "It was a clear and concise report."

Lindsay wasn't surprised that her mother had taken a step back, once she'd had time to reconsider. Cassie had denied she slept with Krew that night, hadn't mentioned him since, and Anita's suspicions were simply suspicions. Moreover, the man she'd once accused without proof was now a hometown hero.

"Lindsay." Eliza's tone held a firm edge.

She jerked her head up.

Gladys leaned close, her voice barely above a whisper. "It's time for your report."

Lindsay scrambled to her feet. Knowing time was tight, she began speaking before she reached the podium. "All your favorite booths will be back in the town square, along with a few new fun activities. In addition to a cow-milking competition for kids, various high school clubs will be putting up homecoming displays in the square."

Once she reached the podium, she relaxed. "The public will be encouraged to vote for their favorite display. To bring together the homecoming theme with the Harvest Festival, the creative use of a hand-crafted scarecrow is to be included in each display. Any questions?"

In the back row, Gladys's hand shot up.

Lindsay inclined her head.

"What's the purpose of the voting?"

"Good question." Lindsay couldn't believe she'd left that out. "Everyone who votes will be entered into a drawing to win a football signed by Krew and his Green Bay teammates. Also, I failed to mention that club members who worked on the winning display will receive tickets for free early admission to this year's Halloween haunted house."

When she saw several puzzled glances, she added, "Numerous teachers at the high school confirmed the tickets are highly prized by the students."

"Thank you, Lindsay." Eliza moved to her side. Her sharp, gray eyes swept over the group. "Any further questions? No? This concludes our meeting. We are adjourned."

Lindsay barely heard the gavel hit the podium. Her entire focus was on her mother, now making a beeline toward her.

"I can run interference." Eliza's voice was a soft whisper in her ear.

"Thanks. I can handle her."

"Around if you need me." Eliza stepped away to answer a member's question just as Anita reached the podium.

"Have you been avoiding me?"

"It's nice to see you, too." Lindsay kept her words light. "I looked for you at church yesterday."

"Len and I—" Anita's cheeks turned a deep, dusky rose. "I slept in."

Was she running a fever? Concerned, Lindsay touched her mother's arm. "Are you feeling okay?"

"I'm fine," Anita snapped, then visibly calmed herself. "I thought you might like to grab a cup of coffee with me. My treat."

Lindsay's doctor's appointment wasn't until the end of the day. Perhaps spending time with her mother would keep her mind off the fact that Owen would be there. "I have time, but don't you need to get back to the shop?"

Anita might have gotten the money to open Crumb and Cake in her divorce settlement from Bernie, but the success of the bakery was due to her own hard work and business savvy.

"I always have time for my favorite daughter." Anita looped her arm through Lindsay's. "And we have lots to talk about."

LINDSAY DIDN'T KNOW what to think when her mother directed them toward the Daily Grind, the coffeeshop where Cassie worked. For her sister's sake, Lindsay hoped Cassie wasn't working this afternoon.

Lindsay stepped inside to the jingle of the door, followed by her mother. It didn't surprise her that the business was quiet. Tourism dropped off after Labor Day.

There was no one behind the counter, but by the time they'd taken several steps, Cassie appeared from the dining area around the corner, coffeepot in hand.

At five feet, eight inches, she and Lindsay were the same height. With similar features and hair the same shade of blond, there was no mistaking they were sisters.

Lindsay thought her sister looked happier than she had in years. Her makeup emphasized the green-blue of her eyes, and the pink gloss drew attention to her full lips. But the bounce to her step and genuine smile on her face erased the hard years from her face.

The smile disappeared when she spotted her mother.

"I wondered if anyone was working."

Lindsay rolled her eyes at Anita's obvious dig. Obviously, her mother had expected her sister to be waiting behind the counter, ready to step up and serve her the second she stepped through the door.

Cassie lifted the glass pot. "Just taking around refills."

"It's nice to see—" Lindsay began.

"Cass, I think I *will* take another doughnut. You—" Dan skidded to a stop. The minister's smile froze as his gaze shifted from Lindsay to Anita. "What a nice surprise."

Anita narrowed her eyes. "Shouldn't you be at the church?"

Dan raised a brow.

"You know." Anita made a circular motion with a hand tipped with bronze-colored nails. "Tending to your flock."

"The secretary can reach me on my cell if any of my flock stops by." Dan's eyes held a twinkle. "I often come here to work on my sermons."

Dan surprised them by slanting a glance in Cassie's direction. "Your daughter has lots of good suggestions."

A knot formed in Lindsay's stomach. When they'd been engaged, Dan had asked her for input on his sermons. She'd put him off.

"Cassie?" Anita scoffed. "I suppose it proves there's benefits to taking a lot of wrong turns."

Two bright patches of color appeared on Cassie's cheeks.

Dan's lips formed a hard line. "We all fall short of the glory of God."

"Whatever." As if bored by the conversation, Anita turned to Lindsay. "I've decided I'm not in the mood for a pastry and coffee. Let's go somewhere else."

Lindsay thought about protesting. Walking out would be incredibly rude to both Cassie and Dan.

What stopped her was the bald hope in Cassie's gaze. She didn't want their mother there.

"It was good seeing you both." Lindsay injected a note of warmth into her tone when she turned to her sister and Dan.

Anita merely inclined her head in a regal nod.

Dan remained by the counter when Lindsay and her mother left the shop.

Anita didn't look back, but Lindsay did.

The pastor put a hand on her sister's arm, his expression intense. Lindsay could see he was attempting to reassure Cassie. It made her happy to know her sister had a good friend in the minister.

"Mom, wait." Lindsay stopped when they reached the sidewalk. She made a big show of looking at the time on her phone. "I forgot I have a meeting with Eliza this afternoon. She's giving me space in her shop for my new business, and we're figuring out the best placement."

Suspicion glittered in Anita's hazel eyes. "If you had plans with her, why did you come with me?"

Because I knew you wouldn't take no for an answer. Because I hoped you'd divert me from thoughts of Owen.

"I had time for a quick cup of coffee, but..." Lindsay allowed her voice to trail off and let her mother fill in the blanks.

"Your sister has a penchant for ruining things." Anita huffed out a breath. "Did she look heavier around the middle to you?"

Puzzled, Lindsay stared at her mother. Cassie was as slender as a willow branch. "No. Why?"

"If that girl is pregnant again..." Anita shook her head, her lips twisting in displeasure. "I know what she'd say, what she always says. It just happened. Unbelievable. With so many birth control options, if a woman gets pregnant, it's because she wanted to have a baby. Or, more likely, it's a way to trap a man."

Lindsay's heart slammed against her ribs, then began beating an erratic rhythm. She didn't dare glance at her mother, fearful what her expression might give away.

When the silence between them lengthened and she sensed her mother's assessing gaze, Lindsay managed a little laugh. "Well, I don't think you have anything to worry about with Cassie. With three kids still at home, plus her job, she doesn't have time to date."

"You don't need to date to get pregnant."

The snide tone pushed all the right buttons. Lindsay had heard enough, had had enough. She whirled and let her anger show. "Cassie has a job. Maybe it's not the prestigious one you've always wanted for your daughter, just like me being a floral designer has never been good enough. But Cass is getting her life in order. I, for one, am very proud of her."

Lindsay was out of breath by the time she finished. Her chest heaved. Her hands shook.

"What bee got in your bonnet?" Anita studied her as a scientist might study a bug under a microscope. "I know Cassie has struggled. And no, I never believed that working for Shirley was enough of a challenge for you."

When her mother laid a hand on her arm, Lindsay didn't know what to think.

"You are a talented woman." Anita met her gaze. "Shirley never gave you the credit you deserve. Though I may not say it often, I'm proud of you."

The flush of pleasure at the compliment was tempered by the disappointment Lindsay knew her mother would experience when she discovered she was pregnant. "Thank you."

"Now." Her mother's eyes sparkled. "Before you head off for your meeting with Eliza, tell me how long you've been dating her brother."

CHAPTER EIGHT

Lindsay resisted the urge to swipe her sweaty palms against her red pencil skirt as she and Owen stepped into her doctor's office.

When he'd met her in the lobby, she'd noticed she wasn't the only one who'd dressed up for the visit. If his still slightly damp hair and smooth face were any indication, Owen had shaved and showered, then pulled on a pair of khakis and a plaid button-up shirt after leaving the Greasy Wrench.

"Dr. Swanson, this is Owen Vaughn."

Thankfully, when Lindsay hesitated, unsure how to explain their relationship, Janice Swanson stepped forward and extended her hand.

"It's a pleasure to meet you, Owen." The doctor was a tall, slender woman in her mid-forties with a choppy bob of silver hair. "I'm happy you could make it. The first ultrasound is an experience most expectant parents never forget."

"I'll be coming with Lindsay to all her visits," Owen announced, a determined jut to his chin.

"That's fabulous." The doctor's expression softened. "While I understand it isn't always possible, I encourage my patients to bring their partners to the visits."

Partner.

As he wasn't her husband, Lindsay supposed partner was as good a term as any.

She glanced around Dr. Swanson's office. The OB-GYN group occupied the second floor of the medical office building on the edge of Good Hope. The wheat-colored walls and pictures with accent colors of red and yellow promoted a feeling of tranquility.

Unlike last week's exam room, which had had no windows, light streamed into the office from the wall of floor-to-ceiling windows. Ignoring her contemporary desk with its sweeping curves, Dr. Swanson motioned to a seating area where an ultra-modern, ivory leather love seat and two matching chairs were casually grouped.

Lindsay sat on the love seat, while the doctor chose one of the chairs angled toward her. She thought Owen might choose the other chair. Instead, he dropped down beside her.

He was stiff and rigid, his jaw clenched so tight that a tiny muscle jumped in his cheek. Lindsay wondered if being in a medical setting brought back memories of all the treatments he'd gone to with Mindy. Visits where bad news had become the norm.

Her heart swelled with sympathy. She rested her hand on his arm and found the muscles rock hard beneath his shirt sleeve.

If he noticed the touch, he gave no indication. His gaze remained firmly fixed on the doctor.

"When Lindsay was here last week, I confirmed the pregnancy." The doctor leaned forward, her posture relaxed, her tone conversational. She was recapping the visit for Owen, Lindsay realized, getting him up to speed and attempting to put him at ease.

"We drew blood for several routine tests. I wrote a prescription for prenatal vitamins."

Dr. Swanson slanted a questioning glance in her direction.

"I picked them up from the pharmacy and started on them that same day." When the doctor had mentioned the importance of extra folic acid early in pregnancy, Lindsay wished she hadn't waited so long to schedule her first visit.

"I knew you'd follow through." The doctor turned to Owen. "There wasn't time for us to squeeze in an ultrasound on Friday. It appears that was for the best, since now you can be here to share the experience with Lindsay."

"Is it necessary?" Owen asked.

"For you to be here?" The doctor hesitated. "While it isn't absolutely nec—"

"No. The ultrasound. Is it necessary?" Owen cleared his throat. "Do you suspect something is wrong?"

Though the question didn't appear to surprise the doctor, it surprised Lindsay.

"It's routine," Lindsay assured Owen.

"In answer to your question, no, I don't suspect anything is wrong. Lindsay is correct. It's routine, and it's safe for both her and the child." Dr. Swanson kept her voice even and her eyes on Owen. "The ultrasound is simply a tool to evaluate the growth and development of the fetus."

Suspicion lingered in Owen's hazel depths. "That's it?"

"As Lindsay came to me at the end of the first trimester, she's far enough along for me to do some further assessment today. I'll look for any fetal anomalies, check the placenta position and the amount of amniotic fluid present. If you want—and your child cooperates—I'll tell you the baby's sex."

"I'd like to know." Lindsay glanced at Owen. "If you don't, you could step out when—"

"I want to know, too." A muscle in his jaw jumped.

"Well, then, let's hope baby cooperates." Dr. Swanson shifted her gaze to Lindsay. "Did you drink the water?"

Lindsay nodded. "Six glasses."

At Owen's questioning look, the doctor explained, "A full bladder changes the position of the uterus so it's easier to scan.

The fluid in the bladder also is a good medium for sound conduction." Dr. Swanson studied both of them for a second. "Any other questions before we get started?"

"Thank you for taking time to explain all of this to me." Owen spoke haltingly. "I've been through this before. But it's been a long time."

A smile broke over the doctor's face. "You have a child."

"I did." Owen's expression went flat. "My daughter died of a brain tumor."

"I'm so sorry. I can't imagine how hard that must have been." The doctor's voice softened. "Was it recently?"

"Last spring." Owen surged to his feet. "Where do you do the ultrasound?"

Lindsay and the doctor stood.

Owen's shoulder brushed hers as they made their way down the hall.

The doctor kept the conversation light. Lindsay didn't expect her to stay for the procedure, but Dr. Swanson told the tech she had time in her schedule.

When the heartbeat filled the room, Owen's eyes widened. "It's fast."

"One sixty is completely normal." The doctor studied the screen. "The measurements indicate we're on target for the end of March."

Owen squinted at the screen. His brows pulled together as if he tried to make sense of the shapes and shadows. "Do you see anything abnormal?"

Lindsay held her breath.

"No. All good." The doctor studied the screen intently. "There *is* something I don't see."

Lindsay and Owen exchanged worried glances.

"What's that?" Lindsay managed to utter when she found her voice.

"A penis." A slow smile lifted the doctor's lips. "Congratulations. You're having a girl."

"ARE YOU DISAPPOINTED?" Lindsay waited until they were outside the clinic and in the parking lot to ask.

Owen turned slowly to face her. Confusion furrowed his brow. "Disappointed?"

"That we're having a girl." Lindsay's hand dropped to her still-flat belly. "A lot of men want a son."

It wasn't only that, but she couldn't bring herself to voice the thought that maybe a boy would be easier on Owen. After all, wouldn't a girl constantly bring up thoughts of Mindy?

He drummed his fingers on the side of his truck, his expression inscrutable. "Why don't you go home and change into something more comfortable? I'll stop by, and we'll go for a drive. We can discuss the visit then."

Common sense told Lindsay to limit her time with Owen. But a drive sounded wonderful. Besides, did she really want to have a conversation about her baby's first ultrasound in a parking lot?

"Unless you already have plans?"

Lindsay shook her head. "Not unless you count watching a tutorial on how to use QuickBooks."

Relief skittered across his face. Pulling out his phone, Owen glanced at the display. "Pick you up in twenty?"

"Make it thirty."

Lindsay opened her car door and was ready to slide behind the wheel when she heard him call out.

"Don't eat. We'll want to celebrate."

Then he was in his truck with the radio blasting.

Celebrate?

Her spirits lifted. Perhaps he wasn't disappointed after all.

~

OWEN CHANGED into jeans and a striped polo shirt before stopping by the Greasy Wrench. He went directly to Wayde Lingstrom, his lead mechanic.

"Everything is under control here." Wayde wiped his hand on a grease rag and studied Owen. "Based on what you're wearing, I'm guessin' you're done working for the day."

Owen slapped the man on the back. "You're an observant guy, Wayde."

"What's the occasion?" Wayde cocked his head. "You've been closing the place down for weeks."

"I've got plans." Owen kept it simple, but the comment only appeared to spike Wayde's interest.

"You've got a date?"

"Is that so strange?"

"Well, yeah. You haven't been out since you and Lindsay split." Wayde walked with him toward the service counter. "Is she anyone I know?"

Owen hesitated, then decided what the heck? "Actually, I'm headed over to Lindsay's apartment."

"Getouttahere. You and Lin are back together?" A smile split the man's thin face. "Mary Jo is going to be super stoked when she hears the news. Neither of us could believe it when you two split."

For a second, Owen wondered if he should tell Wayde he and Lindsay weren't dating. He quickly dismissed the thought.

Contrary to what Lindsay believed, he didn't just care about the baby, he cared about her. He cared about her reputation. He didn't want people thinking he was spending time with her only because she was pregnant with his child.

It would be easier if everyone thought...well, if everyone thought they were in love.

If he could love any woman, it would be Lindsay. But after Tessa left and Mindy died, he'd decided love wasn't for him. Still, he firmly believed marriage was the best solution. It would shield Lindsay and the baby from any talk and also allow his daughter to grow up in a two-parent family.

Lindsay wanted love, but hopefully in time, she'd realize love wasn't all it was cracked up to be and accept they could forge a strong partnership without it.

With a determined tilt to his jaw, Owen continued toward the back of the garage. He stepped outside and walked over to another, smaller building. Unlocking the door, he stepped inside and flicked the switch.

The sight that greeted him always made him smile. The 1967 Pontiac GTO would be at home on any dealership's showroom floor. The muscle car's high-gloss paint gleamed like a finely polished cherry in the fluorescent lights. The silver spokes of the mag wheels provided a nice contrast to the black sidewalls.

The black convertible top was up, but Owen planned to remedy that the second he drove it out of the building.

Owen slid behind the wheel and pushed a remote that raised the overhead door. After rolling down the windows, he pincered a piece of lint off the black leather passenger seat.

The second he turned the key, the engine roared. Owen's smile widened. Motors had always fascinated him. As a teen, he'd developed a particular love for 1960 muscle cars. The Pontiac GTO had quickly become his favorite.

His father hadn't understood—or shared—his passion. Or maybe, Owen thought, the man simply hadn't wanted to encourage his interest in mechanics. Tessa hadn't understood, either, but when he told her a widow in Egg Harbor had a GTO for sale, she'd gone with him to look at it.

The car had been in much the same shape as the ramshackle outbuilding where it had been stored. Though Tess had difficulty seeing the vehicle's potential, when he'd whispered that the price was a really hot deal, she encouraged him to buy it.

They hadn't really had the money, but it was as if she'd realized how many sacrifices he'd made for her schooling and wanted to give something back to him.

How had he forgotten her generosity?

Owen shoved the thought aside and drove the vehicle into the sunshine, the top already retracting.

When he and Lindsay had been together, he'd showed her the car, but they hadn't taken it out. Though Mindy had told him she wished it was pink, she had loved the convertible.

Owen wished his daughter could go on this celebratory ride with them. Mindy would be over the moon knowing a baby girl was on the way. He could see her wanting to fill the baby's dresser with everything pink and frilly.

Tears stung Owen's eyes. When he stopped at the light, he pulled sunglasses from the glove compartment and put them on.

Today was a day for celebration. For the next few hours, Owen planned to avoid glancing in his rearview and only look ahead.

CHAPTER NINE

"This is a beautiful car." Lindsay slipped into the passenger seat, leaned her head back and smiled.

When Owen had texted that he was on his way, she'd grabbed her purse and headed down the stairs. It was too nice a day to spend even ten minutes waiting indoors.

Her jaw had dropped when he'd pulled up in the red GTO. While he rounded the front of the vehicle to open her door, she'd pulled her hair back into a ponytail and put on her sunglasses.

Owen kept the conversation light as they drove through town, the sun warm and the sky a brilliant blue. The tightness that had gripped her chest most of the day began to ease.

Owen cast a sideways glance. "What do you think about driving down Millionaire's Row?"

"I love that stretch of road." Lindsay shifted in her seat to face him. "The view is amazing."

Nodding, Owen veered left at the next intersection.

The waterfront properties built along the road were some of the most expensive homes in the area. David and Hadley Chapin lived on this road. Cade and Marigold Rallis owned a piece of land and hoped to eventually build.

Lindsay cast an admiring glance at a Frank Lloyd Wright-inspired home, then at one with a third-floor crow's nest.

"When Ami and I were young, the cottages along here were small." Lindsay's lips lifted. "We would come here and pick buckets of wild blackberries and thimbleberries."

"When we moved here, no one in my family had heard of a thimbleberry." Owen chuckled. "We didn't even realize thimbleberries and blackcap raspberries were the same."

"I have a fabulous recipe for thimbleberry-strawberry cream cheese pie. It's kind of labor intensive, but it's super good. I—" Lindsay stopped herself just before she offered to make a pie for him.

"My mother once made a thimbleberry pie." Owen grimaced.

"Too tart?" Lindsay ventured.

"None of us could force down more than a bite."

"Thimbleberries are usually too tart to be the only ingredient in a pie." Lindsay cocked her head. "Does your mother like to bake?"

"Not at all." Owen laughed. "I can't recall why she made the pie. Mom was never one for homemaking stuff. Her career as a college professor was her focus. That dedication and single-mindedness explain why she and Tessa get along so well."

Lindsay picked up on the present tense. She hadn't realized Owen's mother and his ex were close. "They stay in touch?"

"Probably." A song that had hit number one a couple of years ago played on the radio. The tune was catchy, with a refrain you couldn't help belting out. Especially when driving down a country road with the sun warming your face and a light breeze on your cheeks.

Lindsay had barely started to sing when Owen switched stations. She turned to look at him, or rather, at his profile.

"I never liked that song." Owen spoke without glancing in her direction. "The bay is calm today."

The water might be smooth as glass, but the muscle jumping in

Owen's jaw told Lindsay he wasn't calm. Something had caused him to tense up. Was it the talk about his mother? From what she knew, he'd had little contact with his family since they moved from Good Hope.

"I read an article recently that said gazing at water makes you calmer and more creative." Lindsay brought the article up in her head. "The research related to oceans, but I think the same would apply to Green Bay."

Owen glanced briefly at the water.

"I think you have to stare at it longer than five seconds." Lindsay spoke in a teasing tone, then narrowed her gaze. "Is that Marigold and Cade?"

Owen must have seen the couple at the same time, because he slowed, then pulled into a dirt driveway leading to an empty lot on a large acreage. The convertible came to a stop behind Cade's truck.

Before Owen cut the motor, the sheriff and his wife were at the car.

"I heard you had a GTO." Cade's gaze held appreciation. "1966?"

"'67."

"What's it got under the hood?"

Lindsay pushed open her door just in time to hear Owen say something about a 389 V-8 and four-barrel carb. Based on Cade's low whistle, she assumed that must be good.

Marigold slipped around the car to greet Lindsay.

"Nice ride." Marigold flashed a bright smile, her gaze lingering on the car. "I adore convertibles. Especially red ones."

When the hood popped open, Lindsay decided she and Owen were staying for a while, which was okay with her. She liked Ami's youngest sister. "I can't remember the last time I rode in a convertible with the top down."

"If you're headed to David and Hadley's, they should be home now." Marigold leaned inside the car to study the dash. "They just left here."

"Actually, we were just out for a drive." Lindsay did her best to keep her voice casual, as if she and Owen driving around Good Hope on a Monday afternoon was a frequent occurrence. "We spotted you and Cade and decided to stop. I hope we're not intruding."

"Don't be silly." Marigold waved a dismissive hand, her gold-tipped nails glittering in the late afternoon sun. The youngest Bloom sister was an adorable pixie with curly blond hair framing an elfin face. "Cade and I come here often, mostly to remind ourselves this land is actually ours."

Lindsay had heard the story from Ami. Cade had inherited a substantial sum of money shortly before becoming sheriff. When he'd fallen in love with Good Hope—and with Marigold—he'd used his inheritance to buy this plot of land.

"I hear David drew up house plans." As that fact had been mentioned recently at several gatherings, Lindsay knew it wasn't a secret. "Are you getting closer to building?"

"The house we'd like to build, one that will do justice to this property, is still outside our budget." Marigold lifted her shoulders in a careless shrug.

Marigold's hair salon did a good business in Good Hope, but according to Ami, it was her sister's premier clients who brought in the big bucks. When Marigold worked in Chicago, she'd developed quite a following, especially among the rich and famous.

Recently, Marigold had started flying to Chicago one weekend a month to see clients. She also continued to do hair for models involved in high-profile fashion-week activities across the country.

"—infertility stuff doesn't come cheap."

Lindsay pulled her thoughts back and focused on the petite blonde. "Infertility?"

"Cade and I have been trying, rather unsuccessfully, to get pregnant."

"You haven't been married all that—"

"I have endometriosis." A look of pain crossed Marigold's face. "That's one of the reasons we started trying to get pregnant right after the wedding."

Lindsay rested a hand on Marigold's arm. "I'm sorry."

"It's crazy how some people who don't want a baby get pregnant without trying, while those of us who really want one struggle."

Not certain what to say to that, especially in light of her own circumstance, Lindsay settled for a sympathetic nod.

"Next up is Clomid and IUI." Marigold held up a hand, two fingers crossed. "Please send prayers and positive vibes our way."

"Will do. And it will happen." Out of the corner of her eye, Lindsay saw the two men step back from the car.

Owen talked with his hands, the way he did when he felt passionately about a topic. Seeing him so animated warmed Lindsay's heart. After Mindy's death, he'd cut himself off from everyone.

Except her.

He'd let her in, accepted the comfort she willingly gave, and in the process, she'd fallen in love.

Once his world had righted and he no longer needed her support, he'd given her the heave-ho.

"Are you two back together?" Marigold's blue eyes sparkled with interest. "I read in the Open Door that you and Owen went on a walk after church yesterday."

Lindsay blinked. "Katie Ruth put that in the newsletter?"

"In the gossip section."

The Open Door, a daily e-newsletter, allowed anyone interested in the day-to-day of Good Hope to stay informed.

"Is it true?" Marigold pressed.

"That we took a walk? Yes, that's true." As she spoke, Lindsay maneuvered her way over the uneven terrain toward the back of the lot.

Lindsay craned her neck back to gaze up at the large stand of evergreens. "These trees are like sentinels guarding your land until you're ready to build."

"You didn't answer my question." Marigold was like a dog with a bone. "Are you and Owen back together?"

Lindsay wished she could demand Marigold go somewhere else to play, like she and Ami used to tell her when she annoyed them. But they weren't children, and this was Marigold's property.

Besides, Marigold didn't mean any harm. She was a friend. A friend who, like most hair stylists, prided herself on being "in the know."

"Owen and I are exploring a relationship." Lindsay chose her words carefully, not wanting to lie, but definitely not ready to share everything. "Where it ends up, time will tell."

"You're good together." Marigold shifted her gaze to Owen and Cade.

As if sensing his wife's gaze, Cade turned and a slow smile lifted his lips.

Marigold blew her husband a kiss.

Cade said something to Owen, and the two men started walking toward them.

When he reached his wife, the sheriff slid his arms around her. "What has you both looking so serious?"

Lindsay sincerely hoped Marigold would not bring up her and Owen's relationship.

"I told Lindsay they just missed David and Hadley. I forgot to mention Brynn was with them." Marigold turned to Owen. "It seems like just yesterday that Mindy and Brynn were giggling together at Seedling meetings."

"They were best friends." Owen's lips briefly tipped upward. "In fact, they loved to tell strangers they were sisters."

"That's adorable." Marigold sighed. "I think everyone should have a sister."

"What made them decide they needed a sister?" Cade's natural curiosity was only one of the things that made him an effective sheriff.

"When I asked Mindy, she told me a sister is always there for you. A sister sees you at your worst and still loves you." Owen cleared his throat. "Tessa had left, and contact between her and Mindy had dried up. Brynn was going through pretty much the same with her own mother."

"Losing a mother tears your heart in two." Marigold's eyes held a sheen, and Lindsay knew she was remembering her own mother, who died when Marigold was young. "Even with sisters who love and support you."

"You were there for Mindy," Lindsay reminded Owen.

"I made a lot of mistakes." Owen's eyes turned troubled. Then he appeared to shake off the melancholy. "But I did my best. Every choice was with her best interests in mind."

Time to change the subject, Lindsay thought. "Do you think David and Hadley will be giving Brynn a little brother or sister soon?"

"Hadley told me the wedding is the first thing on the agenda. She and David have talked about waiting a little bit, not years or anything, but long enough for the three of them to get used to being a family." Marigold's lips curved in a rueful smile. "I won't be surprised if that resolution quickly falls by the wayside. It seems like everyone in Good Hope is turning up pregnant."

Except me. Though Marigold didn't say the words, Lindsay heard them loud and clear.

Lindsay was avoiding Owen's gaze when Marigold let out a whoop. "I almost forgot. I have something for you."

Marigold stuck her hand inside the bag hanging off her shoulder, diving deep.

Owen looked at Cade, who only shook his head.

"Aha." With a cry of triumph, Marigold pulled her hand from her bag. She turned to Lindsay. "Hold out your hand."

When Lindsay complied, Marigold pressed the cards into her palm.

Lindsay turned the deck over. "What are these?"

Marigold's lips curved in a feline smile. "A gift from David and Hadley."

Cade slanted a glance at Owen. "Have fun with those."

Owen stared at the deck, clearly puzzled. "Playing cards?"

"Relationship cards." Marigold's light tone sent up warning flags. "You and Owen need to each answer three questions."

Cade cocked his head. "Did we answer three?"

Marigold ignored him. "Those are the rules. Once you're through with them, you pass them along to another couple."

"David couldn't get rid of them fast enough." Cade offered Owen a pointed glance. "I felt the same."

"They're fun," Marigold insisted.

"Mar-i-gold." Cade gave her shoulder a squeeze.

His wife's lips quirked upward. "Okay, total truth. They're fun unless you're the one answering the questions."

Lindsay stared at the deck, then dropped the cards into her bag.

Compared to what she was facing, a few questions would be a piece of cake.

～

WE DID a lot of talking this afternoon." Lindsay paused outside the door to her apartment. "But you never told me what you think about having a girl."

On the drive back from Millionaire's Row, she'd nearly brought up the subject several times, but decided to wait. Being in a vehicle didn't give her much of an exit strategy should the conversation go south.

When Owen had pulled to a stop in front of her apartment, the question was poised on her lips. Then Owen had flung open his car door and insisted on walking her up the steps.

After unlocking her front door, she faced him and waited for his response.

Before he could respond, the door to the apartment next to hers opened. Cody Treacher, a smart-mouthed twelve-year-old, barreled out the door toward the steps, his mom in hot pursuit.

"You can't tell me what to do." The boy yelled the words over his shoulder. His gaze was on his mother, rather than where he was going.

He hadn't seen Lindsay standing there. That was the only explanation she could come up with for why the hundred-pound boy barreled toward her at full speed.

Seeing what was happening, Owen shoved himself between her and the kid, absorbing most of the impact. Still, the force had Lindsay stumbling backward. Owen's arms stopped her fall.

"I'm sorry." Cody's mother paused for a moment, then continued after her son, who was already at the bottom of the steps.

"Let's go inside." With a supportive arm still around her, Owen pushed open the unlocked door.

Lindsay's heart beat an erratic rhythm. She wasn't sure if it was because of nearly being tackled by a preteen or because of Owen's nearness.

Drawing a shaky breath, Lindsay lifted her face.

Hazel eyes filled with worry locked with hers.

Her breathing hitched.

With fingers that were tender and a bit unsure, Owen brushed a strand of hair back from her face. "You okay?"

All Lindsay could manage was a nod.

His gaze searched her face, and he was silent for a long moment.

She thought he might step back, reassured no harm had been

done. Instead, Owen shifted, gathering her close against him. "If he had hurt you, I—"

Lindsay stopped his words with a finger against his lips. "I'm fine."

He expelled a ragged breath.

"He didn't hurt me." Her heart swelled. Without taking a second to consider the ramifications, she kissed him.

When she pulled back, he studied her for several seconds, his steady gaze shooting tingles down her spine. This was the point where a wise woman would take a step back.

Lindsay stood her ground, knowing she was being reckless but not caring.

His eyes glittered, looking more green than brown. Lindsay saw desire reflected in the hazel depths. He smelled of soap and a familiar, warm, male scent that made something tighten low in her abdomen. His hair was a rumpled mass, brushing the collar of his shirt.

"I want to kiss you." His husky voice had desire sliding like warm honey through her veins.

Lindsay moistened her lips with the tip of her tongue and saw his eyes grow dark. "What's stopping you?"

CHAPTER TEN

Even before their lips melded, she knew the feel of his mouth, the softness, the warmth, the gentleness.

Owen continued pressing his lips to hers teasingly, his mouth never completely pulling away. The dreamy kisses had shivers and tingles spiraling through her body.

A hot riff of sensation traveled up her spine. When she heard herself groan, a low sound of want and need, Lindsay realized this was madness. She jerked from his arms with such force she stumbled.

When he reached out a steadying hand this time, she didn't take it.

It wasn't that she didn't trust him.

She didn't trust herself.

OWEN PUT a hand to his head as if waking up after a dream. Or was it a nightmare?

But the fact that Lindsay stood less than three feet from him, her chest rising and falling as if she'd just finished a long race, told him he hadn't been asleep.

"Would you like to stay for dinner?"

For a second, all Owen could do was stare. He'd expected her to point at the door and order him to leave. It appeared he didn't know Lindsay Lohmeier as well as he'd thought.

"I haven't eaten since this morning." Lindsay took off the band holding most of her hair back. "It won't be anything fancy."

"Ah, sure. Sounds good." Owen shifted from one foot to the other, wondering if he should apologize for the kiss. Then again, she had invited him to kiss her. "Do you need help? I've got a few skills."

The relief that skittered across her face told him she was no more eager than he to discuss what had just happened. Sweeping difficult topics under the rug had become a habit while they were dating.

Lindsay moved to the small kitchen adjacent to the living room. Pulling out a pan, she filled it with water and set it on the stove. "Is spaghetti okay with you? I don't have any sauce, but I have shredded parmesan and butter."

"That works." He glanced around the familiar kitchen with its blue gingham curtains, white cabinets and appliances. "How can I help?"

He knew his way around this kitchen. When they'd been together, they'd spent more time at her apartment than at his house.

"There's a bag of broccoli in the freezer." As she pulled a box of spaghetti from a drawer, she gestured with one hand. "You could stick it in the microwave."

Owen did as she asked, setting the timer for five minutes. He'd eaten at her place plenty of times and knew she loved to cook and bake. But when he'd retrieved the broccoli, he'd noticed her freezer was nearly empty. He wondered if he'd find the shelves of her refrigerator also bare.

He hoped she wasn't scrimping on food in order to save money. Owen understood what it was like being tight on money. During the early years of his marriage, he and Tessa had lived paycheck to paycheck. Eating everything in the cupboards to avoid going to the grocery store before he got paid was a common occurrence.

The last thing Owen wanted was for Lindsay to live that life. Since he knew she'd refuse any offer of financial help, he'd have to make sure to take her out for meals or have her over to his place, where they'd use his groceries, not hers.

His spirits lifted at the thought. Yes, that was an excellent solution.

"Would you mind setting the table?"

The kitchen was postage-stamp-sized, so when she turned from the stove, she was right there.

He dropped his gaze to her mouth, to red lips that reminded him of ripe strawberries and tasted just as sweet.

For a second, heat flared in her eyes, then disappeared, like a candle that had been suddenly extinguished.

"I'll get the plates on the table." He slipped past her. Unable to resist touching her, he gave her shoulder a squeeze. "Like I said, anything I can do to help."

He meant every word.

It wasn't until Lindsay was setting the plates of spaghetti and steamed broccoli on the table that Owen noticed the bright blue stoneware canister on a nearby side table.

While Lindsay filled their glasses with water, Owen removed the lid to reveal tiny scraps of folded paper. Gazing down at the rainbow of colors, his heart gave a lurch.

Feeling Lindsay's eyes on him, Owen replaced the lid. "It's a gratitude box." He didn't bother to hide his surprise. "Mindy had one."

Lindsay, who'd taken her seat across the table from him, lifted her napkin and placed it on her lap with careful, precise movements. "Ami keeps one, too."

Owen told himself to let it drop, but the question came out before he could swallow it. "What will you write on that scrap of paper today?"

"That's easy." Red lips curved. "I'm grateful for a healthy baby."

Owen gave a jerky nod, then busied himself sprinkling parmesan on the mound of spaghetti on his plate.

"We never did talk about how you feel about having another daughter."

Another daughter.

The words pricked his heart, drawing blood.

He lifted his spoon, twirling the spaghetti around his fork, using the spoon the way his mother had taught him.

"I never cared if the baby was a girl or a boy. All that's important is a healthy child." His fingers tightened around the fork. "Did you think the sex would make a difference to me?"

Lindsay lowered her fork. "I knew the baby's health would be the most important thing to you."

"Then why ask if it made a difference?"

"I'm worried our baby being a girl might prove difficult for you."

He raised a brow, not following, but determined not to jump in and put words in her mouth.

"Because of Mindy." Lindsay sighed the words. "With comparisons."

"I'm sure there will be comparisons as our child grows and develops."

"It could be painful." Lindsay hadn't yet taken a bite of her dinner, and her pallor worried him. "For you. You'll constantly think of Mindy."

When the first bite of pasta hit her lips, relief coursed through him. He waited until she'd stabbed a broccoli floret to respond.

"Mindy is never far from my thoughts." Owen hesitated. "Thinking of her doesn't always hurt."

He gestured toward the gratitude jar. "Fin initially told Mindy that Ami had one. Mindy made me go out and get one that same day. I tried to get her to use one of the canisters in the cupboard, but that wouldn't do."

Her lips curved. "I bet I know why."

"It wasn't pink," they said in unison, then laughed.

Lindsay's brows pulled together. "I don't think I ever saw a jar at your house."

"Mindy kept it in her bedroom." The door to which Owen kept firmly closed.

"Other than being pink, what does it look like?" Lindsay stabbed another floret.

"It's actually a wooden box with figures of various princesses etched in pink on top of the lid." The night of the wedding, Mindy's last night on earth, she'd taken time to write something down. "Every night, without fail, she'd put something in there."

Lindsay's gaze grew assessing, but before she could ask another question, he took himself off the hot seat.

"What about you?" Owen shifted his chair just enough that the blue canister was out of his direct line of sight. "How do you feel about having a girl?"

"A boy would have been fine with me." Lindsay's lips curved ever so slightly. "But I'm glad she's a girl. It seems it'd be easier for a single woman to raise a girl alone than a boy."

Her words scraped the sides of his heart.

"You won't be raising her alone," Owen reminded her. "We'll be raising her together."

"You're right." She reached for her water glass. "Of course, you're right."

They ate in silence for a couple of minutes.

"I'm glad we were able to discuss this issue in such a calm

manner." Lindsay met his gaze. "Everything I read says open communication is key."

Something in what she was saying made Owen uncomfortable, like an itch between his shoulder blades that he couldn't quite reach.

"The whole reason we're spending time together is so we can be better parenting partners. I'd say today was a successful use of our time."

Use of our time? Was that how she classified their outing today?

What about the kiss? Had that been on her checklist? A test to see if there was still any sizzle between them? Owen told himself not to be ridiculous. Romance didn't play a part in any of this.

"I made up a list of parenting questions." Lindsay bit her lower lip. "It might be good for us to discuss one or two each time we're together."

"Are there many questions?

Her forkful of spaghetti hovered in the air. "Quite a few."

Which meant lots of reasons for them to be together. Owen nodded. "Sounds like an excellent plan."

OWEN TOLD himself to wait until Lindsay contacted him, but he couldn't get her empty freezer out of his mind. Then, like an angel from heaven, Gladys arrived at the garage with a sack of Honeycrisp apples.

The former stage star had presented the fruit to him with a dramatic flourish, announcing they were a token of appreciation for taking such excellent care of Frank's car.

Owen had been ready to start a transmission rebuild when she'd swept through the door. Still, they'd talked for nearly fifteen minutes. A comment she made about Lindsay being crazy about Honeycrisp apples had him leaving work early.

Owen slid behind the wheel of his truck, a sack of apples on the passenger seat and one in his hand. Biting into the shiny red fruit had memories surging.

An apple had been in his hand the day he and his mother had stopped at a Minneapolis fire station. Though only three years old at the time, Owen recalled that day vividly.

He remembered running toward the fire truck, excited to be so close to one of the big engines. When he turned to ask his mom if he could climb on it, she'd disappeared. Vanished without a trace. He was able to tell the firefighters his name was Owen, but nothing else.

Owen tossed the apple into the plastic bag he kept in the truck for garbage. It struck him as fitting. That day, his mother had discarded him like he was a piece of garbage.

Thankfully, Owen had become adept at keeping memories and feelings at bay. This afternoon was about Lindsay and making sure she had everything she needed. Which was why, on the way to her apartment, he made a quick stop at the market. He emerged minutes later with a full sack of groceries. Owen would have bought out the store, but believed he stood a better chance of her accepting one bag.

If she balked, he'd insist the apples were from Gladys and the groceries were his way of saying thanks for letting him attend the ultrasound on Monday with her.

His body hummed with anticipation on the drive to her apartment building. Not because he thought he'd get another kiss, but with the hope he could convince her to go out to dinner with him. Muddy Boots had their meatloaf on special tonight.

He took the steps to the third level, a bag in each arm. Setting them down, he knocked on the door. After several seconds, he knocked again. Still no answer.

The food in the bags would keep, but—

The door suddenly swung open. Lindsay stood there, a towel wrapped around her head and wearing nothing but a short, silky robe.

"Owen." Her gaze shifted to the sacks at his feet and her brows pulled together. "What are you doing here?"

"Gladys stopped by—"

Those were all the words he got out before Lindsay grabbed the handles of the paper sacks and motioned him inside. She smelled wonderful, some sort of lemony scent that was new. Or at least new to him.

She inclined her head. "You said something about Gladys?"

"Gladys?" Owen tried to corral his thoughts but finding her nearly naked had short-circuited his brain.

Tiny droplets of moisture dotted her skin. A damp tendril of hair had escaped from the towel and curled against her cheek. If those signs weren't enough to tell him he'd interrupted her shower, the way the silk robe clung to her bare skin confirmed it.

He'd been in that shower with her, he recalled. Once. Just once, they'd shared the small space.

"You said something about Gladys," she prompted, cinching the belt of her robe tight.

"She brought apples by the garage." He forced himself to keep his gaze on her face. "She mentioned Honeycrisp are your favorite."

Lindsay had set down the bags. She bent over to glance inside. A smile bloomed on her lips. "I love them. But she gave the apples to you."

"I have plenty at home." The suspicion in her eyes had him continuing, "My neighbor went to the orchards with his kids last weekend and brought some back for me."

"That was nice of them." Lindsay cast a quick glance in the other bag and lifted a head of cauliflower. "Did Gladys also give you this?"

"I stopped by the store and picked up a few staples." When he saw a protest forming on her lips, he made his tone persuasive. "You did something nice for me. I wanted to do something nice for you."

Puzzlement blanketed her face. "What I did I do?"

"You let me come with you to the ultrasound appointment."

She rolled her eyes. "That's a stretch, but thank you. I-I haven't been to the store lately." Her hand rose to the towel encircling her hair. "Have you eaten dinner?"

He shook his head.

"Give me fifteen minutes to get dressed and dry my hair, and I'll whip us up something."

"I have a better idea." The last thing Owen wanted was for her to use her precious food to feed *him*. "It's meatloaf night at Muddy Boots. Let me take you out to dinner."

Her look turned wary. "Why?"

"You mentioned you have lots of parenting questions to ask me."

"What does that have to do with eating out?"

"Ask anyone." He forced a light tone. "Conversation always flows more easily over meatloaf."

CHAPTER ELEVEN

Stepping into muddy boots, Lindsay was surprised to see her sister and youngest nephew standing at the counter.

"Cassie." Lindsay gave her sister a hug and tousled Axl's blond curls. "What are you doing here? Where are K.T. and Braxton?"

"The boys are working on homecoming displays." Cassie gave her youngest son's hand a swing. "Axl and I are trying to decide which pie to buy. Then I'm headed home to make dinner."

Lindsay's eyes went to the clock on the wall.

Cassie's chin jutted up. "I just got off work."

"That's great." Owen spoke in a hearty tone.

Cassie blinked.

Owen gave the toddler a poke in the ribs that had the boy giggling. "Since you haven't eaten, you and Axl can join Lindsay and me for dinner."

Her sister started shaking her head even before Owen finished. Owen shot Lindsay an *I need some help here* look. Since Cassie was her sister, it fell to Lindsay to do the encouraging.

Lindsay scooped Axl up into her arms. "C'mon, Cass. I hardly ever get to see you and this little cutie. Besides, meatloaf is on special. It's the good kind, not Mom's hideous recipe filled with broccoli."

"Hers is pretty awful." Cassie laughed, then slanted a glance at Owen. "Are you sure you don't mind me interrupting your date?"

"We don't mind." Lindsay spoke in a firm tone that brooked no argument.

She ignored Owen's curious look. No doubt, he was wondering why she didn't correct her sister about this being a date. The truth was, she wasn't sure herself.

The hostess, a teenager Lindsay vaguely recognized from church, showed them to a table, then brought over a booster seat for Axl.

The second they sat down, Cassie slipped several cars from her purse. It wasn't long before Owen and Axl were zooming the brightly colored metal cars across the table.

He would do well with a son, too, Lindsay thought.

The waitress had just dropped off their drinks when Axl threw his car to the table with a clatter. "I have to go to the baffroom." The boy spoke loudly.

A couple in a nearby booth chuckled.

"Now." The boy's tone took on an urgency. "I have to go potty *now.*"

Not having success with pushing back from the table, he rocked back and forth in his booster seat in an attempt to free himself.

"I heard you." Cassie stilled the motion of the seat with a firm hand. "There is no need to yell."

"I can take him." Owen stood. "If that's okay with you."

"Sure." Cassie tucked a long strand of hair back from her face in a nervous gesture. "If you don't mind."

"No trouble at all." Owen shot Lindsay a wink. "We'll be back soon."

Owen lifted the boy from the booster. "C'mon, sport."

"He's a nice man." Cassie watched as her son and Owen headed to the restrooms, the child's hand firmly clasped in his.

Lindsay nodded. "Yes, he's very nice."

"I lied to you." Cassie's gaze shifted to her hands.

Her heart slammed against her ribs. What had her sister gotten herself into now?

Lindsay took a sip of water. "What about?"

"I didn't just get off work." Cassie blew out a breath. "I was at a psychologist's office."

Lindsay frowned. "Is one of the boys in trouble?"

When Clint Gourley had been in the house, Cassie's two older boys had had some behavioral issues. But once Cassie kicked Clint out, things seemed better.

"No." Cassie cleared her throat. "I didn't go there about the boys. I went there for me."

Lindsay didn't like to pry, but the way she figured it, if Cassie didn't want to talk about it, her sister wouldn't have brought it up. "What's going on?"

"I don't like who I am."

Lindsay inhaled sharply, then covered it with a cough. She lifted her tumbler of water and took another drink. Cassie hadn't had an easy life, but Lindsay thought she'd been doing better.

As if she could read her mind, Cassie smiled. "Seeing Dr. Gallagher is a positive step."

"Then I'm glad." Lindsay reached across the table and covered her sister's hand. "I hope you know you can count on me."

Cassie's fingers curved around Lindsay's for a second, then she pulled back. "I know."

Lindsay forced herself to breathe normally. "What made you decide to see a counselor?"

"Clint contacted me. He asked me to come to the prison. He wanted me to bring Axl."

"What did you tell him?" Despite a thousand hummingbirds beating against her throat, Lindsay sounded calm.

"I told him no." Cassie's gaze was steady. "I almost said yes. Even after all that happened, I almost said yes. That scared me."

"You did the right thing."

"This time. I want to be a good mother. I don't want to make more mistakes." Cassie's lips trembled for a second. "I spoke with Dan. He thought it might be helpful for me to meet with a professional. He suggested Dr. Liam Gallagher."

Lindsay had never met the man, but she remembered Hadley mentioning him. "Isn't he a child psychologist?"

"Kids are his specialty, but his practice includes adults."

"What are you two looking so serious about?" Owen scooped the little boy up and deposited him back into the booster.

"Just sisterly stuff." Cassie turned to her son. "Did you wash your hands?"

The boy nodded vigorously. "I went potty *and* poopy."

"That's fabulous." Cassie shifted her attention from her son to Owen. "I owe you."

"It was no trouble." Owen lifted his glass of tea and smiled at the boy, who'd grabbed two cars and was reaching for a third. "He's a good kid."

Cassie ruffled her son's hair. "I want to do right by him."

"That's what it's all about." But Owen's gaze now rested on Lindsay, not Cassie. "Doing what's best for your child."

"How do they make those potatoes?" Owen asked once they'd paid the bill and said good-bye to Cassie and Axl. "I can't recall tasting anything so good."

"They're an Ami Cross special creation. You take a baked potato out of its skin, mash it up, add butter and cover the potato with creamed corn." Lindsay slowed her steps to the truck, not in a hurry for the evening to end. "The bacon, onions and peppers that top the meatloaf while it cooks are added to the corn."

Owen's eyes lit up. "Can you make them?"

Lindsay nodded.

"I could bring over the ingredients one night, and we could make dinner together."

"With sourdough bread and meatloaf, too?"

"Of course." He grinned. "And cherry crisp with ice cream for dessert."

"It's a deal." Though everything in Lindsay warned her to keep her distance, Cassie's words kept circling.

Her sister wanted the best for her children, just as Lindsay wanted the best for her baby girl. That meant she and Owen needed to be cordial and on the same page.

They walked in silence, but neither stopped when they reached the car. The warm air held the tangy scent of drying leaves mixed with pungent evergreen. Streetlights added a golden glow, while banners hawking the Harvest Festival gave a cheerful feel to the business district.

"We haven't discussed our parenting question yet." Lindsay was tempted to let it go, but reminded herself this was the sole purpose of her spending time with Owen.

"We could wait, do it next time?"

Lindsay shook her head.

"Okay." Owen's warm smile had her knees going to jelly. "Lay one on me."

"I don't have the list with me, but I remember one of them was, 'Where does help from the grandparents fit into our plan?'" Lindsay didn't want to lead with her mother. "Let's start with your parents. You mentioned once that they were involved with Mindy's care when she was an infant."

"They lived in Good Hope at the time."

"You said your mother watched Mindy while you worked and Tessa was in class."

"My mother was finishing her dissertation. Mindy's birth came at a good time."

Lindsay's heart gave a ping. As opposed to this baby's birth.

She dug deep, determined to get through this discussion without giving way to emotions. "Do you anticipate they'll come back to Good Hope for our child's birth?"

Owen frowned. It was apparent he hadn't even considered the possibility. "I never thought of inviting them."

Lindsay felt her face warm. She waved a hand. "That's okay. It isn't as if—"

He captured her hand in his, and her breath lodged in her throat. "If you want us to discuss these questions, we need to discuss, not shut down when the conversation gets difficult."

The heat infusing her face spread. Diverting from a controversial or possibly contentious topic had become a specialty of hers.

"You're right." She swallowed past her embarrassment. "I've played the peacemaker between my sister and mother for so long it's become second nature."

"I can't speak for them, but between us there's no reason to avoid touchy subjects." He gave a little laugh. "And my parents are definitely a touchy subject."

He resumed walking, and Lindsay fell into step beside him. With a comment like that, the ball remained in his court.

"I love them." Owen shook his head. "But they wanted a different life for me than the one I pursued. They ask about the business, but it's only for form."

He paused for so long, Lindsay wasn't certain he was going to say more. They crossed the street to the town square, where they continued their walk under branches heavy with leaves of gold, orange and red.

"I'm not saying they aren't interested in my life. But usually when I mention the garage, they always manage to bring up how well my sisters are both doing. It feels dismissive. When Tessa—" He stopped himself. "Doesn't matter."

Lindsay looped her arm through his. "Tell me."

"When Tessa was here, it was different." Owen slanted a glance in her direction. "My parents admired her drive and her passion for success. That's why I have no doubt they'll love you, too."

Passion for success? Those weren't words Lindsay would use to describe herself. Little ice prickles of alarm skittered across her skin. Did Owen see her as a driven career woman?

She considered setting him straight, thought about telling him that she'd gone into business for herself only because she saw no other options. But she remained silent. The last thing she wanted was for him to worry she couldn't earn enough to care for her child.

"As far as them coming back when the baby is born, I doubt it." He gave her arm a squeeze. "Will it bother you if they don't? I mean, you'll have your mother and sister. And, of course, me."

The flash of a smile didn't erase the worry in his eyes.

Lindsay ignored his question, swallowing against the rising lump in her throat. "Cassie will be a good resource, but she's busy with her own kids and her job."

"What about your mother?" Owen's voice remained neutral, a huge accomplishment considering he'd been on the receiving end of her mother's sharp tongue many times.

"She'll insist on being involved." Everything in Lindsay went cold at the thought. "She'll sweep in and take over and complain how I'm not doing anything right and I'll feel even more inept."

The rapid rush of emotion rising inside her had her continuing instead of clamping her mouth shut. "Then she'll rush off, and I'll be there alone with a baby who'll be crying because she feels my stress and—"

"Let me make one thing clear." Owen turned her head to face him with a gentle, warm hand on her cheek. "You won't be alone. I'll be there. If Anita proves a problem, I'll speak with her."

Lindsay shook her head. "My mother. My responsibility."

"Then we'll speak with her together." Owen's eyes held reassurance and a warmth that beat off the chill. "You're not in this alone, Lindsay. We're a team. A family. That means neither of us is going down this path alone."

Lindsay hesitated. Owen appeared sincere, but it was clear he hadn't looked far enough down the road ahead. "You'll always be an important part of your daughter's life."

"I hear a 'but' in there." Though his tone held a light, teasing quality, a wary watchfulness had invaded his hazel eyes.

"*But* we won't be a family. Not in the traditional sense, anyway." Even as her heart cracked open and began to bleed, Lindsay reminded herself nothing good came from holding on to old dreams. "You'll be busy building your own life, apart from me and our daughter."

When he opened his mouth to speak, she lifted a hand. "In time, you'll fall in love and get married."

He started shaking his head before she finished speaking.

Stubborn man, she thought with more than a little exasperation.

"You will," she insisted. "I want that for me, too."

Puzzlement filled his eyes. "You want me to get married?"

Just the thought had the crack in her heart splitting wide open. When tears pushed against the backs of her lids, Lindsay determinedly blinked them back.

"I was referring to me. I hope one day to find someone special. A man I'll dearly love who will love me back just as much."

If she never found that special guy, that was okay, too. She would always have her family, her friends and her career. This spring, she would have a baby girl to shower with love.

No matter how she looked at it, she was incredibly blessed.

After what seemed an impossibly long moment, Owen nodded. "I want that for you, too."

The second the words left his mouth, Owen wondered how a simple parenting conversation had gotten so far off track. While he wished Lindsay only the best that life had to offer, did they really need to be talking about her future with another man?

Their baby should be her focus and his.

If she wanted to talk marriage and family, he had solid arguments in favor of *them* forging a family unit. While thoughts of love obviously appealed to Lindsay's romantic nature, what about friendship and mutual respect? That was a far better foundation for a successful marriage than love.

He nearly brought up that point, but the determined gleam in Lindsay's eyes had him swallowing the words.

In business, Owen had learned the value of knowing when to push a point and when to let the other person come to a necessary realization in their own time.

Eventually, Lindsay would see that the arrangement he'd proposed was the best option. Not only for them, but for their child as well.

CHAPTER TWELVE

The parking spot, reserved for visitors to Good Hope High, gave Lindsay a front-row seat to the mass exodus. The principal had been right. Staff and students didn't hang around on Friday afternoons. Once the bell sounded, they poured out the doors.

Seeing three girls walking together, arms looped, brought memories of her own high school days. She, Eliza and Ami had been inseparable.

A wave of yearning for those simpler days washed over Lindsay as she slipped from her car and headed inside. She checked in with the office, then returned to the entryway to wait for Owen. Fifteen minutes later, she watched him park next to her car and hop out.

She thought he'd come straight from work, but his sweater and jeans told her he'd stopped home to change. Either that, or he'd been doing paperwork all day.

He moved in long, confident strides up the walkway, the wind pushing his sandy hair in a dozen directions at once. When he drew close to the school and spotted her standing inside the glass entryway, his lips curved.

Lindsay felt a tiny flutter deep in her belly. A visceral reminder that she needed to guard her emotions. She wasn't yet immune to his charms.

Pulling open the door, he stepped inside.

His eyes held an admiring glint. "You look nice."

"Back at you." Lindsay kept her tone light. "I was surprised when Eliza said you'd been assigned to help me with this project."

"I think the assignment may have been at Gladys's instigation."

Lindsay inclined her head. "What makes you say that?"

"When Gladys dropped off the apples, we got to talking about homecoming. It came up that I was on the championship team with Krew." Owen shrugged. "She asked if I was involved with any of the planning. I told her no."

"A red cape in front of a bull."

"What?"

"Gladys believes everyone in Good Hope should be involved in community activities." Lindsay's lips quirked upward. "Saying you weren't, well, it was like waving red in front of a bull."

"I don't mind." Owen rocked back on his boot heels and glanced around. "Especially since being on the committee means I get to see you."

Lindsay tamped down the surge of pleasure, reminding herself the only reason he wanted to be with her was the baby.

"We're here today to check on the progress of the homecoming displays." Lindsay's tone turned businesslike. "I need to make sure the clubs are on track."

Owen's gaze returned to the endless hall. "Where are the displays being stored?"

"In the gym."

"Let's take a look at them." He flashed a smile. "Then you can tell me how I can help."

"I'm not sure there's much for you—"

"Being here brings back so many memories," Owen interrupted and started down the hall. As he walked, his sweeping gesture encompassed the shiny floor tile in a speckled tan pattern and the lockers that lined both sides of the hallway. "How do they do it? Even after being filled with kids all day, the aroma of floor wax and cleaning solvent comes through."

He was gazing at her so expectantly that Lindsay obediently sniffed. Her lips curved. "Just like perfume."

"Not a scent I'd suggest." He winked. "Just sayin'."

Lindsay laughed. "I'll keep that in mind."

Somehow, his palm ended up against the small of her back as they meandered down the hall. "I can't believe we never talked back in high school."

"You were a year older," she reminded him.

"That isn't much." He studied her face. "Of course, you were way out of my league."

Lindsay made a scoffing sound. "I was in Cooking Club. You were a football player."

"Anyone could have been on the team. If a student had a pulse, they were welcomed with open arms."

"You won the big game when you kicked that field goal."

"How do you remember that?"

Lindsay shrugged. "I thought you were cute."

Something in his eyes softened. "I wish I'd gone up and talked to you."

Their gazes held for several long seconds.

She waved a hand. "Not meant to be."

"Back then."

Lindsay opened her mouth, then shut it. There was no point in covering old ground. Owen knew the score. They would never be more than a man and a woman with a baby in common.

"Tell me about the displays."

His request diverted her attention back to the task at hand.

"Each high school club was encouraged to do one." Lindsay held up her hand and began ticking off her fingers as they continued to the gym. "National Honor Society, Future Business

Leaders of America, Chess Club, Cooking Club, Math Club and Photography Club."

"Other than the Cooking Club, those are all ones my dad pushed."

Lindsay cocked her head. "Which ones did you join?"

He grinned. "The Football Club."

Then, before she could ask, he added, "My parents weren't fans of physical sports. They preferred academic pursuits."

"You were a rebel."

"It was more a survival thing." His eyes turned dark. "If I hadn't asserted myself, my father would have cheerfully run my life. With only the best intentions, of course."

Lindsay understood parental expectations and pressures all too well. "I'm guessing they didn't want you to be a mechanic, either."

"My dad was a college president. My mother was also an academic. The thought of their son being 'blue-collar' horrified them." He offered a humorless chuckle.

"I bet they're proud of you now. I mean, you're a very successful business owner."

"I'm a mechanic." He met her gaze, his tone flat. "I saw the same judgment in your mother's eyes when we dated. She wants more for you than a man who works with his hands."

"Don't get me started on my mother." Lindsay jerked open the gym door, but waited for Owen before stepping into the cavernous room. "Believe me, if I dated a primary-care doc, my mom would be disappointed he wasn't a specialist."

Owen laughed and followed her across the gym to the far wall.

She paused in front of a scarecrow contemplating a chess move. She wasn't sure how it related to homecoming, unless that part was yet to be added.

Lindsay moved to the next display. A scarecrow wearing a chef's hat stirred a big pot. The sign read, "Stirring up a victory."

"Let me guess." Owen pointed a finger. "Cooking Club."

"Ah, the memories."

"Now I know where to give the credit for those fine meals you made me."

"They did turn out well. Most of them, anyway." Some of her favorite memories of the months they'd dated centered around Friday-night dinners.

After shopping for ingredients, they'd prepare a meal together. Well, actually, she'd cooked and he'd helped by doing whatever she told him to do.

Over the dish-of-the-week and a glass of wine, they'd shared what had gone on in their lives during the week. For dessert, they'd made love.

When they'd split, Lindsay missed the conversations as much as the physical closeness. Only recently had it hit her they'd barely scratched the surface of what made each other tick. Had they kept things superficial, knowing they wouldn't stick?

Owen glanced at the rest of the displays. "When do they have to be completed?"

"October twentieth. They'll be on display the week before homecoming."

"Homecoming is late this year," Owen murmured.

"We scheduled it for when the Packers have a bye week in the hopes Krew can make it. We decided to start the Harvest Festival a week earlier than normal to match homecoming. Not exactly tradition, but it will work out." Lindsay fingered the tassel of the National Honor Society's scarecrow. "If we'd known he'd rupture his spleen in September and be off on medical leave, we would have scheduled it sooner."

"Once homecoming is over, it'll be the holidays." Owen's brows pulled together. "Then it will be a new year."

A sense of dread gripped Lindsay. Something was obviously on Owen's mind. If she was reading him correctly, whatever was bothering him didn't have a thing to do with homecoming.

"I need to ask you something."

Her heart flip-flopped. She managed a careless wave. "Ask away."

"When are we going to let people know about the baby?" Owen cleared his throat. "And, you know, tell them we're back together?"

Back together.

Lindsay bent over and inspected a scarecrow holding a brand of camera popular during their high school years. When she straightened, she was in full control of her emotions.

"We're not back together." She kept her tone matter-of-fact. "As far as any public announcements, I'd like to keep this pregnancy between us for a while longer."

Startled surprise crossed his face. "Why wait?"

"Right now, I don't have time to deal with my mother and her extreme disappointment." As that was all she planned to say on the matter, Lindsay spun on her heel and headed toward the gymnasium door.

Owen quickly caught up to her, slipping past her to hold open the heavy door.

They continued down the hall, their footfalls the only sounds as they strode down the deserted corridor.

"I bet Anita would find it easier to accept the news about the baby if you told her we were getting married."

"Possibly." When he raised a brow, she amended, "Probably. But we aren't, and I can handle my mom."

"Getting married makes sen—"

"Stop. Will you just stop?" Her voice came out sharper than she'd intended, but she'd had enough. "I've given you my decision. The answer is no. I won't marry you."

Owen lifted both hands, palms out. "Just hear me out. Two minutes. Give me two minutes."

Making a great show of looking at her watch, Lindsay pursed her lips and gave a go-ahead nod.

"I married the first time for love. I was head over heels for

Tessa. She seemed to feel the same about me. Within a few years, our marriage fell apart." Owen paced the width of the hall. "I now believe it isn't a lack of love, but a lack of friendship that sinks most marriages. I see friendship being the key. It's the spark that makes marriages last."

"I happen to agree with you."

"You do?" Hope filled his hazel eyes. "So you'll—"

"I believe couples who marry should be friends. Hopefully, best friends. But while friendship alone may be enough for some women…" Lindsay shook her head. "It's not enough for me. I want love, as well."

Owen's gaze searched her face, and Lindsay willed him to see she meant every word. This wasn't some game she was playing.

After a moment, he rubbed the bridge of his nose as if fighting a headache. "Okay. If that's how you feel, we need to discuss joint custody."

Lindsay inhaled sharply, one hand rising to her throat. "A baby's place is with her mother."

"A baby's place is also with her *father*." Owen emphasized the word. "I've cared for an infant, and owning an established business gives me flexibility."

He wanted to take her baby.

Okay, so maybe that wasn't fair. But Lindsay had assumed she'd have full custody. She twisted her fingers together. "Is this a threat, a way to try to get me to marry you?"

"Do you really think I'd stoop that low?" Hurt underscored Owen's shocked tone. "I want to be a father to our child, Lin. I still believe the best way to do that is for us to marry. But if you aren't interested in marrying me, sharing custody of our daughter seems a logical next step."

While on the surface his request appeared reasonable, Lindsay wasn't about to agree without more information. "I'll look into it. Constantly moving back and forth from one house to another seems like it would be hard on a baby. But maybe I'm wrong."

"I'll be interested in hearing what you find out." Owen reached out and touched her arm. "Thanks for being so open."

Lindsay ignored the heat of his fingers against her skin and kept her tone even. "Married or not, we're in this parenthood thing together."

Their exchange was so civilized, so businesslike that Lindsay wanted to weep. When she'd dreamed of one day having a baby, she'd never imagined needing to have a custody talk with her child's father.

Then again, having a baby with a man who didn't love her had never been part of the dream.

CHAPTER THIRTEEN

The general store in Good Hope had been owned by Eliza's family for generations. The commercial Italianate building sat next to the Good Hope Market and contained everything from bug repellent and fishing lures to a full-service pharmacy.

When Eliza's grandmother had died, instead of giving the business to her son—who had no interest in remaining in the community—she'd left it to her beloved granddaughter.

"This place is as close as we come to a Good Hope institution." Lindsay stood at the counter with Eliza and gazed down the aisles. "It hasn't changed much since I was a kid."

Eliza's fingers absently stroked the side of the ornate cash register that had sat on the same counter for generations. "When something isn't broken, why fix it?"

Lindsay gestured with one hand to the shelves housing batteries, webbing for snow shoes and other assorted necessities. "Are you sure you want a floral shop messing with the ambience?"

Eliza snorted out a laugh, then sobered.

"Change is a part of life." Eliza searched her face. "How are you holding up, Lin? This has to be difficult."

Was Eliza talking about the pregnancy? About the fact that she was thrust back into interacting with the man who'd dumped her? Or the loss of her job and the start of a new business? Any and all applied to her current situation.

"It's been a challenge." Lindsay had read somewhere that when you said something aloud, your ears heard the comment and that reinforced the thought in your brain. "But I'm excited about the direction my life is taking."

To add extra weight to the words and imprint the comments fully in her brain, she added a smile.

Though the skeptical look in Eliza's eyes told Lindsay she wasn't fully convinced, she slowly nodded. "You're a strong woman. I have a feeling that one day you'll look back and say getting pregnant and quitting your job were the best things that ever happened to you."

Old habits died hard, and Lindsay struggled not to argue, to assert she wasn't strong at all. That inside she was still that nine-year-old scared-to-death swimmer in Green Bay, furiously dog-paddling as the waves pushed her farther from shore.

On that particular occasion, her father had rescued her. She remembered clinging to him, weeping when she realized she was safe in his arms. But he was gone now, and her mother, though a lovely woman in many ways, would be the type to stand on the shore and chide her for letting herself drift out so far.

Just like she'd felt in the waves that day, Lindsay felt battered. Too many changes. Too fast. She wished she still had a job at the Enchanted Florist. At least that would be familiar and—

"Kyle and Beck will move the units on Wednesday."

Lindsay jerked her attention back to her friend.

"Kyle said he'll put together a counter where you can take orders." Eliza gestured carelessly toward the back of the store. "There isn't room for another office, so you and I will share."

When Lindsay opened her mouth to say that she didn't need office space and was absolutely not going to crowd Eliza in the small—heck, tiny—office in the back, Eliza raised a hand, palm out. "If you're worried we'll be tripping over each other, don't be. My husband does a lot of bidding from home, so I do most of my paperwork there. I enjoy spending time with Kyle."

The sharp edges to Eliza's face softened, the way they always did when her husband's name found its way to her lips.

"You understand what it's like to navigate change."

Okay, so perhaps Lindsay could have smoothed the transition a bit, but she couldn't take the extra seconds. If she had, Eliza might have brought up something else about the new business.

Right now, all the *wonderful* changes in her life were beginning to stress her out. Adding to that stress was Owen's request for joint custody.

Eliza arched a brow. Even with a plain green bib apron pulled around her trim waist, her friend was a beautiful woman. She'd always been pretty, but since she'd met Kyle, happiness radiated from her like rays of the sun.

Lindsay had no doubt that if she'd told Eliza that, her friend would fix a steely gaze on her and Lindsay would dissolve into a puddle at her feet.

"What specific change in my life are we discussing?" Eliza prompted.

"When your dad sold the house out from under you last spring." Lindsay couldn't believe Eliza even had to ask. "When Kyle bought it and moved in."

Eliza's lips curved into a slow smile. "I was furious at my father. And at Kyle when he insisted on moving in. Then when his sister came to live with us…"

"Don't forget Katherine," Lindsay reminded her. "When she returned to Good Hope, Kyle invited her to live with you."

"I was ready to explode." Eliza gave a little laugh. "The routine I'd once embraced disappeared. I was forced to accept a new normal."

She waited while Eliza rang up a customer and the bells over the door jingled his departure.

"You were comfortable with your routine." Lindsay had always considered that was one of the many things she and Eliza had in common.

"Too comfortable. I'd gotten in a rut."

Lindsay sighed. "I miss my rut."

Eliza pinned her with steel-gray eyes. "What haven't you told me?"

Hedging wasn't an option. Eliza would get it out of her. Besides, sharing her troubles with friends always made her feel better. "Owen wants joint custody."

Eliza waited. "And?"

"Isn't that enough? He wants to take my baby from me."

"She's his baby, too." Eliza reminded her, as if Lindsay needed reminding. "Owen loves kids. He was a stellar dad. Frankly, I'd be surprised if he didn't ask for joint custody. Are you saying you want to keep the baby from him?"

"No, but—"

"Why won't you give the guy a chance to step up and do the right thing?"

"You think I should marry him." Disappointment added a heaviness to Lindsay's words.

"That isn't what I said." Eliza searched her face. "I realize this is difficult for you."

"The only reason Owen wants to marry me is because he feels obligated." Lindsay cleared her throat. "Remember, he broke up with me."

"I remember."

The softly spoken acknowledgment had Lindsay's heart lurching.. "At first, it was just friendship between us."

"That was when you were still engaged to Dan."

"It wasn't until after I ended my engagement that things began to heat up. But Owen was grieving."

"You held back."

"I didn't trust his feelings." Lindsay shifted awkwardly from one foot to the other. "He had just lost his daughter."

Eliza nodded, her eyes never leaving Lindsay's face.

"For years, I'd felt this sizzle whenever Owen was nearby. Nothing came of it." Lindsay moistened her lips with her tongue. "Nothing probably would ever have come of it. Then I was in the right place at the right time."

Lindsay thought back to the days after Mindy's death and the months following. Their relationship had built slowly before exploding like fireworks over Green Bay in July.

Eliza inclined her head. "Are you saying it was simply the situation?"

"We never should have gotten sexually involved. It was too much, too fast." Emotion welled up, and when she spoke, her voice was thick. "I believe Owen likes me, but in many ways we're still strangers."

Lindsay thought about how only recently they'd shared information about their backgrounds. "There was this strong sexual pull. I wanted so much to be close to him that I let myself believe that us sleeping together meant more than it probably did."

When Eliza didn't comment, Lindsay shrugged. "That's pretty much where we stand."

"Your relationship never had a fair chance." Eliza's expression turned pensive. "With Owen grieving, it wasn't the time to build anything lasting."

Despite tears stinging the backs of her eyes, Lindsay forced a light tone. "Now it's too late."

"It's not too late." Eliza never pulled punches, and she didn't start now. "Give the guy a second chance. Give yourself that second chance, as well."

"You think I can't do this on my own." Despite telling herself the only thing that mattered was what she believed, the thought stung.

Eliza laughed. "Oh, puh-leeze. You're one of the strongest

women I know. I absolutely think you can do this on your own. And you won't be alone, because you'll have all of us to help you."

Lindsay swallowed hard.

"If you don't want Owen, I'll support you." The look Eliza gave her was as steady as the clasp of the hand she rested on Lindsay's shoulder. "All I'm saying is be sure of how you feel before making any final decisions."

Before Lindsay could respond, the bells over the door sounded and several women walked into the store.

"Let's continue this in the back." Eliza made a come-on gesture, and Lindsay reluctantly followed her.

On the way, Eliza caught the attention of the pretty strawberry-blonde stocking shelves. "Jackie, I'll be in my office."

Jackie White straightened, resting a hand against the shelves to steady herself. She nodded. "I'll watch the cash register."

"How long has Jackie been working for you?" Lindsay asked, eager to change the subject.

"She started shortly after school started." Eliza added in a matter-of-fact tone, "She's a good employee."

Coming from Eliza, it was high praise.

"She and Cory had a rough go of it." Lindsay shook her head. "I remember when they were going to lose their house. Until a mysterious someone made that large donation to the Giving Tree that covered their back payments."

"Neighbors helping neighbors." Eliza's lips curved. "That's what the Giving Tree is all about."

"Was it you?" Lindsay asked, wondering why she hadn't made the connection before.

Eliza gestured to a chair, then took a seat behind her desk. "Was what me?"

"Did you donate the money and designate it to go toward their past-due house payments?"

Eliza shook her head. "I wish I had, but it didn't even occur to me. I was too self-centered."

"You were not." Lindsay rose instantly to her friend's defense.

"I was." Eliza made the comment without apology. "That's what I meant about change. Sometimes difficult changes bring out the best in us."

"You really think so?"

"I do. I'd become comfortable in my selfishness." Eliza gave a little laugh. "I rarely empathized with someone else's plight. I hate to say it, but I was like your mother in that regard. I still have the tendency, but Kyle keeps me grounded."

Lindsay mentally picked her way through everything Eliza had said. "Do you think I'm selfish?"

She waited for the instant denial.

"It doesn't matter what I think." Eliza studied her through lowered lashes. "Do *you* think you're self-centered?"

Didn't Eliza realize that selfishness and self-centeredness were two different things? But Lindsay wasn't about to argue semantics.

Was she self-centered? The impulse was to say no, but because it was Eliza who'd asked, Lindsay carefully considered her response. "I think it's more the whole rut thing. Take my apartment. I don't love it there. My neighbors are loud, and the landlord ignores needed repairs for months. But the rent is cheap and moving can be a hassle, so I've stayed."

"And your job at the Enchanted Florist?"

"Same. I liked it, especially the design part, but I didn't love it," Lindsay admitted. "Shirley is a micromanager. Despite all the years I'd been there, she didn't fully trust me to do my job."

"You quit. That came from inner strength."

Lindsay shrugged. "I suppose it did."

"The baby will propel you out of your rut." Eliza met her gaze. "A child causes you to look at everything differently. Even though Kyle's sister, Lolo, isn't my child, the time she spent with us opened my eyes. Things are never as black-and-white as they appear. When you've never walked in someone else's shoes, it's easy to be judgmental."

When those smoky eyes settled on her, Lindsay wondered if Eliza was thinking of Cassie. Both Lindsay and her mother had judged—and condemned—Cassie's choices. Though Lindsay was still convinced she'd have handled the situation better than her older sister had, she was ashamed now by her lack of compassion.

Lindsay dropped down into the wooden chair next to the desk, mentally overwhelmed and physically exhausted. Over these past couple of days, though her body had craved sleep, she'd found herself lying in bed trying to make sense of her life and coming up empty.

In this single conversation with Eliza, she'd experienced a roller coaster of emotions. At the peak on second, feeling proud of herself for quitting her job. The next second, plunging toward the abyss, ashamed for drifting through life.

Lindsay had once thought there wasn't anything she couldn't tell Eliza. But there was one revelation about the person she'd been that she would keep to herself.

She hadn't been strong, not like Eliza thought. Instead, Lindsay had spent the past ten years waiting for Prince Charming to ride up on his white horse and rescue her from the monotony of her life.

Well, that fairy tale ended today.

The thought of waiting for a man—any man—to save her no longer held appeal.

She would chart her own course.

She would build a good, happy life for herself and her child.

Most important, she would be strong enough to ensure that her daughter grew up surrounded by nothing less than real love.

CHAPTER FOURTEEN

"When you invited me for dinner, you didn't mention it was a party." Lindsay glanced around Eliza's parlor, a large, spacious room that managed to hit the right note between warmth and elegance.

"Wherever Sarah Rose is, it's a party." Ami set the one-year-old on the floor, and the toddler made a drunken beeline for Eliza.

Almost from the time she was born, Sarah Rose had adored the one woman who hadn't wanted anything to do with her.

Much like the kitty she'd had as a child, Lindsay thought. Her mother hadn't been fond of felines, but Snookums had loved her. Okay, she'd loved rubbing up against Anita's legs and depositing cat hair on her clothes.

Her mother had never grown to love the cat.

Eliza, on the other hand, clearly doted on Sarah Rose. She scooped the toddler up into her arms and pretended to toss her back to her mother.

Sarah Rose, glossy dark curls pulled into two high pigtails, squealed with laughter.

"I'm going to let go and you'll fly like a bird." Eliza spoke in the teasing voice adults used with children.

Ami held out her arms. "Fly to Mama, sweet girl."

Instead of giving the child to her mother, Eliza deposited the squirming toddler into Lindsay's arms.

"Sounds like a party." Kyle's amused voice came from the doorway.

Lindsay turned with Sarah Rose in her arms. "That's what I just told your wife…"

Her voice trailed off when she saw it wasn't just Kyle and Beck traipsing into the room, but Owen as well.

Slowly and with great care, Lindsay placed Sarah Rose on the floor.

"Mama." Instead of Ami, the girl ran to her father, her arms outstretched.

"Mama?" Lindsay shifted her gaze to Ami, then to Beck.

"I'm Mama, too." Beck crouched down and received a big hug and sloppy kiss.

"We're working on Dada." Ami's face glowed at the sight of the two dark heads together. Sarah Rose might have her mother's green eyes, but her hair was as dark as walnut.

Behind Beck, Owen shifted awkwardly from one foot to the other. Though he spoke to Eliza, his gaze kept sliding to Lindsay. "Kyle invited me for dinner. I hope I'm not intruding."

"I told you, we'll have plenty." Kyle spoke before Eliza could respond. "Beck and I couldn't have gotten those refrigeration units in place without your help."

"You're not intruding," Eliza assured him, while slanting an apologetic glance in Lindsay's direction. "It's good to see you again, Owen."

Lindsay inclined her head slightly, letting her friend know she didn't have a problem with Owen being here.

Between the time Eliza had invited her over, not only had Ami and her family been added to the guest list, Katherine had appeared, along with Ruby and Gladys.

Apparently, when Katherine had heard Eliza planned to have

Lindsay over and was bringing out the fondue pots, she'd not only invited herself, but also her two friends.

The three women had disappeared into the kitchen, grocery sacks in their arms, immediately after they'd arrived.

Lindsay glanced around. "Where is Katherine?"

"She and her friends are getting everything set up in the dining room." A smile danced in Eliza's gray depths. "They chased me out of my own kitchen."

As Eliza explained, Lindsay watched Kyle sneak up behind his wife and wrap his arms around her waist. Eliza's lips curved as she turned to gaze up at him.

Kyle kissed her softly on the lips, and the newlyweds exchanged a smile filled with such love and promise that Lindsay had to look away.

The only trouble was, when she did, her wandering gaze connected with Owen's.

Something in the mechanic's hazel eyes had Lindsay's heartbeat quickening. Still, she managed to keep her tone even. "How'd you get roped into helping these two?"

She jerked a thumb in the direction of Beck, who was cooing over his little girl, and Kyle, who was cooing over his wife.

Owen crossed the short distance to her. "I ran into Katherine as I was leaving work. She mentioned Beck and Kyle needed help getting your refrigeration units moved and installed at the General Store."

The fact that he'd shown up to help didn't surprise her. Owen was always helping someone. What surprised Lindsay was that he'd run into Katherine near the Greasy Wrench. She wondered what Eliza's cousin had been doing in that part of town.

Before she could ask, Katherine appeared in the doorway leading to the dining room. "Prepare to be wowed."

"Did she really just say 'prepare to be wowed'?" Lindsay spoke in a low tone, leaning close to Owen so as not to be overheard.

Feeling eyes on her, Lindsay swiveled her gaze.

In the doorway, Katherine had been joined by Ruby and Gladys. Though Lindsay told herself it was only her imagination, the three appeared to be focused on her and Owen.

With big smiles on their faces.

~

"Wow." Owen's eyes widened as he took in the table.

Lindsay elbowed him. "You did not really just say that."

"Katherine promised we'd be wowed. She was right." Owen's gaze was riveted on the largest display of shrimp Lindsay had ever seen.

When Eliza had waved her guests into the dining room, Ruby had blocked Lindsay by asking a question about her mother. This slight delay had put Owen at her side when they stepped into the parlor. If Lindsay hadn't known better, she'd think she and her baby's daddy were being deliberately thrown together.

Even if that was the case, Lindsay wouldn't complain. She needed someone to hang with this evening. Other than the three older women, everyone else was part of a couple.

Seeing her friends so happy only emphasized the emptiness of her own life. Besides, Owen had done her a big favor in helping Beck and Kyle install her refrigeration units. No, she couldn't be rude.

"I don't know where to start." Lindsay found her attention drawn to the far end of table and the fondue pots of cheese. She loved cheese, any and all kinds.

"There are so many choices." Owen appeared equally over-whelmed by the selections. "It all looks good."

Ruby, obviously sensing Lindsay's interest in the cheese, pointed. "The white pot contains Emmentaler and Gruyère. I rubbed a clove of garlic around the inside of the pot."

Lindsay cocked her head.

Ruby lowered her voice as if imparting a secret. "It gives a hint of the flavor without being too much."

"What's in the red pot?" Owen asked.

"Beer and cheese," Ruby confided. "The other is pimento cheese."

Unable to resist, Lindsay strolled toward that end of the table, skirting her friends congregated around the main-course pots.

Owen and Ruby followed her.

"I've done fondue, but this is a-ma-zing." Lindsay breathed out the word as she took in the soft pretzel bites, bell peppers, celery and assorted bread cubes.

"We thought most would start with the cheese fondues, not that it matters." Ruby gestured to the couples filling their plates at the other end of the table. "It appears the shrimp is a hit."

"They look good." For a second, Owen looked as if he might join the throng. "What's in those pots?"

Though Owen hadn't specifically asked her, Lindsay answered, "Some kind of broth or oils would be my guess."

Ruby nodded approvingly. "Specifically, roasted garlic broth and coq au vin."

Out of the corner of her eye, Lindsay saw Ruby catch Gladys's eye and give her friend the thumbs-up.

Assuming Gladys was the one in charge of the main course, Lindsay flashed her own thumbs-up.

For a second, the older woman appeared startled, then smiled.

"I've only had fondue one other time." Owen turned to Lindsay. "The chocolate fondue at your apartment."

Ruby's eyes lit up. "Sounds like fun."

"Oh, it was fun." Recalling the night of gluttony, Lindsay gave a little laugh. "We dipped brownie cubes and mini cupcakes in chocolate."

"Don't forget the marshmallows."

"Chocolate and strawberry marshmallows." Lindsay brought a

hand to her stomach, but her smile couldn't have gotten any wider. "Sugar overload."

The light in Owen's eyes told her the memory was as pleasant for him as for her. They'd had some really good times, which was why she'd been stunned when he told her he didn't want to see her anymore.

Lindsay's smile slipped away. She turned to Ruby. "Do you recommend the garlic broth for the shrimp?"

Food and weather. Both safe topics. Once she'd depleted the food questions, Lindsay would bring up the recent warmer-than-normal temperatures.

Before answering, Ruby shifted her gaze between her and Owen. The look in her eyes might be assessing, but her voice remained mild when she answered. "Shrimp and scallops for the roasted garlic broth and bites of chicken and cubed beef for the coq au vin."

"When Eliza asked me over, I expected one fondue pot, maybe two." Lindsay forced a laugh. "Instead, I find myself at a fondue feast."

The only thing Lindsay could figure was Katherine and her friends were take-charge women. They must have heard the word *fondue* and decided to go all out.

It was incredible how, in such a short time, they'd created this wonderful, festive atmosphere. Three months ago, Lindsay would have wanted the evening to never end. Now, she didn't know how long she'd be able to stay and make polite conversation.

At the moment, she was finding it difficult to even look at Owen. His comment about their private fondue party had brought the memories flooding back. She blinked rapidly as tears flooded her eyes.

Darn hormones.

Keeping her face averted, Lindsay blurted, "Excuse me, please."

Then she did what she'd sworn she wouldn't do.

She bolted.

⮜

"I SHOULD LEAVE, TOO." Owen turned to go, but Ruby's hand on his arm stopped him.

"Lindsay will be back." The older woman looped her arm through his, the grip as steely as an NFL lineman's. "The direction she took leads to the restroom, not the front door."

"Oh." Owen shifted from one foot to the other. "I didn't know."

"I bet she's hungry. Why don't you get a plate for her?" Ruby met his gaze, concern in her eyes. "She looked a bit peaked to me."

Peaked?

Owen had thought Lindsay looked extra pretty tonight. Even dressed casually in jeans and a sweater the color of newly mown grass, she was by far the loveliest woman in the room. He hadn't taken his eyes off her since he'd first stepped into the parlor.

Had he missed the pallor? Was Ruby right?

He recalled how, when they'd been together, she'd often got so caught up in what she was doing that she forgot to eat. She simply couldn't continue that practice. Not with the baby coming.

Ruby shadowed him to the buffet table, and he took the china plate she held out.

Even as he added veggies to the plate, his gaze kept drifting to the hallway. Was Lindsay feeling sick? Was that why she'd made such an abrupt exit?

"I should check—"

"There she is."

While he and Ruby watched, Katherine caught Lindsay's attention and motioned to her.

But before Lindsay reached Katherine, Eliza intercepted her.

Owen, only a few feet away, remained where he was and watched the curious byplay.

"I saved a place for you," he heard Eliza tell her friend.

"Lindsay is sitting at my table." Katherine's smile might have been pleasant, but her tone brooked no argument. "You see her all the time. Ruby and I are eager to hear her plans for her shop."

When Eliza hesitated, Katherine added, "With my background in finance and accounting, I'll be able to give her some business tips."

Owen waited for Eliza to remind her cousin that while Katherine had an accounting background, Eliza ran her own shop, putting her in the perfect position to offer advice to someone launching a new business.

"I'd love to sit with you and Ruby, Katherine." Lindsay bestowed a warm smile on the woman.

"Wonderful. It's settled." Katherine turned to Eliza and made a shooing gesture. "You have guests to tend to, my dear."

"We'll catch up later." Lindsay gave Eliza's arm a squeeze and followed Katherine to a small table festively decorated with bright red napkins. "Will Gladys be joining us?"

The question carried easily to where Owen stood. He assumed the answer was yes. In Good Hope, it was often said if you saw one woman, the other two weren't far behind.

Before Katherine could answer, Ruby grabbed his arm and tugged him forward.

"Actually"—Katherine smiled broadly as Ruby's fingers dug deeper into his forearm—"the seats at this table are already taken. Owen is joining us."

∼

"IS THAT OKAY WITH YOU, LINDSAY?" Owen paused, his free hand on the back of the chair. "If you'd prefer to catch up with Gladys, I understand."

He was giving her an out, Lindsay realized.

Owen was willing to find a spot at another table. But where would that be? Lindsay knew how it felt to be the only single in a group of couples.

"Of course it's okay with me."

"I got these for you." Owen shoved a plate of veggies at her. "You're probably hungry."

When Lindsay took the china plate, her fingers brushed against his. Electricity zipped up her arm.

Lindsay resisted the urge to sigh. She'd hoped this connection would dull over time. So far, that hadn't happened. "You're very considerate."

Ruby patted Owen's back. "He's also a fine man."

"And a real hottie," Katherine added, her eyes twinkling.

Lindsay swore she heard Owen groan.

Not wanting to see the look in his eyes, she averted her gaze and took a step.

Katherine and Ruby inhaled sharply.

"You're leaving?" The horror in Katherine's voice both puzzled and amused Lindsay.

"Just to get some cheese sauce for the veggies." Lindsay slanted a glance at Owen. "Want to help me?"

Relief skidded across his face. "Sure."

Once they reached the buffet table and were out of earshot of the two older women, Owen turned to her. "Is it just me, or are they acting strangely?"

He didn't have to say who the "they" were, not when his gaze flicked briefly to the table they'd recently left.

Lindsay added a dollop of pimento cheese to her plate. "I think they're simply trying to be good hostesses. You know, making sure everyone is happy and getting along."

Those beautiful hazel eyes met hers. "We're getting along."

"Yes," she agreed. "We are."

His shoulders relaxed as he added beer cheese to the plate he picked up. "The crazy thing is, this is Eliza and Kyle's place, not their home."

"You and I have known these women for years." In addition to the cheese, Lindsay added pumpernickel bread cubes to her plate. "Does anything they do surprise you?"

Owen chuckled. The last of the tension between them dissolved.

"That looks good." Ami appeared on the other side of the table. She took a red pepper strip from Lindsay's plate and dipped it in the pimento cheese.

"Hey." Lindsay slapped playfully at her hand. "Get your own."

Ami laughed. "Why is it that what someone else has always looks better than what's on your own plate?"

Lindsay thought of Ami and Beck, of the home and the love they shared. Yes, what was on other people's plates often did look better.

"Thank you for helping Beck and Kyle." Ami shifted her attention to Owen. "It sounds as if those refrigeration units were a lot heavier than they looked."

"Beck and Kyle could have handled it." His gaze slid to Lindsay. "But I was happy to help. I'm happy to help in any way I can."

Ignoring Ami's speculative glance, Lindsay lifted her plate. "This all looks so good. I can't wait to dive in."

Before they could head back to the table, Gladys wandered over.

"Can I interest anyone in a glass of wine?" Gladys held a bottle of one of Eliza's highly prized vintages in one hand and a bottle of sparkling grape juice in the other.

"I adore that particular red, but I have to say no." Ami glanced longingly at the bottle, then sighed. "Sparkling grape juice is more my speed these days."

"That's right. You'll have another little one, come spring." Gladys smiled warmly. "There's no greater blessing than a child."

After the older woman had poured some of the juice into a glass, she shifted her focus. "What about you two?"

Gladys knew Lindsay loved wine. If she turned down a glass,

the astute older woman would know something was up. Gladys could ferret out a secret from fifty paces.

"I'm going to stick with the sparkling grape juice tonight." Owen spoke in an offhand tone that Lindsay guessed was anything but casual. "C'mon, Lin, hop on board the sparkling grape train tonight."

Gladys shot Owen a sharp glance. "Lindsay can have wine if she wants."

"Of course she can," Owen said smoothly. "It's her decision."

I'll help in any way I can.

Lindsay smiled and managed to keep the relief from her voice as she turned to Gladys. "Sparkling grape juice for me, as well."

CHAPTER FIFTEEN

Throughout dinner, the two older women kept up a lively conversation about recent events in Good Hope. It was odd, Lindsay thought, how the ones they mentioned happened to be all ones she and Owen had attended together.

It was nice reliving those times. Because everyone at the table had been there, conversation flowed easily. By the time they reached the dessert phase of the evening, Lindsay had completely relaxed.

"Does it seem strange not to be working?" Katherine directed the question to Lindsay.

Owen jumped to her defense before Lindsay had a chance to respond. "It takes a lot of planning on the front end to get a business off the ground."

"It isn't the same as getting up and going to a job every day." Katherine's gaze returned to Lindsay.

"It's definitely different," Lindsay admitted. "I've already started to lose track of what day it is. They blur together."

"Tell me about it," Ruby piped up. "If it wasn't for cards on Monday and Wii bowling on Wednesday, I wouldn't have a clue what day it is."

Katherine nodded at her dear friend's statement, but the gaze she settled on Lindsay was all business. "Unless you've got a secret trust fund, you're going to need to start bringing in money."

"I know." Lindsay chewed on her bottom lip, her earlier calm disappearing as icy fingers traveled up her spine. "While I'd love to work exclusively on weddings, until I get established, I'll accept any business that comes my way."

Katherine nodded approvingly. "What steps have you taken so far?"

"I've contacted wholesalers and set up accounts." Lindsay pushed her dessert plate to the side, her stomach tensing at the thought of everything she'd done and everything still needing to be done. "I've also ordered the accessories I'll need."

Owen cocked his head. "Accessories?"

"Vases, ribbons, pruning equipment," Lindsay explained.

"What about your seller's permit?" Katherine asked.

"I applied. I haven't heard anything yet." Lindsay twisted the napkin in her lap around her finger. "They said it can take up to three weeks."

"Sometimes they require a security deposit." Katherine's eyes never left Lindsay's. "It can be substantial."

A knot formed in the pit of Lindsay's stomach. "Up to fifteen thousand dollars."

Ruby's blond brows formed a perfect vee. "Why would they ask for a deposit?"

"I wouldn't worry about a deposit." Owen shot Lindsay a reassuring smile. "From what I understand, it's usually only required if you have a history of not paying your taxes."

Lindsay hoped Owen was right. She took a calming breath, releasing it slowly. In the past two weeks, she'd discovered something about herself. She was a floral designer at heart, not a businesswoman.

Unlike her friends, she didn't look forward to dealing with the financial aspect of running a business. Dreaded it, in fact.

Simply requesting the required permits and tax forms, not to mention contacting wholesalers, had made her palms grow damp and head swim. Yet, pride had her sitting a little taller. Instead of throwing up her hands or diving into a pint of Ben & Jerry's, she'd persevered and done what had to be done.

Making this business a success was her only way to give her baby a good life.

"What's your business structure?" Katherine lifted a piece of pineapple with her fork and brought it to her lips.

For a second, Lindsay felt a stab of panic, then realized this was something she'd researched and understood. "Sole proprietorship."

Katherine nodded approval. "At this point in your venture, that makes the most sense."

"I'm grateful to Eliza for giving me space in her store." Lindsay glanced across the room where her friend stood at the table perusing the dessert selections.

Kyle was behind his wife, arms looped around her waist. While Lindsay watched, he stole a strawberry from her plate and popped it into his mouth. Eliza swatted at him, pretending to be annoyed, but the smile on her face gave her away.

Sighing, Lindsay pulled her attention back to the conversation and found Katherine staring at her with an unreadable look in her eye. Both Owen and Ruby were focused on dipping pieces of fruit into the chocolate on their plates.

Lindsay fluttered a hand in the air. "What was I saying?"

"How grateful you are to Eliza for giving you space."

To her surprise, it wasn't Katherine who answered, but Owen. Apparently, he wasn't as absorbed with his food as she'd thought.

"Yes, well, it was extremely generous." Lindsay's earlier panic over taking this big step outside her comfort zone resurfaced. She determinedly shoved aside the worries. "If I'd needed to rent a location, I never could have done it."

Then it struck her how that sounded. As if she was taking

advantage of her friend, when nothing could be further from the truth.

"I'm going to pay Eliza rent." Lindsay hesitated. "Once I get on my feet."

"She won't take your money." Ruby swirled a bright red cherry in the chocolate sauce, making a pattern on her plate.

If Anita Fishback had seen Lindsay do that, the plate would have been snatched away and she'd have received a stern lecture on playing with food.

Lindsay lifted her chin. "I'll make her take it."

"She won't." Ruby quit playing and popped the cherry dripping with chocolate into her mouth.

"She will," Lindsay insisted. "Believe me, I can be as stubborn as Eliza."

"Friendship is all about give-and-take." Ruby gestured with her head toward Katherine. "Look at me and this one. I take and she gives."

Lindsay widened her eyes, but before she could respond to the outrageous boast, Katherine chortled.

"Friends make your problems their own." Ruby's blue eyes were serious. "Give Eliza a chance to be a good friend. Don't take her desire to help away from her."

Katherine's gaze shifted to Owen. "This one here is another friend you can count on for help."

Lindsay's heart quit beating. What did Katherine know? Had Eliza told her about the baby? As quickly as the thought surfaced, Lindsay brushed it aside.

She trusted Ami and Eliza implicitly. They would never betray her confidence.

Owen's expression stilled, and his fingers had a death grip on the fork.

"No one pressured him to help Beck and Kyle carry in those refrigeration units. Here's to three good men." Katherine lifted her glass of wine in a mock toast, then her gaze pinned Lindsay. "Owen volunteered because he wants to be a good friend."

Ruby gave a decisive nod and added, "It's the Good Hope way."

~

IT MIGHT BE the Good Hope way, but Owen didn't believe for a second that Lindsay would allow him to do more than the bare minimum. That's why he was surprised when, at the end of the evening, she asked if he could help move some furniture out of her spare bedroom to make room for an office.

Katherine and Ruby nodded their approval at the question and his agreement to come over the next morning. Owen was feeling pretty good about how the evening was going when Eliza's brother showed up. Ethan paused by the dining room colonnade.

In his dark pants and sweater, he looked like one of those male models in a fashion magazine. Owen resisted the urge to glance at Lindsay. He wasn't sure he wanted to see her reaction.

Ruby glanced at her friend. "What's Ethan doing here?"

Katherine didn't appear surprised to see her cousin. "The boy lives here. Eliza told me he was out for the evening."

"Did he have a date?" Lindsay's tone gave nothing away.

This time, Owen couldn't help but glance in her direction. She'd move her plate back in front of her, and her eyes were on the fruit she was spearing with her fork.

Ruby and Katherine exchanged glances.

Katherine spoke first. "I guess I don't know."

"It's something we should know." Ruby's cryptic comment had Katherine nodding.

"What are you two cooking up?" Gladys appeared at the edge of the table.

"Just wondering who Ethan is dating." Katherine shot a pointed look at Ruby. "*If* he's dating."

"He's your cousin, not mine," Ruby reminded Katherine. "His dating status is something you should determine."

It was a curious interchange that Gladys appeared to understand completely. When she shifted her attention to Owen, those pale blue eyes sharpened.

"Lindsay invited Owen to come to her apartment in the morning." Katherine's lips tipped up in an approving smile.

"It might be easier if he simply spent the night." Gladys cackled.

Lindsay felt her cheeks warm. "Owen is coming to move furniture. I told him he didn't have—"

"I want to help. In your condition, you shouldn't be moving heavy furniture."

Like three bloodhounds who'd caught an especially juicy scent, the three older women snapped to alert.

"Condition?" Gladys's voice reverberated with excitement. "Does this mean you're—"

"I have a *back* condition." Lindsay emphasized the word and flashed Owen a look that told him he was lucky he wasn't six feet under right now. "A herniated disc."

Owen was ninety-nine percent sure Lindsay didn't have any issues with her spine, had never had an issue, but he gave her props for quick thinking.

The gleam in Gladys's eyes disappeared, and she relaxed her stance.

"In addition to knee issues, my son, Frank, has experienced his share of spine problems." Gladys pointed a finger at Lindsay. "You let Owen move that furniture. I don't want to hear that you lifted a single piece. Understood?"

"Don't worry. I'm not about to take any risks." The promise in Lindsay's voice reassured Owen.

Despite knowing he'd be in for a rigorous day, Owen couldn't help but look forward to the morning.

His mood took a nose dive when Ethan strolled over. He'd

visited briefly with his sister and brother-in-law before making a beeline for their table. Was Lindsay the draw?

The wealthy bachelor flashed the smile that always had the single females in Good Hope swooning. This time, his smile appeared directed at his cousin and her two friends. "What are you three plotting?"

"Plotting?" Katherine brought bony, bejeweled fingers to her chest, her expression entirely too innocent. "Whatever would we be plotting?"

Ethan snagged a chair from a nearby table, spun it around and sat. "Let me think. World domination? A liquor license for Muddy Boots? Or perhaps something that involves these two?"

He jerked a thumb in the direction of Lindsay and Owen.

"How did you—" Ruby began.

One look from Gladys had Ruby falling silent.

"There's a story here." Ethan snagged a slice of apple from his cousin's plate and popped it into his mouth. "I'm not leaving until I hear it."

"You're right." Katherine emitted a trill of a laugh. "We were securing free labor for Lindsay."

Shifting his gaze, Ethan bestowed that heart-stopping smile on Lindsay. Her cheeks pinked, and Owen fought the urge to throttle Ethan.

It wasn't that he was jealous, merely protective. After all, everyone in Good Hope knew that Ethan was a player. As far as Owen knew, he'd never stuck with the same woman for more than a couple of months.

The fact that the same could be said of him was something Owen chose not to examine too closely.

"Lindsay needs furniture moved at her apartment. Owen volunteered." Katherine gave him an approving smile.

"He's going to have to move everything himself," Ruby added. "Lindsay can't help."

At Ethan's look of confusion, Katherine sighed. "She suffers from a slipped disc."

Owen wasn't certain a herniated disc was the same as a slipped disc, but he didn't bother to correct the woman. It didn't really matter, as Lindsay didn't have either condition.

Ethan fixed his gaze on Lindsay. "I didn't realize you had trouble with your back."

She shifted in her seat. "It isn't something I talk about."

If Ethan noticed she hadn't really confirmed his comment, it didn't show. His expression turned thoughtful. "What needs to be moved?"

She ticked off the items on her fingers. "A bed. A small nightstand. Oh, and a dresser."

"What are you doing with them?" Absently, Ethan picked another piece of fruit from his cousin's plate.

"Donating them to a Giving Tree recipient." Lindsay took a sip of sparkling grape juice. "There's a family not far from me who needs bedroom furniture for their son."

"I'll help." Ethan turned to Owen. "Maneuvering those items down the outside steps won't be easy."

For a second, Owen wondered how the man knew where Lindsay lived, much less that her building had outside steps. Then he remembered the *date*. A muscle in his jaw jumped. "Not necessary."

Ignoring the brusque tone, Ethan turned to Lindsay. "I can be over at eight. Unless that's too early?"

She shook her head and smiled at Ethan. "Eight works."

Sensing this was a battle he couldn't win, Owen would accept the guy's help. But there was no way Ethan was going to be there alone with Lindsay.

If Ethan planned to be there at eight, Owen would be there at seven thirty.

LINDSAY MIGHT HAVE SPENT the past ten years hopping out of bed at six thirty, but since quitting her job, she'd given herself permission to sleep in. Last Friday, she hadn't crawled out of bed until nearly nine.

The overwhelming fatigue that dogged Lindsay early in her pregnancy might have eased its grip, but she still found herself yawning in the midafternoon. According to the books on pregnancy she'd devoured, the tiredness would be history in another month.

Which was good, Lindsay thought, because launching a business demanded long hours.

Since Owen and Ethan planned to arrive at the ungodly hour of eight a.m., Lindsay set her alarm and rolled out of bed at seven. She pulled on a striped sweater in bright jewel tones, then tugged on her favorite blue jeans.

The pair, which had once been relegated to the back of her closet for being too big, now fit perfectly. Lindsay smiled when the zipper slid easily up.

Tomorrow, she'd officially enter the second trimester, but other than a slight swell low in her abdomen, no one would guess she was pregnant by looking at her.

Lindsay couldn't stop thinking about this tiny being nestled inside her. Right now, it was the size of a lemon. And according to the experts, in a couple of weeks she'd feel this little one move. She wondered how—

A knock interrupted her thoughts and had her glancing at the clock.

7:28.

After checking the peephole, she opened the door and greeted Owen with a cheery, "Good morning."

"Good morning." Owen stepped inside. While it wasn't cold outside, it was windy. His hair stood up in sandy tufts.

Lindsay wondered if he remembered that the plaid flannel shirt he wore today had been one of her favorites. "You're early."

"I've been up since six. I've been driving around your block for the last hour."

Lindsay widened her eyes. "Seriously?"

"Naw, just kidding." Owen gestured to the short hall leading to the living room. "If you show me what needs to be moved, we can get started."

"Ethan won't be here until eight," she reminded him.

"We don't need him." When she didn't immediately answer, he shot her a smile that had her knees turning to jelly. "Do we?"

"I guess not." She hesitated. "I mean, I'm certainly capable of helping."

Owen's eyes reflected his horror. "Not in your—"

Lindsay arched a brow. "Not in my condition?"

The tips of Owen's ears turned red. "I'm sorry about that, and with Gladys of all people..."

Lindsay waved a dismissive hand. "We covered it."

"Thanks to your quick thinking." Owen held up a hand, fingers lifted in the Boy Scouts salute. "I won't make that mistake again."

"I know." Lindsay touched his arm, then immediately pulled her hand back and cleared her throat. "Let me show you what you'll be moving."

She strolled ahead of him down the short hall, conscious of his muscular body only inches behind her. Though she recalled Owen telling her he wore cologne only on special occasions, she swore she caught a faint whiff of the lime scent she loved.

Seconds later, Lindsay reached her destination. With him still too close for comfort, she stepped inside the spare bedroom. Despite it being the size of a matchbox, she'd managed to cram not only bunk beds, but a nightstand and a three-drawer dresser into the room. "Cassie's boys sleep here whenever they need a place to stay."

Owen glanced around and rocked back on his heels, his expression inscrutable. "I assume you'll be converting it into a nursery."

"Maybe." Lindsay gazed at the room that was smaller than most walk-in closets. "For the time being, it'll be my office."

"What about the baby? Where will she sleep?"

"I'm thinking of going with a co-sleeper bassinet, instead of a crib." Lindsay kept her tone offhand. "Ami and Beck used one for Sarah Rose and swear by it."

Puzzlement blanketed Owen's face. "I don't even know what that is."

"Think of it as a bassinet that attaches to the side of the parent's bed." Lindsay felt her cheeks warm as she continued. "If she wakes during the night and wants to nurse, I'll be right there."

Owen frowned. "I thought having a baby sleep in bed with you was dangerous."

"She'll be in her own *bassinet*," Lindsay emphasized the word. "She won't be in bed with me."

"Mindy always slept in a crib," Owen murmured, then cleared his throat. "What if the boys need a place to crash?"

The abrupt change of subject had Lindsay's head spinning. Apparently, he was done discussing the baby. Unfortunately, he'd picked a sensitive topic for the switch.

Though his voice held no judgment, Owen was aware of the turmoil in Cassie's home. He also knew Lindsay provided a haven for the boys when troubles in the home escalated.

The worst situation had occurred several years earlier when Lindsay had taken in her niece for months in order to protect her from Cassie's live-in boyfriend.

Lindsay still hadn't fully forgiven her sister for putting a guy above Dakota's welfare.

"I'll always make room for my niece and nephews." Lindsay would sleep on the floor before she'd turn them away or leave them in an unsafe situation. "The boys will be happy with an air mattress on the floor, as long as I make them chocolate-chip pancakes in the morning."

"I'd sleep on the floor for those pancakes of yours."

Lindsay laughed. "They are amazing."

A knock sounded at the door.

"Looks like I'm not the only early one." Owen sounded disappointed.

Last night, she'd been relieved when Ethan had volunteered to help move the furniture so she wouldn't have to be alone with Owen.

Now, as Lindsay slipped out of the bedroom, she realized she didn't have anything to fear from Owen. The only thing she had to fear was leftover longings for a life that could never be hers.

CHAPTER SIXTEEN

"That wasn't so bad." Owen gazed at the furniture stacked in the back of his pickup, ready for delivery to a family in need.

"It makes a difference when you have two men." Ethan pushed up the tailgate. "Are you sure you won't need help unloading this stuff?"

"According to your sister, there are people at the house where this is going who will help."

"If they aren't there, text me." Ethan's gaze met his. "I have a meeting at noon, but I'm free until then."

"Thanks, Ethan." Owen held out his hand.

"I was happy to help." Ethan gave Owen's hand a shake.

"I misjudged you."

Eliza's baby brother had been just enough younger that Owen had had little contact with him growing up. Owen had judged Ethan based on his money and his success. Based on what he'd observed this morning, he'd been wrong.

"We got off on the wrong foot." Ethan gestured with his head toward Lindsay, who'd started down the steps of her third-floor apartment. "If I'd known you and Lindsay were involved, I'd never have agreed to escort her to the wedding and reception."

"We're not—" Owen stopped, not sure how to describe what was between him and Lindsay. "Lindsay and I are friends."

The phone in Ethan's pocket emitted a sound that reminded Owen of the *Law & Order* chimes. Pulling it from his pocket, he glanced down. "Looks like the meeting has been moved up. I have to go."

Lindsay strolled up. "Pancakes and coffee are on the table."

"Thanks, but I'm going to take a rain check." Ethan lifted a hand. "Take care of that back, Lindsay."

Without waiting for a reply, Ethan slipped behind the wheel of his truck, and the engine roared to life.

"What am I going to do with all the pancakes?" Lindsay wailed as Ethan's taillights disappeared from view.

Impulsively, Owen slung an arm around her shoulders. "Hey, you still have me."

A look he couldn't quite decipher crossed her face. "Yes, I guess I do."

The only trouble was, she didn't look very happy about it.

LINDSAY TRIED TO CALM HERSELF. She'd been certain today's mail would include her seller's certificate. After all, it had been nearly three weeks since she'd submitted her application. Instead, the handful of mail held only bills and a circular promoting sales at the Good Hope Market.

It would be okay, she reassured herself with false heartiness. Lindsay was still feeling out of sorts when she received a text from Owen asking if she was free this evening.

She wasn't sure why the text pricked her temper. Maybe because she hadn't heard a peep from him since he'd helped her move the furniture last week. Not that she expected them to be in daily contact.

This wasn't like last spring when they'd spoken or texted every day. Whatever was between them now was a totally different animal. Still, hearing from him at five o'clock on a Friday night rubbed her the wrong way.

Did he really think she'd be waiting around, hoping to hear from him and eager to get together? When she found herself wanting to tell him to come over, she informed him she already had plans.

She *did* have plans. With herself and the television. She didn't mind spending a Friday night alone. She'd certainly had a lot of practice.

Even in her younger years, she'd never been a partier. A movie, a bowl of popcorn and an early bedtime would round out this evening. The phone rang while she was trying to decide if she was in the mood for a romantic comedy or an action movie.

She smiled at her sister's name on the display.

"Hey, Cass." Lindsay put the phone on speaker and settled back in the chair, her hand on the remote. "How are you?"

"That piece of junk I call a car won't start. I have to get to work." Cassie's words tumbled out, and Lindsay heard the panic. "I'm supposed to be there at six. Ryder is counting on me."

Ryder Goodhue owned the coffee shop where Cassie worked. Recently, he'd started turning over some of the day-to-day supervision to her sister.

"What about the person watching Axl?" Her sister had numerous babysitters on speed dial, so Lindsay wasn't ever sure who was watching her youngest nephew. "Can she give you a lift?"

"The boys are watching him tonight." Cassie's voice turned pleading. "Please, Lin, can you give me a ride? I'll figure out a way to get home."

"No worries. I'll be right there." Tossing the remote aside, Lindsay hopped up from the couch, then glanced down. Normally, she wouldn't consider going out sans makeup and in the soft flannel pj's she'd pulled on for a "movie night" at home. She reassured herself this would be only a quick trip in the car.

Cassie was in the driveway next to her rusted-out foreign compact when Lindsay pulled up. The second Cassie's seat belt was buckled, they were on the move.

"I have another favor to ask." Cassie lifted a hand when Lindsay cast her a suspicious glance. "Feel free to say no."

"What is it?"

"K.T and Braxton were begging to go to the high school tonight and work on the homecoming displays." Cassie gave a little laugh. "They're desperately hoping their club wins the free early-entry tickets to the haunted house."

The puzzle pieces fell into place. "You'd like me to watch Axl."

"And maybe drop off the boys at the high school." Cassie shot her a hopeful smile. "They can ride their bikes if they have to, but it'd be nice if someone—meaning you—could give them a lift."

"Sure." Lindsay wasn't sure why Cassie was acting like any of this was a big deal. She liked helping her sister. "I can do that."

"Thank you. Thank you." Cassie flung her arms around Lindsay. "You're the best sister."

"Hey, I'm driving here." But Lindsay couldn't help but smile as she pushed her sister back with one hand.

It was good to see Cassie excited about work and the boys interested in school activities. For years, Lindsay had worried about her sister and her nephews. Now it seemed life in Cassie's household had settled into an easy rhythm.

Perhaps, seeing the psychologist had helped. Maybe it was Dan's support. Or even Ryder giving her a job and boosting her confidence with added responsibilities. Whatever it was, Lindsay hoped it continued.

After dropping off her sister, Lindsay headed back to the house. She came to a full stop at the lights and was careful not to speed. The last thing she needed was Cade, or one of his deputies, to pull her over. She couldn't imagine offering her license and registration to an officer of the law while wearing pink pajamas covered in frolicking monkeys.

She released the breath she must have been holding when she pulled into Cassie's driveway. The door was unlocked, and Lindsay stepped inside without knocking. Braxton glanced up from an iPad while K.T.'s eyes remained focused on his sketch pad. Axl sat on the floor, eating Cheerios straight out of a family-sized box.

The house Cassie called home was a white single-story with peeling paint and leaky windows covered with plastic. The inside wasn't much better, although Lindsay noticed that Cassie was doing a better job of keeping it clean.

Other than the Cheerios scattered on the floor, the worn rug looked like it had been recently vacuumed, and there were no dishes in the sink. The two Rottweilers were gone, taken by Clint when he moved out.

"I hear you two need a ride to the high school." With that one sentence, Lindsay captured her nephews' attention.

Braxton lifted a dark brow. "Does this mean you'll watch the brat?"

Despite the term, Brax's tone held affection.

"That's right." Lindsay shot a glance at Axl, then refocused on her eldest nephew.

Braxton's hair was shaved up the sides, while the rest had been left long. The jet-black strands on the top were bleached. It was a new look for the computer geek, but it suited him.

K.T., a talented artist, had also altered his hairstyle since Lindsay had last seen him. Instead of brushing his shoulders, it was now a short messy mop that suited his thin, angular face. The strands she remembered being streaked with violet were a rich, chestnut brown.

Both boys wore jeans with holes and graphic T-shirts with sayings Lindsay wasn't sure she wanted to read.

"Awesome." K.T. scrambled to his feet. "What about Axl?"

"Were you zoned?" Braxton set aside the iPad Lindsay had given him last Christmas. "Aunt Lindsay said she'd watch him."

Lindsay crouched down beside the little boy who was shoving cereal into his mouth as if he expected the box to be snatched away any second. "Hey, buddy. Want to go for a ride in the car?"

It took only a minute for Braxton to transfer the car seat from Cassie's beater to Lindsay's vehicle. Then only another ten or so minutes for them to reach the high school. Lights blazed from every window, and the parking lot was full.

"All this activity can't be from club members working on displays." Lindsay pulled her brows together. "What's going on at the school tonight?"

"All-school play." Braxton slung his backpack over his shoulder and stepped from the car. "Appreciate the ride, Aunt Lindsay."

"Yeah." K.T. slammed the back door. "Thanks."

"Wait," Lindsay called out when they turned to walk away.

"What is it?" Braxton shifted impatiently from one foot to the other, casting quick glances at the school.

"Do you have the phone with you?" Lindsay knew Cassie provided the boys one cellphone with limited minutes to share.

K.T. patted his jeans pocket. "Right here."

"When you're ready to come home, let me know, and Axl and I will pick you up."

"No worries." Braxton waved a hand. "We can catch a ride."

"Text me when you're ready to leave. We'll discuss possible options then." She shifted her gaze from one boy to the other. "Understand?"

K.T. only shrugged, but Braxton nodded. "Sure."

"Have fun." Lindsay knew it was silly, but she didn't immediately drive off. She wanted to make sure they were safely inside the building before she left.

She smiled when Braxton deliberately bumped K.T. and his brother immediately shoved him back. Despite their different interests and personalities, the boys were good friends. A friendship that had helped them survive some difficult times.

The boys had just disappeared inside the school when a tapping sounded on her car window.

Lindsay whirled, then smiled and rolled down the window. "Gladys. Hello."

"Babysitting tonight?" Gladys glanced into the backseat to where Axl sat, slamming two red foam cars together.

"Cassie's car wouldn't start, so I took her to work. The boys are working on homecoming displays, and this little guy"— Lindsay gestured with her head toward the backseat—"is my date this evening."

Gladys, resplendent in an ice-blue caftan with silver swirls, cocked her head. "What about Owen? Is he helping you?"

"Not this evening." Lindsay found herself both amused and disturbed by the older woman's assumption that she and Owen were joined at the hip. "Owen mentioned something about getting together, but I was busy."

No need to tell Gladys that the babysitting gig had been a last-minute addition to her plans.

"What about you?" Lindsay tried to deflect. "Are you here to help with the homecoming displays or to watch the play?"

"The play." Gladys answered, then immediately shifted gears. "You mentioned Cassie's car. What's wrong with it?"

"No idea." Lindsay shrugged. "All I know is when she went to leave for work, it wouldn't start."

"That must have been frustrating." A thoughtful look stole over Gladys's face. "Especially with her and the boys sharing one vehicle."

Lindsay nodded. "That's why I'm praying whatever is wrong is something that can be easily fixed."

"Owen is a whiz with cars. You should have him look at it."

"I suppose." Lindsay spotted Ruby and Katherine coming up the sidewalk, headed straight for Gladys. "Well, it looks as if your friends have arrived. Enjoy the play."

"You enjoy your evening as well." Instead of rushing off,

Gladys remained on the sidewalk while her friends joined her. Shoulder to shoulder, the three women watched her drive away.

"Well, Axl," Lindsay said to the boy in the backseat. "It looks like it's just you and me tonight, buddy."

"Car," Axl called out, seconds before the foam roadster hit her in the back of the head.

OWEN PULLED to a stop at the curb in front of Cassie's house and cut the engine. Lindsay's import sat in the driveway, parked behind her sister's hunk-a-junk.

He, or one of his mechanics, had worked on Cassie's vehicle numerous times in the past couple of years. Owen wondered what he'd find wrong this time.

Gladys had told him she thought it was likely the battery, but that had been replaced right before Christmas last year. He still didn't understand why Lindsay had had Gladys call him instead of simply contacting him herself.

In ground-eating strides, Owen covered the cracked sidewalk to the sinking concrete stoop that functioned as a front porch. His heart picked up speed at the thought of seeing Lindsay.

He couldn't believe it had been more than a week since he and Ethan had moved the furniture for her. The last eight days had been crazy busy.

Colton, one of his transmission specialists, had been out with a new baby, leaving Owen to pick up the slack. He'd arrived home late every night, too tired to do anything but crash.

With Cody back on the job today, Owen had been able to leave the garage on time. He'd hoped to spend the evening with Lindsay, even if he had to answer parenting or relationship questions in the process.

When she'd texted back that she already had plans, he'd wondered if that was an excuse.

Was she pissed she hadn't heard from him? That made no sense considering she was the one who'd made it clear she wasn't eager to pick up where they'd left off. Owen didn't want that, either.

Too close, too fast came to mind when he thought of those four months after Mindy passed away. What he and Lindsay were building now was different. She was having his baby. They were forging a partnership, not having a romance.

Still, he'd missed seeing her, talking with her, laughing with her. Owen opened the rickety aluminum storm door and rapped on a wooden door with peeling varnish.

After several seconds, it opened. Lindsay stood with Axl riding her hip. The pink pajamas she wore were something Mindy would have loved. Lindsay's face was shiny clean, her hair pulled back with two pink, heart-shaped clips.

She was obviously spending the night. He wondered why she would stay instead of driving the short distance to her apartment. Cassie's house was so small, it barely accommodated her and her three boys.

"Owen." Lindsay bit her lower lip, drawing his attention to her mouth. "What are you doing here?"

Pulling his gaze from those luscious lips, he gestured with one hand. "Mind if I come in for a second?"

She hesitated for only the briefest of moments before stepping aside to let him enter. Once he was inside, Lindsay shut the door, then gave it a second push with her backside to get it to latch.

When she turned back to him, her blue eyes were watchful. "To what do I owe this honor?"

Not exactly the response he'd hoped for. Especially when he was so wholly glad to see *her*. "Ah, you, ah, you asked me to come."

He nearly groaned aloud. He sounded like some awkward teenager.

"I told you I had plans for tonight." She spoke slowly and distinctly, as if he was someone who had difficulty understanding.

He frowned. "You told Gladys your sister's car wouldn't start."

She offered a grudging nod of agreement. "Gladys thought it might be the battery."

"I replaced the battery last winter."

"Why are we talking about the car?" Lindsay puffed out her cheeks, then exhaled. "I want to know why you're here."

"The car is why I'm here." Well, part of the reason, anyway, and the only reason he'd own. Owen felt his frustration surge. Couldn't she look a little happy to see him? "Gladys said you wanted me to come over and check what's wrong with it."

"Where would she get that idea?"

"From you."

Lindsay shook her head. "Not from me."

Owen blew out a breath. "Are you telling me you and Gladys never discussed Cassie being without wheels?"

Lindsay started to shake her head again, then stopped. A look of chagrin crossed her face. "I did say I took Cassie to her job because her car wouldn't start. Gladys may have mentioned something about having you look at it."

A smile tugged at the corners of Owen's lips. Now they were getting somewhere. "And?"

"I may have given her the impression that would be a good idea." Lindsay stepped to the side as Axl barreled past her and flung himself at Owen.

"The mystery is solved." Owen swung the child up and gave a good-natured chuckle. "I don't think either of us is surprised that Gladys Bertholf played a starring role in this drama."

"I'm sorry you came all the way out here for nothing." Lindsay's voice held genuine regret.

Owen went from amused to confused in seconds. "Did someone already fix the car?"

"No." Lindsay glanced around, as if hoping to find the answer she sought in the shabby furniture and thrift-store lamps. "But I don't know that Cass has the money for repairs. And right now, I don't have any extra to lend her."

Lindsay's cheeks pinked with the admission.

"Cassie is practically family." Owen waved a dismissive hand. "I won't charge her."

"She's not your family," Lindsay protested.

"Cassie is my daughter's aunt." Owen swung Axl down to the floor.

When Lindsay opened her mouth, Owen held up a hand. "Just give me the keys and let me take a quick look."

Lindsay hesitated, then moved to a hook screwed into the side of a kitchen cabinet. Slipping the keyring off of the hook, she crossed to him. "Promise you won't do any major repairs before Cassie gets home."

Owen curled his fingers around the keys she placed in his outstretched hand and smiled. "Hey, I'm a mechanic, not a miracle worker."

CHAPTER SEVENTEEN

"Are you sure you can't sit for five?" Lindsay glanced around the dining area of the Daily Grind. For the first time since she'd arrived, there was no one waiting at the front counter.

Cassie's gaze did the same sweep. Though she glanced longingly at the empty chair, she blew out a breath. "I better not."

Lindsay took a sip of her very excellent decaf vanilla latte. "Is Ryder that strict?"

"I don't think he'd mind. He's a good guy." Still, Cassie remained standing. "This job might not seem like much, but I like it. Ryder has given me more responsibility, and I want to be worthy of his trust."

"I understand." Lindsay smiled at her sister. "It's just nice to spend time with you."

"It's very nice, especially without Axl throwing foam cars or pitching a fit about something." Cassie chuckled, then sobered. "I wish Owen could have come with you this morning."

"He's working." Even if he hadn't been, Lindsay wasn't sure she'd have invited him.

When she'd picked up Cassie from work last night, in Cassie's car, her sister had been speechless. Though Lindsay had repeated what Owen told her, that a loose battery cable had taken two minutes to tighten, Cassie wanted to repay them both. She'd issued an invitation for them to stop in at the Daily Grind for a coffee and doughnut, her treat.

"Well, be sure and tell him my offer has no expiration date." Cassie turned to a couple who'd gotten up to leave at a nearby table. "Thanks. Come back and see us again soon."

"We will." The woman slipped an arm through her boyfriend's arm, an easy gesture that spoke of comfortable intimacy.

Lindsay's heart burned with envy.

The couple hadn't even walked out the door when Cassie was clearing their table. "I forgot to mention that Mom and Len stopped in last night."

Lindsay started to say she was surprised the two were still together, but stopped herself. Nothing about her mother really surprised her.

"Really?" Lindsay set down her cup. "Anything interesting going on with them?"

"She tried to pump me about you and Ethan Shaw." Cassie's gaze turned curious. "Doesn't she know you're with Owen?"

"You know Mom." Lindsay chuckled. "She has high aspirations for us."

"Not for me. Not anymore." Cassie's smile faded, and for a second, a haunted look filled her eyes. "I heard Krew is coming back for homecoming."

Cassie's expression gave no indication what she was feeling, but Lindsay had a good idea. "I'm surprised she brought him up. She hasn't mentioned him in years."

"It was Len who brought him up." Cassie twisted the dishrag around her finger. "Not Mom."

"How do you feel about him being back in Good Hope?"

Cassie's face remained carefully blank. "It doesn't matter to me. Mom was always the one who insisted he was Dakota's father. She saw his money-making potential and went with it."

"You liked him."

Cassie's blue eyes narrowed. "I didn't know him."

The words were cold enough to cut glass.

"What I meant was, most of the girls in this town were half in love with him." Lindsay kept her voice light. "Heck, I was only in seventh grade and I thought he was hot."

Lindsay was rewarded with a reluctant smile. There was more she could say, but nothing would be served by trying to get Cassie to admit she'd crushed on the football star who'd been a senior when she was a lowly freshman.

But Lindsay remembered the way her sister's eyes had followed Krew when she thought no one was looking. It had been a puppy-love kind of thing. Sweet and innocent. A couple of months later, everything had changed for her sister. Cassie never had a chance to be a teenager before she was propelled feetfirst into motherhood.

The bells over the door jingled.

Cassie shifted her gaze. "Duty calls."

The relief in her sister's voice told Lindsay that while she hadn't intended to make her sister uncomfortable, that's exactly what she'd done.

Lindsay shifted her gaze to the door, curious to see if she knew the latest customer.

Dan strolled in, looking very unministerlike in jeans and a caramel-colored sweater. Tousled and windblown, his normally carefully arranged hair went in a dozen directions.

Cassie's smile widened when she saw him. Seconds later, she was laughing at something he said.

Lindsay pushed back her chair, intending to make a quick exit, when a light brushing of butterfly wings deep in her lower abdomen stopped her cold.

She dropped her hand to her belly. The doctor had told her to expect movement sometime in the next month. She'd never thought it would be this soon.

Remaining absolutely still, Lindsay willed it to happen again.

"Do you mind if I join you?"

The question was like a splash of cold water. Lindsay jerked her head up to find Dan standing beside the table, a cherry Danish in one hand, a cup of coffee in the other.

"Please." When her voice came out raspy, Lindsay cleared her throat and tried again. "I'd like that."

Dan pulled out a chair and took a seat. "Beautiful day."

"I love this time of year. I don't know if I could live somewhere without a change of seasons." Lindsay figured they could talk about the weather for a few minutes, then she'd make her excuses and head home.

"You and I were dating this time last year." Dan's hazel eyes, the same color as Owen's but somehow profoundly different, studied her. "I heard you and Owen are back together."

Lindsay hesitated. What did she say to that? Was there a special place in hell for those who lied to a minister?

"We've been spending time together." The truth, Lindsay told herself. She'd seen a lot of Owen over the last three weeks, the past week excluded.

"I'm glad." He forked off a bite of Danish and brought it to his mouth.

"You are?" When they'd been together, Dan had been jealous of her friendship with Owen. Which was all it had been at the time. "Why?"

"You're good together." Dan took a long sip of coffee and studied her over the rim of the cup. Then he smiled, a slow, easy smile that reminded her why she'd once been attracted to him. "You and Owen are a far better match than you and I ever were."

What did she say to that? Thankfully, she was spared the need to respond when Katie Ruth burst into the shop. The pretty blonde's gaze frantically searched the dining area.

When she spotted Dan, relief flooded her face. Then she saw Lindsay and stopped midstep. For a second, Lindsay saw herself featured in the e-newsletter for the second time in as many weeks. Only, this time she'd be linked to her former fiancé.

After only a momentary hesitation, Katie Ruth was on the move, crossing the dining area to Dan in long, purposeful strides. "Why aren't you answering your cell?"

The blonde shot a censuring look at Lindsay as if she was to blame.

Lindsay lifted her hands, palms up. If Katie Ruth thought she and Dan were having some intimate tête-à-tête, she was dead wrong.

With puzzlement furrowing his brow, Dan slipped his phone from his pocket. A second later, he shook his head in disgust. "It's dead. I must have forgotten to charge it last night."

He looked up, meeting Katie Ruth's gaze. "Is there a problem?"

"Please." Lindsay gestured to an empty chair. "Join us."

Lindsay winced when a startled look skittered across the blonde's face. The last thing she wanted to do was give the false impression there was anything more than friendship and respect between her and Dan.

"Thanks. I can't stay." Katie Ruth leaned forward, pressing her palms against the table as she lowered her voice. "I was at the church helping Marnie in the office when the call came in. There's been an accident out on Highway 42 and Wieker Cliff Drive. It's a bad one."

"That road leads to the barn where the haunted house will be held," Lindsay offered.

Katie Ruth pressed her lips together for a second before expelling a ragged breath. Only then did Lindsay remember that Katie Ruth was not only active in YMCA youth programs, she headed the youth programs at First Christian. These were kids she probably knew.

"Apparently, two cars filled with teenagers collided." Katie Ruth swallowed, then cleared her throat. "From what I understand, one slammed into the back of the other without braking."

Dan's gaze sharpened. "Injuries?"

"Multiple." Worry filled Katie Ruth's vivid blue eyes.

"Any...fatalities?" Lindsay didn't remember speaking, but the voice was hers.

"I don't know." Katie Ruth lifted her hands, let them drop. "Several ambulances are on their way to the scene now."

Dan pushed to his feet. "Have the parents been notified?"

"Marnie just said the deputy who called thinks you need to be there."

"Thanks for finding me, Katie Ruth." Dan's hand touched the woman's arm. "You went above and beyond."

A touch of pink colored the woman's cheeks.

"My car is out front," Katie Ruth told the minister as they headed to the door.

Two cars filled with teenagers.

Lindsay thought of her nephews. How many times had she seen Braxton and K.T. riding around town with their friends, packed like sardines into one old car or another?

Trying to appear casual, Lindsay strolled to the counter.

"What had Dan and Katie Ruth rushing off?" Cassie asked.

Lindsay followed Cassie's gaze, and together they watched Katie Ruth's SUV jerk backward out of the parking spot. Then, with a squeal of tires, it shot like a rocket down the street.

"Something about Dan being needed...somewhere." Lindsay waved an airy hand and fought to keep a nonchalant expression.

"I hope no one is hurt." The genuine caring in Cassie's voice had Lindsay's heart twisting.

"I need to get going, too." Lindsay paused as if a question had just popped into her head. "Are Braxton and K.T. watching Axl today?"

"K.T. is home with him." Cassie shrugged. "Braxton is hanging with friends. I think they were going to check out the progress on the haunted house."

A ball of ice formed in the pit of Lindsay's stomach.

"Why?" Cassie asked curiously.

"No reason." Somehow, Lindsay managed a smile. "Thanks for the latte."

Lindsay cursed her decision to walk to the coffee shop this morning. Thankfully, she didn't live far. Once she was out of Cassie's sight, she began to jog. She'd made it a couple of blocks when a familiar red truck pulled to the curb.

Owen rolled down his window and leaned out. "Need a running partner?"

Without answering, Lindsay opened the door and slid into the passenger seat. "I need you to take me to Wieker Cliff Drive and Highway 42."

Even before she finished speaking, he'd put the truck in gear and they were on the move.

"What's going on there?" His voice was low and soothing.

Lindsay swallowed past the sudden lump in her throat. "I think Braxton was in an accident."

WITH SIRENS BLARING, the ambulance came up fast behind them. Lindsay's heart gave a solid thump as Owen wheeled the truck to the side of the road and stopped.

Only when the vehicle disappeared from sight, did he pull back onto the highway. Though Owen didn't speed, he pushed the limit.

They'd just passed Gibraltar Bluff Road when a police cruiser, positioned across the southbound lane of the highway, forced them to stop. Lindsay recognized the deputy, but couldn't recall his name.

"We've got an accident up ahead." The young man wore mirrored sunglasses and a grave expression. "Until the scene is cleared, the road is closed. You need to turn around."

Unfastening her seat belt, Lindsay leaned across Owen. "Can

you tell me if my nephew Braxton Lohmeier is one of the injured?"

"Are you the boy's guardian?"

Before Lindsay could respond, the radio pinned to the deputy's left shoulder squawked. He lifted a finger and listened. "Copy that."

Lindsay waited impatiently until the man's attention returned to her. "My sister is his mother, but—"

"If her son is one of the injured, she'll be notified." The deputy made an impatient, sweeping motion with his hand. "You need to turn this truck around. Now."

Owen obligingly slipped the truck into gear just as Lindsay shoved open her door.

The second her feet hit the asphalt, she bolted. She'd spotted Cade up ahead, clipboard in hand.

"Ma'am. Stop. You can't go—"

Lindsay ignored the deputy's shout and aimed for where the sheriff stood, engrossed in a conversation with Bob Tidball.

Though her attention remained on Cade, Bob was impossible to ignore. A redwood among normal mortals, the man towered over the sheriff. Over the years, the muscle Bob had developed as a semipro linebacker had given way to a Santa Claus softness. The only difference between him and Saint Nick was the absence of white hair and a beard. The belly was definitely there, and Lindsay could vouch that it jiggled when he laughed.

The coroner wasn't laughing now.

For a second, Lindsay's knees grew weak. She stumbled, but caught herself and continued on. Behind her, she heard Owen call her name. But what had Lindsay's heart picking up speed was the sound of the deputy's footsteps growing closer.

By the time she reached Cade, her breath came in ragged pants. She leaned over, putting her hands on her thighs, fighting for breath.

"Lindsay." Cade placed a hand on her shoulder, concern deepening his voice. "What's wrong?"

The question had barely left his lips when Owen and the deputy skidded to a stop beside them.

"I'm sorry, Sheriff." The deputy cast a censuring look in Lindsay's direction. "I made it clear she needed to go back to town. Instead, she took off running."

"It's okay, Aaron." Cade waved away the deputy's obvious distress. "Lindsay is a friend."

The sheriff turned to Owen, who had moved to Lindsay's side. Unlike her, Owen didn't appear the least bit winded. "What's going on?"

"We—" Owen began.

Lindsay pushed herself upright and found her voice. "Braxton. Is he injured?"

Cade's gaze sharpened.

Lindsay knew he could easily cite some kind of confidentiality statute, but she prayed he wouldn't go that route.

After several long seconds, Cade lifted the clipboard. He scanned the list of names. When he lowered his hands, the gaze that met hers was strong and steady. "Braxton isn't on the list."

"Meaning?" Owen asked.

"He wasn't in either car."

Lindsay blinked away the tears suddenly clouding her vision. "You're positive?"

"Yes." Before Cade could say more, Bob cleared his throat.

Cade shot Lindsay an apologetic look. "I'm sorry, things are a little crazy right now."

"Someone died." Lindsay's heart swelled, making breathing difficult. While the nephew she loved was safe, someone else's child hadn't been as lucky.

"We have two fatalities." Cade's expression remained composed, but she saw the pain in his eyes.

"Sheriff Rallis." Another deputy, this one standing near one of the ambulances, motioned to Cade.

"I'm glad Braxton is safe." With a squeeze of her shoulder, Cade strode off.

Lindsay barely remembered the walk to the truck. She remembered only Owen's supportive hand on her arm.

Owen kept the conversation light on the drive back to town. Only when he'd pulled into her apartment parking lot and shut off the engine did he bring up the accident. "Shouldn't you call and let Cassie know Braxton wasn't involved?"

Lindsay shook her head. "She doesn't know there was an accident."

"I'm sure she's heard about it by now." Owen's hazel eyes remained hooded. "If she hasn't, it won't take long for word to spread."

"You're right." Lindsay pulled out her phone. After a short conversation with her sister, she slumped back against the seat. "Cass *had* heard."

"Now she can relax." Owen reached over and patted her hand. "You can both relax."

The warm reassurance in his touch had tears clouding her vision. "I was so scared."

"That's understandable." Owen's voice reminded her of crushed rock over whiskey. "When you love someone, you don't want anything bad to happen to them."

"It's a good reminder how those we love can be here one day and gone the next." The second she spoke the thoughtless words, Lindsay wished she could pull them back. Who was she to lecture Owen on the importance of making each day count?

He, more than most, knew just how quickly things could change.

"You're right. There are no guarantees." Owen's eyes were somber. "Still, life goes on. In the spring, you and I will welcome a daughter into our lives."

"Yes." Lindsay's lips curved. "Before you know it, she'll be here."

"This probably isn't the best time, but I've been wondering what you discovered in your joint-custody research."

Lindsay stiffened, then recalled her conversation with Eliza. Owen, she reminded herself, was simply being a proactive dad. "I'm happy to go over it with you, but I don't have my notes."

He smiled. "The high points will do."

Tapping a finger against her lips, Lindsay thought for a moment. She mentally brought the research she'd done into some semblance of order in her head. "The main pro was the child has the influence of both parents and both are able to make legal decisions."

"What about the cons?" Owen's gaze remained on her face. "You had concerns."

"It was as we—or rather, as I—thought. The stress of going back and forth can be difficult, especially for small children."

"Oh." The word came out on a long exhale.

"But all the articles said shared parenting is becoming the norm."

Owen slowly nodded. "I appreciate the information."

"Is joint custody something you're still planning to pursue?" Though it was difficult, Lindsay kept all judgment from her voice.

"I want to be a strong presence in my daughter's life. That will never change." Before Lindsay could ask whether that was a yes or a no, he continued. "But I can assure you that I will never try to take our child from you."

Her heart suddenly squeezed tight in her chest. Without thinking, she reached over and placed her hand on his arm. "Thank you."

"Another thing." He paused for a second before continuing. "As we move forward, I'd like to focus on the present and not let what happened in the past impact our current relationship. As much as that's possible, anyway."

"Sleeping with you was a mistake." Lindsay kept her tone matter-of-fact. "It's funny how in retrospect things that were impossible to see at the time become clear. I mean, you were still grieving."

It had taken distance and a conversation with Eliza to bring that much-needed clarity.

"We got too close, too fast," Owen agreed.

She waved a hand. "Totally agree."

A muscle jumped in Owen's jaw. "If you're willing, I'd like us to use the next six months to build on our earlier friendship."

Though Lindsay knew what he was suggesting would undoubtedly be best for the baby, she hesitated. "How do I know you won't one day just up and decide we're getting too close again?"

Owen's eyes took on a faraway look before refocusing on her. "I won't make choices based on what *might* happen in the future, which is what I did in July."

Lindsay wasn't certain how that answered her question, but when she opened her mouth to ask, he waved a hand and continued. "You and me, we've been given a second chance. Not many people get do-overs."

There was something in his eyes she hadn't seen before. A kind of steely determination.

"This time, I won't blow it." Owen turned his body to face Lindsay's, pulling her gaze to his. "What do you say?"

CHAPTER EIGHTEEN

Lindsay's breath caught in her throat.

Owen stared at her, waiting for her response.

"I want—" Her voice cracked. "I want..."

Swinging her gaze away from Owen, she shoved open the door. "I want to walk."

She knew what he was asking. He was asking her to put her heart on the line again.

Lindsay thought of all the times she'd condemned Cassie for being a fool over a man. She slammed the car door and mentally offered up an apology to her sister.

"Lindsay?" Owen appeared at her side. His voice, as smooth as honey, broke through her thoughts. "Would you mind if I hold your hand while we walk?"

Instead of saying no—the only sane, responsible answer—she shrugged as if it didn't matter to her one way or the other. Lindsay knew she shouldn't let him touch her. Not with her feelings so raw and close to the surface.

The feel of his hand on hers had her heart tripping. His was a strong hand, callused and used to labor, but gentle, too. An image of his callused palm caressing her bare skin sent a sudden shiver up her spine.

As they strolled down the sidewalk, she remembered the intimacy they'd shared. If the number of times they'd made love *had* been an indication of the depths of his feelings, he'd never have been able to walk away from her the way he had.

Apparently, she wasn't the only Lohmeier female to confuse lust with love. If it wasn't so sad, it'd be funny.

Could she trust him now? Could she trust her own judgment?

Logic and emotion wove together in a tight ball, making it difficult for her to tell where one ended and the other began.

There was so much Lindsay wanted to say to him, so much she needed him to understand, but where to begin? It was important to voice her feelings clearly. But with him so close, she was having difficulty concentrating.

Lindsay stopped beneath a large oak and blurted, "Are you proposing this because you hope in the end I'll agree to marry you?"

Those hazel eyes, framed by dark lashes, didn't leave her face. "I won't lie. I believe us being married is the best thing for our daughter. But I also want to build a strong relationship with you."

"You weren't interested before." Lindsay could have cheered when her voice stayed even, giving no indication of her inner turmoil. "I can only assume all of this is because of the baby."

"Things are different now."

Lindsay raised a brow at the nonanswer.

"We're going to have a baby. For her sake, we need to be true partners. Which means knowing and trusting each other." Owen raked a hand through his hair. "I won't lie. Letting someone in is difficult for me. I've spent most of my life never letting anyone get too close. But if you're willing to give me another chance, I promise I won't hold back."

Hold back.

An accurate description of their prior attempt at a relationship.

"I never trusted your feelings for me." The admission, spoken in the light of day, was somehow freeing. "You broke up with me with no warning."

The swell of pain told her the wound she thought had scabbed over was still raw and bleeding. "Do you know how that made me feel?"

She didn't wait for his response.

"It made me feel worthless. It made me feel used." She spat the words as anger surged.

"That wasn't my intent. I—"

"Intent be damned. You hurt me, Owen, and now you're asking me to forget it happened and trust you."

When her voice broke, she pressed her lips together.

He reached for her then, but she held up her hands and backed away.

Owen's gaze shifted down the block, to the row of small homes with postage-stamp-sized lawns before returning to her. "Building trust will be an uphill climb for both of us. But I believe it's worth the effort."

While he sounded sincere, a tiny voice inside her head—one that sounded suspiciously like her mother's—told her she'd be a fool to agree.

Was she playing the fool?

"How did you feel after you broke up with Dan?"

Startled by the unexpected question, Lindsay responded without thinking. "Relieved."

His gaze, strong and steady, remained riveted on her face. "No regrets?"

"None."

"That's when you know a decision is right." He took a step closer, the light breeze ruffling his hair. "When I think back to breaking up with you, I have nothing but regrets."

She wanted to believe him. Dear God, how she wanted to believe him.

"I'm sorry I hurt you." He blew out a long breath. "I got scared. I pushed you away. I'm not proud of how I behaved, and I'd give anything to go back."

This time when he reached out, Lindsay let him enfold her in his arms. After a moment, she laid her head on his shoulder.. "Is this the right thing, Owen? Or are we just opening ourselves up to more heartache?"

She didn't expect an answer. Or so she told herself.

"It's worth the risk." His arms tightened around her. "It's definitely worth the risk."

ON SATURDAY, Owen was convinced he and Lindsay had come to an understanding. They would forge a strong relationship.

One day at a time.

On Sunday, he arrived at church early, eager to see her. When she didn't show, he texted and discovered she was spending the day with her sister.

Shoving aside his disappointment, he listened with half an ear to the sermon, then went out for breakfast at Muddy Boots. Being surrounded by friends was pleasant, but Owen found himself watching the door, hoping Lindsay would walk through it.

On Monday, he still hadn't heard from her. Thankfully, things were hopping at the garage. He'd just finished entering a supply order when a knock sounded on his office door.

Owen swiveled in his chair. David Chapin stood in the doorway, ready for business in dark gray chinos and a long-sleeved blue shirt. But then, Owen couldn't recall ever seeing the architect look anything but professional.

Rising, Owen rounded the desk to greet his friend. "It's good to see you. What brings you around these parts?"

David jerked a thumb in the direction of the bays. "Oil change and tire rotation."

"Can I interest you in a cup of coffee while you wait?" Owen gestured to the Mr. Coffee on the side table. "Fresh pot."

"If I'm not interrupting—"

"I just finished ordering supplies. I could use the break."

"In that case, I'd love coffee." David smiled. "I was running late this morning. There was no time to grab a cup before I left home. Brynn is a stickler about getting to school on time."

"Mindy was the same way."

An awkward silence descended. Owen shifted from one foot to the other, then gestured to the small round table used for one-on-one meetings with his mechanics. "Have a seat."

As David pulled out one of the orange plastic chairs, Owen moved to the pot and grabbed two mugs. "Do you like anything in yours?"

"Just black." David leaned back in the chair. "The stronger the better."

Owen slanted a glance at the architect as he poured. "Late night?"

David nodded. "Hadley and I were finalizing last-minute wedding stuff."

"That's right around the corner."

"It is." David's gray eyes took on a soft glow. "I can't wait."

Owen lifted a brow, coffeepot in hand. "Can't wait for the wedding? Or for it to all be over and done with?"

"Both." David chuckled. "Though I must say, this time the process has been remarkably free of stress. With Hadley, it's not about the spectacle, but about celebrating the start of our new life with family and friends."

As Owen carried the mugs to the table, he wondered if the spectacle comment was a jab at David's first wedding. People still talked about the open-top tent and fireworks.

David wrapped his fingers around the mug. "I hear you and Lindsay are back together."

Owen hesitated for a split second. "We are."

"I never understood why you two broke up. You seem good together."

Owen shrugged.

"How do you like the cards?"

"Cards?" Owen let the warmth of the mug seep into his fingers.

"Marigold told Hadley that she gave Lindsay the deck of relationship cards." Owen must have still appeared clueless, because David prompted, "You'd taken the GTO out. You and Lindsay stopped and—"

"Oh, that deck of cards." Owen hadn't given them a second thought. He took a long sip of coffee. "Lindsay dropped them in her bag. She hasn't mentioned them since."

"Be grateful. Some of the questions can be difficult." David waved a dismissive hand. "Seriously, the premarital questions are easy by comparison."

"Do you complete those online?"

"I wish. No, it's done at the church. In-person premarital counseling is required for anyone wanting to be married at First Christian." David's lips lifted in a rueful smile. "It isn't as bad as it sounds. Dan strongly believes in the importance of identifying potential issues before they become problems."

Owen chose his words carefully. "Are you and Hadley having issues?"

"Not at all. But I agree it's important for the bride and groom to look at previous relationships and see where they may have fallen short." David shifted in the chair. "Otherwise, more than likely, the same behavior will be repeated in the current relationship."

Though Owen hadn't known David's first wife well, he remembered the time she'd brought in her BMW and pitched a fit when they told her the part needed to fix it was on back order. "He's having you look at your interactions with Whitney?"

"Yes. Be forewarned, if you decide to get married there, you'll be asked to look at your relationship with Tessa." David's gaze grew thoughtful. "Again, not a bad thing. A marriage takes two. When it falls apart, each party has usually contributed in some way."

Owen gave a reluctant nod. He accepted that he bore some responsibility for the failure of his marriage. "It makes sense that fixing what you can about yourself only makes any future relationship stronger."

"Hadley said I was inspired by that session." David chuckled. "I went home and made a list of things I plan to do differently in this marriage."

"I bet you'd have made those changes anyway," Owen told him. "Or, they were probably things that wouldn't ever come up because Hadley isn't Whitney."

"Maybe. But reading the items on my list made me more aware and more determined to be the best husband possible." David's gray eyes turned solemn. "We have Brynn to think of, too."

Owen nodded. "Kids add an extra wrinkle."

"Hadley and I want Brynn to see what a healthy relationship looks like. It was difficult for her when her mother moved to Florida. You understand. You went through the same thing with Mindy."

A tightness filled Owen's chest. Mindy had suffered greatly when Tess had moved out. Then, when his ex-wife had quit coming to visit...

His heart had ached for his daughter each time her mother would say she'd pick her up, then cancel at the last minute. After watching Mindy cry herself to sleep one too many times, he'd told Tessa to stay away.

She'd argued with him, but he'd pointed out she was only

hurting their daughter more by waltzing in and out of her life. Tessa had done as he asked.

Owen told himself that had been for the best, but he was no longer sure. Mindy had never stopped missing her mother and hoping for her return.

"I've made my share of mistakes," Owen heard himself say, his voice seeming to come from far away. "They aren't ones I want to repeat."

"Do you think you and Lindsay might one day take a walk down the aisle?"

"I'd like to," Owen admitted. "But after our time apart, she's not sure she can trust my feelings for her. That's on me."

Owen wasn't sure why he was sharing so much with David. They were, at best, casual friends. Perhaps it was because they'd each had a wife who'd not only left them behind, but left their child, as well.

"Mr. Chapin." Wayde stood in the doorway, keys dangling from his fingers. "Your car is ready."

"Thanks." After the mechanic tossed him the keys, David downed the rest of the coffee and stood. "I can't believe we spent this entire time talking about weddings."

"Getting married again is a big step."

"This time, I have no doubts." David smiled. "I looked at Hadley this morning and I knew I'd do everything in my power to make her happy. That's when you know it's right. When it's not about you, it's about them."

CHAPTER NINETEEN

"Lindsay."

The shout of her name had Lindsay turning to see her former boss cross the street and make a beeline straight to her.

Shirley, owner of the Enchanted Florist, was a tall woman in her early fifties. Auburn hair, styled in a layered bob, flattered her square face. The smile on her red lips couldn't quite disguise the lines of weariness edging her brown eyes.

Now that Lindsay had a better idea of what was involved in running a floral shop, she understood why the woman seemed perpetually stressed.

"It's good to see you." Shirley's gaze took in Lindsay's long-sleeved jersey dress in muted earth tones coupled with brown ankle booties. "You're looking well."

"Thank you." The woman's assessing gaze made Lindsay glad she'd dressed up for her noon meeting at Eliza's house. Though it would just be her, Eliza and Ami, Eliza always looked so, well, so perfect.

As her blasted seller's certificate had yet to be issued, she'd had plenty of time to get ready. She'd taken her time this morning, doing her makeup in a way that made her eyes look large and even more blue. She'd even pulled out the special foundation that hid the scar on her cheek.

"It's nice to see you." The warmth in Lindsay's voice appeared to surprise Shirley. But Good Hope was a small town. Her path and Shirley's would continue to cross in the years to come.

Besides, after shedding a few tears, Lindsay had concluded Shirley had done her favor. For a number of years, Lindsay had needed to step outside her comfort zone. Without a push—or kick in the pants—she'd likely have stayed put. Though it wasn't flattering, Lindsay viewed herself as one of those birds that had to be shoved out of a nest in order to fly.

"How have you been?" Shirley posed the question with what appeared to be genuine interest.

For a second, Lindsay thought about replying with a simple *fine*. After all, what was there to say? Since her business hadn't yet gotten off the ground, she had nothing to report. And she wasn't about to bring up the pregnancy, though she knew the time was drawing near to announce to the Good Hope world that she was having Owen's baby.

Yet, cutting a conversation short, especially when someone had deliberately sought you out, wasn't the Good Hope way. Besides, she had plenty of time before she needed to be at Eliza's home.

"I've been keeping busy." Lindsay paused then brought up the elephant in the room. "I suppose you heard I'm starting my own floral business."

The smile remained steady on Shirley's lips. "Someone may have mentioned that to me."

"Floral design has always been my passion." Lindsay met the woman's gaze head on. "I'm excited to start this new chapter in my life."

When Shirley said nothing, Lindsay felt compelled to fill the silence.

"I understand the Enchanted Florist is, at heart, a family business." Lindsay kept her tone light. "It was only natural that once the twins got older, you'd want them to be more involved."

Shirley huffed out a breath. "Kids nowadays are eager for more responsibility, even when they aren't really ready to take it on."

Even though it had been only a few weeks since Lindsay stepped away from her duties at the Enchanted Florist, it appeared there was already trouble in floral paradise.

The first couple of days after she quit, Lindsay would have rejoiced at the knowledge. When she'd walked out the door, she'd wanted nothing more than for Shirley's business to suffer.

Perhaps the fact that she'd soon be a mother herself had given Lindsay new perspective. While she didn't appreciate how Shirley had treated her, she understood the woman's desire to increase her daughters' roles in the business.

"I'm sure the girls will find their way. In no time at all, they'll be seasoned veterans." Lindsay's lips turned up. "Remember my first job as a designer? I did the wedding and reception flowers for that bride in Egg Harbor."

"She told you what she wanted and made it clear she wouldn't welcome any input from you or me." Shirley chuckled. "You gave her what she asked for."

"She'd picked all strong-smelling flowers for the reception tables." Lindsay shook her head. "She was furious with us when the guests complained."

"You gave her what she wanted," Shirley reminded her.

"Even if she didn't want to hear it, I should have warned her." That was one lesson Lindsay had never forgotten. "Now, I'd speak my piece. If she still wanted those flowers, well, she couldn't say she wasn't fully warned."

"The twins will need to learn that lesson."

"They will." Lindsay placed a hand on Shirley's arm. "They're smart girls, and you'll be there to guide them."

"That's kind of you to say."

Lindsay didn't know what to think when Shirley's eyes took

on a sheen. "It's been a difficult couple of weeks. We have so many orders, and the girls are, well, inexperienced."

"All that business is a good thing."

"It is," Shirley agreed. "Except when you can't keep up."

A few heartbeats of silence followed.

"If you need help, and it works with my schedule, I'd be happy to lend my expertise to get you over the hump." The offer was out of Lindsay's mouth before she could stop it.

Shirley's eyes widened. "You'd do that? After what I did to you?"

"You didn't do anything except give me a much-needed kick in the backside to get me to follow my own dreams." Lindsay grinned. "I'd be happy to help. But I'm warning you. I don't work cheap."

LINDSAY'S EMOTIONS were in a tangle as she climbed the steps to Eliza's front porch. The more she thought about her former employer's predicament, the more she realized Shirley had only herself to blame.

Though returning to the Enchanted Florist made financial sense, it somehow felt as if she'd conceded a battle before a single shot had been fired.

Before even launching her new business, she'd put herself back under Shirley's thumb. Heaving a sigh, Lindsay raised a hand to knock.

The door swung open before her knuckles touched the thick oak.

"I'm happy you could come by on such short notice." Eliza's megawatt smile had Lindsay taking a step back. "Come in. Come in."

Though her friend was dressed in her trademark black, the

sparkle in her eyes and the wide smile were definitely not what she expected from Eliza.

"I'm not sure why we're meeting." Lindsay studied her friend, whose text had seemed deliberately vague. "Does this have something to do with the homecoming displays?"

"Ami is in the parlor. She brought over cherry pie cookies. It's a new recipe." Eliza waved a perfectly manicured hand. "I've already had one. I think she's got another winner."

The woman's flushed cheeks, broad smile and happy chatter were worrisome signs. "Who are you, and what have you done with Eliza?"

Her friend's trill of laughter only added to Lindsay's unease. Other than on her wedding day, she'd never seen Eliza so, well, so joyous.

Ami sat on the divan sipping a glass of lemonade. Eliza quickly filled a crystal tumbler for Lindsay. After handing it to her, Eliza commandeered the throne chair. This, at least, was expected behavior.

Lindsay smiled at Ami. "Eliza said you brought some new cookies for us to try."

Ami gestured to a box on the coffee table. "I wanted to put them on a plate, but Eliza told me not to bother."

Okay, this was downright creepy. Eliza had never been one to eat cookies directly out of a box. The puzzled look in Ami's eyes seemed to agree with Lindsay's assessment.

With Eliza munching happily on a cookie and Ami appearing content to sip lemonade, Lindsay took a stab at getting the party, er, the conversation started.

"I ran into Shirley on my way here." Lindsay quickly summarized their interaction, then added, "I agreed to put in a few hours each morning at the Enchanted Florist until my business takes off."

"Have you lost your mind?" Eliza set down her glass with a

decided thump. Her gray eyes narrowed and flashed. "Why would you do that after the way she treated you?"

Warmth flooded Lindsay. Here was her friend, the woman she knew and loved.

"I need money," Lindsay admitted. "Since leaving the Enchanted Florist, I have lots of expenses but zero income. Don't worry. She's making it worth my time."

"Why don't you just bend over and ask her to pretty please kick you again?"

"Eliza." Ami shot the brunette a warning look.

Eliza waved away the rebuke and turned to Lindsay. "You should have told her that if she has too much business, you'd be happy to take it off her hands."

"It does seem like you're taking a step backward." Ami coupled the comment with an apologetic smile.

"It made sense at the time." Lindsay sighed. "But right now I feel like one of those kids who graduate from college with high hopes only to move into their parents' basement a couple months later."

"It's not at all the same. You're only helping Shirley temporarily," Ami insisted. "You need money, and she needs the help. Win-win."

"Way to talk out of both sides of your mouth, Ami." But Eliza's chiding words held no bite. "Bottom line, Shirley doesn't deserve help. If I was Lindsay, I'd never have gone back."

"You might if you needed money bad enough," Ami told Eliza. "If you recall, I went to work for Beck at Muddy Boots to earn money for my store's furnace."

"You went to work for Beckett Cross because you thought he was hot and you wanted in his pants."

"You behave." Ami swatted her friend's arm. She couldn't contain her laughter.

Eliza smirked and took a bite of cookie.

Lindsay rolled her eyes, but felt herself settle at the teasing banter. "Well, Shirley is definitely not hot."

"How much do you need?" Eliza leaned over as if intending to pull her phone from her bag and make a financial transfer right then. "The money can be in your account today."

Ami lowered her cookie, her gaze settling on Lindsay. "I can lend you whatever you need."

"Thank you both, but you're doing enough already." Lindsay softened the refusal with a smile as her heart swelled with love for these two women who always had her back.

When Eliza opened her mouth to protest, Lindsay lifted a hand. "Forget Shirley. We've wasted enough time talking about her. I want to know what has you so giddy."

Shock skittered across Eliza's face, followed by a haughty expression. "I don't do giddy."

"Today, you do." Ami's teasing tone and smile were infectious. "C'mon, spill. What has Eliza Kendrick ready to burst into song?"

Lindsay expected Eliza to stall, perhaps make them beg.

Instead, a Cheshire cat smile lifted her friend's lips. "Kyle and I are pregnant."

Ami squealed and launched herself at Eliza, nearly upending her glass of lemonade.

"You're going to have a baby?" Lindsay choked out the words.

Eliza returned Ami's hug, then sat back and grinned. "Well, I don't plan to give birth to a dog."

Lindsay snorted out a laugh.

Ami clasped her hands together. "I'm so very happy for you and Kyle."

"It's wonderful news." Caught up in her friend's joy, Lindsay didn't take time to identify the emotions battering her heart. "Tell us all. We want the deets."

"Well, we'd been trying for a couple of months." Eliza's smile turned wicked. "That's been a whole lot of fun."

"Did you do a home pregnancy test?" Ami circled a hand,

showing Lindsay that she wasn't the only one eager for details. "Beck and I were super nervous when we did ours. My hand was shaking so much I nearly dropped the stick in the toilet."

"It was the same with us." Eliza's lips curved in remembrance. "Kyle didn't go into work. Once we had the results, we celebrated into the night."

Eliza ended with, "We took flute glasses of club soda to the porch swing. While gazing into a sky filled with a million stars, we discussed our hopes and dreams for our baby."

Lindsay thought of the test she'd done in the privacy of her bathroom and the panic that had gripped her when it came back positive. She shook off the memory and visualized Eliza's scene. "That's so romantic."

Eliza nodded, her expression turning dreamy. "It was."

A pang of longing had the next question stumbling out. "Did Kyle go with you to the doctor when you confirmed the pregnancy?"

"He wouldn't have missed it." Eliza let out a happy breath. "The second we left the office, we called his parents. Lolo is overjoyed at the thought of being an aunt. Once school is out, she's determined to come and help with the baby. She made sure we knew she's a Red Cross-certified babysitter."

Eliza paused as if realizing she'd been babbling. "Sorry. It's just that a couple years ago, I never imagined being this happy."

"You and Kyle should enjoy every moment." Ami's eyes went soft. "Beck was over the moon the first time we found out we were pregnant. I thought maybe he'd be a little calmer this time around, but he's just as excited."

Eliza's gaze shifted from Ami to Lindsay. "The cherry on top of this very fabulous sundae is that our children will grow up together. They'll be classmates and friends."

"We'll do playdates, and once they're in school, we'll sit together during programs and sporting events." Ami clasped her hands together. "It will be absolutely wonderful."

"I've already started thinking about how I'm going to decorate the nursery." Eliza's voice shook with eagerness. "Of course, we want to find out the sex of the baby first."

"You could do what Beck and I did and decorate in primary colors," Ami suggested.

As the two women debated the merits of various color schemes, Lindsay sat back and listened. She didn't have the time or the money to decorate a nursery. Heck, she'd be lucky to be able to afford a crib.

Still, dreaming of shopping with her friends for baby items had a smile forming on her lips.

"How does that sound to you, Lin?"

Lindsay had lost track of the conversation when her mind had wandered, but to admit as much might squash the buoyant mood in the room. "It sounds wonderful."

"You've got something spinning in that head of yours." Eliza wagged a finger. "What is it?"

Lindsay smiled and settled her gaze on Ami. "I was thinking Eliza and I are lucky to have you and Prim."

Ami inclined her head, puzzlement furrowing her brow.

"You're experienced mothers. You'll be there to give us tips on how to navigate those early days with a newborn." With a start, Lindsay realized she'd also have Owen. He was an experienced father.

While she wished she'd had an excited husband beside her when she found out she was pregnant, wished she could have rejoiced instead of worried when the test was positive, she chose to be thankful for all the good things in her life.

"Prim and I will certainly help in any way we can." Ami's lips curved. "Those first couple of weeks can be harrowing. But holding the new life you created with the man you love, well, there is nothing quite as wonderful."

The new life you created with the man you love...

While she and Owen might not be married, their baby girl

would grow up knowing she was deeply loved. Not only by her mother, but by her father, too. A man who wanted to be in his child's life so badly that he was willing to marry a woman he didn't love.

"I'd like to propose a toast." Lindsay lifted her glass of lemonade high. "To our children. May they grow up healthy, happy and surrounded by love."

Her phone buzzed only seconds later.

"It's Shirley," Eliza deadpanned, "telling you not to forget to wear that hideous uniform when you come in."

Chuckling, Lindsay pulled the phone from her bag and brought up the text.

"Who's it from?" Ami asked.

"It's from Owen." Lindsay smiled. "Asking me out to dinner."

CHAPTER TWENTY

Owen wove his way through the crush of people to where Lindsay stood by the exterior door to Bayside Pizza.

"They said it'll be thirty minutes," he told her. The sheer number of people standing around made Owen wonder if the hostess had underestimated the time. "Is that okay, or would you prefer to try somewhere else?"

"I don't mind waiting." Lindsay moved closer, as if to ensure he could hear her over all the voices in the small waiting area. "This is odd. They're never this busy on a Monday."

"I asked the hostess. Apparently, they're running some kind of special." Owen slipped his arm around her shoulders. Because it was crowded, he told himself. "I gave them my number. They said they'd text if we wanted to wait outside."

"In that case, why don't we take a stroll down by the water?" She stood so close he could smell the sweet scent of her lemony shampoo. "I know you like to walk."

After Mindy died, she'd taken many long walks with him. She'd listened as he'd shared his anger, pain and overwhelming sorrow. They had become good friends during that time. But there was still much more to learn, to discover, about her.

Owen held the door open. He took Lindsay's arm as they navigated the steps, then headed in the direction of the shoreline. "Tell me about your day."

"Not much to tell." She shot him a sideways glance and smiled. "What about yours?"

When he opened his mouth to mention David had stopped by, Owen stopped himself. Time for that later. "Did you spend the day at home, or did you go out?"

He feared that without direct questions, she might try to redirect the conversation back to him.

"I spent some time at Eliza's house."

"Details." He offered a teasing smile. "Toss me a bone."

She rolled her eyes, but her lips quirked upward. "Okay. Because the weather was nice, I walked to her house."

"That's a good start." He continued to stare expectantly.

With an exaggerated sigh, Lindsay continued. "I ran into Shirley on the way. Or rather, Shirley crossed the street to intercept me."

"Enchanted Florist Shirley?"

"The one and only." Lindsay's quick smile faded, and beneath his fingers, he felt her arm tense.

Owen felt a surge of anger. If that woman had deliberately upset Lindsay... "Was she nasty?"

Lindsay blinked. "Nasty? Oh, no. It was all good. We had a nice conversation."

Though he sensed that was the truth, there was more she wasn't saying. "What did you speak about during this *nice* conversation on this *nice* day?"

"We talked about floral design. And the girls. Her twins," she clarified, as if noticing his confusion. "I guess the shop is super busy, so much so they're having difficulty keeping up with orders. I believe, though she didn't exactly come out and say, it's because the twins aren't as quick to complete projects as they'll be once they're seasoned designers."

"She should have considered that before kicking you to the curb." The way the woman had treated Lindsay still rankled.

"She didn't exactly kick me to the curb," Lindsay corrected. "I quit."

"You quit when she gave away your duties to her kids. *And* cut your pay," he added.

"The girls are her family, Owen. Her loyalty is to them, not to me." One hand dropped to her midsection.

He stared as the fabric of her dress molded against a little pouch of a belly. *His* baby, he thought with a surge of emotion. *Their* daughter.

"I told her I'd help her out."

He jerked his gaze back to her face. "What?"

Lindsay lifted her chin. "I said I'd help her out in the mornings until my business takes off. It's a good deal for both of us. I need money. She needs help."

The defensive edge to her voice surprised Owen. It was almost as if she expected him to second-guess her decision and argue with her. While Owen didn't appreciate the way Shirley had treated her, if Lindsay wanted to help the woman out, that was her business.

He smiled and gave her arm a squeeze. "I'm sure she's grateful."

"Yes." Lindsay cleared her throat. "Anyway, after speaking with Shirley, I went straight to Eliza's home. Ami was there. We enjoyed cherry pie cookies and fresh-squeezed lemonade."

"Now you're making me hungry," he teased.

"You wanted details." Her eyes twinkled in the waning light. "Not ten minutes after I arrived, Eliza sprang the news that she and Kyle are pregnant. She's due the beginning of May. They're super excited."

Something in the way she delivered that last statement had Owen wondering if it was aimed at him. His initial response to the news of their pregnancy had been far different than how he felt now. "You and I, we're super excited, too."

Lindsay's startled gaze flew to his. "We are?"

"I can't speak for you, but I'm super excited."

Her smile started slowly. By the time it reached her eyes, her entire face glowed. "I'm super excited, too."

His gaze locked with hers, and he couldn't look away. That same intense connection that had caused him to take a big step back from her in July wrapped around him now like a tight glove.

"Eliza and Kyle haven't been married very long." Owen picked up a stone and flung it out over the water. It skipped several times, then plopped into the bay. "I take it they were trying to get pregnant?"

"Yes. They wanted a baby." Lindsay thought for a moment. "When I was leaving, she mentioned something about them not getting any younger and wanting more than one. I don't think they'll wait long before trying for a second child."

Owen thought of Eliza with her perfect wardrobe and mile-high heels. "I'm having difficulty seeing Eliza as the maternal type."

It was a mistake. The off-the-cuff comment had Lindsay's back stiffening. Not surprising, since Lindsay was fiercely protective of her friends.

"Eliza is a warm, caring person." Lindsay bit off the words. "She'll be an amazing mother. When Lolo stayed with them, Eliza was incredibly good to her."

"Whoa. It was simply an observation. I meant no disrespect." Kyle raised his hands. "I know she's your friend, but you have to admit Eliza can come across as prickly."

"It's her persona." A smile tugged at the corners of Lindsay's lips. "Her I'm-running-the-show-and-you-better-not-cross-me face is the one she shows the world. Inside, she's really a big marshmallow."

Not about to touch that comment, Owen released the other stone in his hand. Instead of skipping across the water, this one plopped and sank. "Kyle and Eliza are both busy people."

When he didn't continue, Lindsay cocked her head.

"Have they given any thought to what they'll do once the baby comes?"

"You mean in regard to childcare?"

He nodded.

"They've got that figured out." Lindsay squatted down and let the rocky sand sift through her fingers. She straightened and dusted off her hands. "Eliza is already hot on the nanny hunt. Though she and Kyle frequently work from home, there are times when he needs to be on a job site and she needs to be at the store. Katherine will help out when she can, but she has her own life."

"I wouldn't think a nanny would be easy to find in a community as small as Good Hope." Owen deliberately kept his tone light. "Not to mention how will they know the unknown nanny will take good care of their baby?"

With all the reports of people abusing defenseless children in their care, it was his greatest concern. Granted, none of those stories had occurred in Good Hope, but the knowledge didn't ease his worry.

"Eliza and Kyle are willing to pay top dollar for the right person." Lindsay gave a little laugh. "Trust me. Whoever they pick will be screened within an inch of her life."

They walked in silence for another minute.

"Do you realize"—Owen paused to pick up another stone —"our baby will likely arrive more than a month ahead of theirs, and we haven't had a single conversation about childcare?"

Though he hadn't meant it as criticism, Lindsay visibly bristled. "It's on my list of parenting questions. There hasn't been time—"

"You're absolutely right. We've both been busy." Owen offered an easy smile. "But we have time now."

Not only didn't she smile back, but two lines formed between her brows. "What do you think we should do?"

Owen nearly groaned aloud. This was why he'd rarely

spoken up in school. One saving grace was his conversation with David that morning had gotten him thinking about his first marriage and his lack of support of Tessa and her career.

His wife had been in college when Mindy had arrived. Tessa had given birth on Tuesday and returned to school the following Monday. Taking a few weeks off to care for their daughter hadn't been an option.

Instead of empathizing with the difficult position she'd been in, he'd resented her being gone so much. Instead of being supportive, when she *had* been able to eke out a few hours with Mindy, he'd questioned her parenting skills.

Shame flooded him.

"Owen." Lindsay touched his arm, her voice soft and filled with concern. "What's the matter?"

"Nothing." His chuckle sounded more like a croak. Owen cleared his throat. "I haven't given the matter much thought. Why don't you kick off the discussion?"

"You're not getting off that easy, mister." Lindsay's tone held a teasing lilt. "You brought up the topic. You go first."

Owen shifted from one foot to the other and went wide. "I see us being in the same boat as Eliza and Kyle. I have my business. You'll have yours. Should we join the nanny hunt?"

Owen kept all judgment from his voice, though the thought of leaving their infant with a stranger—even a fully vetted one— made him feel a little sick. But he accepted that finding a caregiver was necessary.

"Having someone come into the home can be pricey. I'm thinking we'll have to drop her off, either at someone's home or at a center." Lindsay blew out a breath. "The day care that recently opened in the Living Center might be a possibility. They take infants, but give priority to teachers and other school personnel. I'm hoping if we get on a wait list, by the time the baby is born, they'll have a space for her."

Owen shoved his hands into his pockets. "Are you thinking of taking any time off?"

"You know how it is when you're building your own business." Lindsay's gaze shifted to the water. "Taking time off, much less during peak wedding season, is tantamount to business suicide. The floral shop will be my bread and butter. I can't fail."

The determination in her voice took him by surprise, until he realized that she and Tessa had more than him in common. Lindsay would likely have the baby one week, then need to jump back into an insanely busy life the next.

This time, however, *his* situation was different. When Mindy had been born, he'd been growing his business. The money from the Greasy Wrench had been critical to keeping a roof over their heads. Now, ten years later, the business was firmly established, and he had a crew of men and women he could count on.

"Most centers won't take infants until they're six weeks old." Owen kept his tone conversational, not sure what she'd think of his offer. "I can clear my schedule so I can be home with her until she's old enough for day care."

"You'd do that?" Surprise lit Lindsay's eyes even as her brow furrowed. "Take off that much time?"

"If you're agreeable, I'll make it work." *Supportive*, he told himself, *make sure she understands you support her career*. "I know how important getting this new business off the ground is to you."

"Thank you, Owen." Relief blanketed her face. "Seriously, I can't tell you how much this means to me."

"It's not a hardship. I'm looking forward to spending time with our daughter." As he voiced the words, he realized just how much he meant them.

Lindsay clasped his arm, her eyes intense and so very blue. "The thought of leaving her with a stranger when she's so little, well, I was concerned. So, thank you for taking away that worry."

"Parenting is a partnership." His eyes never left her face. "I'm just doing my part."

"There are so many things still to work out. Not only about the baby." Lindsay's gaze searched his face. "We still have to figure out *us*."

Sensing her rising distress, Owen shifted, gathered her close and kissed her temple. "That will work out, too."

Tilting her head back, she studied him for a long moment. "I'd nearly forgotten just how nice you are to have around."

The sentiment soothed like balm on an open wound. Despite all that had happened between them, she was still happy to have him in her life.

"I'm not going anywhere," he vowed, twining the strands of her hair loosely around his fingers.

Her eyes darkened to a deep blue. "Good."

Without warning, she wrapped her arms around his neck and kissed him on the mouth. Her lips brushed over his for only a second, but it was still a kiss.

Owen's heart gave a solid thump against his chest.

When she stepped back and looked at him with a bewildered expression, he smiled reassuringly and trailed a not-quite-steady finger along the line of her jaw, then up the faint scar slashing across her cheek. "You're so lovely."

She shook her head. "I'm not."

"Let me be the judge of that." He studied her with an intensity that had bright patches of red blooming on her cheeks. "Your eyes are amazing. In all the time I've known you, I still haven't figured out what color they are."

"They're blue." Her blush deepened, and she looked away, but not before he saw desire reflected in eyes the color of storm-tossed seas.

"They're also gray and a little green." He let his gaze drop to her mouth.

He heard her breath catch, then begin again. She moistened her lips with the tip of her tongue, and his mouth went dry.

"I want to kiss you." His voice was a hoarse and throaty rasp.

Unexpectedly, Lindsay laughed, a short nervous burst of air. "What's stopping you?"

She'd said the same thing before, then pushed him away. Owen let the question hang in the air for several seconds before his mouth closed over hers. Her hands rose to his shoulders, and she pressed against him, so close that the beating of his heart mingled with hers.

Owen reveled in the pleasure of the contact, in the warmth of her mouth against his lips. Though they'd kissed before, made love before, this felt new and fragile.

He took it slow, pressing his lips lightly to hers, teasingly, his mouth never pulling away.

As they continued to kiss, her hands dropped from his shoulders. She curled her fingers in the fabric of his shirt, pulling him closer.

Owen slid his tongue lightly over her lips, and when she opened that sweet mouth, a dizzying barrage of sensual images of the two of them together flashed before him. When they came up for air, need was a stark, carnal hunger. "Let's go—"

A jarring ring cut off his words.

Lindsay released her hold on his shirt and stumbled back.

Owen reached for her.

She shook her head. "Check your phone."

He made no move to pull it from his pocket.

"You better look." Her breath came in little puffs, and bright spots of pink dotted her cheeks. "It could be important."

Retrieving his phone, he glanced at the display. "It's Bayside. Our table is ready."

"Saved by the bell," Lindsay quipped, but something in her eyes told him he wasn't the only one disappointed by the interruption.

Owen raised a brow. "One more kiss for the road?"

She laughed, a joyous sound like the tinkling of a thousand bells. "Better not. I don't think either of us would be able to stop at one."

Conceding the point, Owen extended his arm.

They walked back to the restaurant, leaning into each other like old friends, enjoying the renewed closeness.

Only when they reached the steps of Bayside Pizza did Lindsay release his arm.

She pushed at her wind-tangled hair. "Do I look okay?"

"Beautiful." Owen couldn't resist. Leaning over, he kissed her softly, wishing—not for the first time—he'd turned off the ringer on his phone.

CHAPTER TWENTY-ONE

Lindsay finished off her second slice of pizza and reached for a third. If her mother had been sitting across from her, Anita would have slapped her hand and warned her about getting fat.

Telling her mother that she'd eaten light all day never made a difference. But it wasn't her mother across from her, it was Owen, and he was smiling. The warmth and desire in those hazel eyes had her losing track of what she'd been about to say.

"Wh-what were we talking about?" she stammered.

"You were telling me about Cassie."

"That's right." A lump formed in Lindsay's throat. She sipped her drink to dispel it. "When Cassie got pregnant, I wasn't there for her. Not the way I should have been."

"You were very young."

"I was twelve, almost thirteen. Old enough." Guilt flooded her. "I wanted to be supportive, but I didn't know how. I didn't understand how it could have happened. As far as I knew, my sister had never been on a date."

Owen lifted *his* third slice—not that she was counting—but didn't take a bite. "How did your mother react?"

"She was stunned." Lindsay's heart picked up speed as she

recalled that long-ago night when Cassie had called them all into the living room. "Bernie went ballistic."

Owen finally bit into the pizza. He chewed thoughtfully, his watchful gaze never leaving her face. "Bernie was your stepfather."

"Bernie Fishback, the Bagel King." Lindsay rolled her eyes. She'd done her best to forget the man her mother had impulsively married after her father's death. "Marrying him was the biggest mistake my mother ever made."

Owen set down the half-eaten slice and picked up his tumbler of tea. "What was he like?"

"On the surface, nice. Underneath, a bully." Lindsay's teeth found her bottom lip. "When Cassie announced she was pregnant, Bernie exploded. He called Cassie horrible names."

A muscle in Owen's jaw jumped. "Where was your mother when this was happening?"

"Right there. She stood there and let that vile man spew his venom." Lindsay dropped the pizza back to her plate, her appetite gone. "Mom was shocked. I get that. She'd had high hopes for Cassie. I get that, too. But she shouldn't have allowed Bernie to talk to her child that way."

Lindsay shuddered. "Cassie began to sob. I couldn't take it anymore. I stepped in front of her and told Bernie to shut up, to leave my sister alone."

For a second, Lindsay was back in their old living room, the one decorated with Bernie's money. Her stomach pitched.

"Did he?" Owen prompted, his voice a low rumble. "Did he stop?"

"He backhanded me." Lindsay's hand rose to her face, recalling the explosion of pain. "He hit me so hard it knocked me off my feet."

Owen's eyes flashed. "The son of a—"

"It brought Mom out of her stupor. She ordered him out of the house and called the sheriff. Bernie had poked the bear, and she was out for blood." Lindsay's lips lifted in a sardonic smile. "She filed for divorce and used the money from the settlement to open Crumb and Cake."

"All's well that ends well." Owen's sarcastic tone didn't hide his rage.

"It was a long time ago." Lindsay's gaze settled on a couple a few tables over. The woman couldn't take her eyes off her date. The guy couldn't take his eyes off his phone. "Mom never loved Bernie. Not really. I think she married him for a whole lot of wrong reasons that seemed right at the time. Her experience taught me a valuable lesson."

Smart man that he was, Owen obviously saw where this was headed and didn't appear eager to travel that path. "It was that way with me and Tessa. We were in love and marrying felt right. It ended up being a huge mistake. Except, as painful as the divorce was, I'd do it all over again, because otherwise I wouldn't have had Mindy."

Lindsay wondered if he still loved Tessa. Could love end as easily as flipping a switch when you left a room? "Tessa has done well for herself professionally."

Everyone in Good Hope knew the Slattery family had never done anything to support Tessa or Krew. In fact, it was amazing both kids hadn't ended up in prison.

"Tessa had an intense drive to succeed." Owen's lips lifted, telling Lindsay not all memories of their time together were bad. "The woman had great instincts."

Lindsay forked off a bite of pizza but didn't bring it to her mouth. "How so?"

"She was a master at qualifying for grants and scholarships." He paused as if not certain how to explain. "Like, if she were in your situation, she'd know every small-business grant for entrepreneurs available." Owen cocked his head. "Have you thought about seeing what grants are out there?"

Lindsay tightened her fingers around the fork. Now that he

mentioned the possibility, she recalled reading something about such grants. "I haven't looked into it, but I will. Thank you."

"Happy to be of help." Grinning, he lifted a slice of pizza to his mouth and munched happily.

The food Lindsay had eaten sat in the pit of her stomach like one of her mother's leaden matzo balls. Anita might be a master baker, but the woman was a horrible cook.

Lindsay didn't know if Tessa excelled at cooking, and she wasn't about to ask. No doubt, if Owen's ex had pursued the culinary arts, she'd be a master chef by now.

"Did you and Tessa ever connect in high school?" The second the question slipped past her lips, Lindsay wished she could pull it back. The last thing she wanted to do was spend the evening talking about the woman who'd broken Owen's heart.

"I kissed her one night at a beach party. There was always lots of kissing at the bonfires." Owen waved a dismissive hand. "Along with the consumption of endless amounts of alcohol."

"Ami and I attended just one of those parties." Breathing suddenly became difficult. "She lost control of the car on our way home, and we hit a tree."

Lindsay didn't need to elaborate. The accident had been big news in the tightly knit community.

"That's where you got this…" Owen trailed a finger down the scar on her cheek.

Lindsay sat back, suddenly self-conscious. "I-I have makeup that does a good job covering it, but it's expensive. I reserve it for special occasions."

Grasping her hand, Owen brought it to his mouth and pressed a kiss into the palm. His gaze never left her face. "You survived injuries that nearly took your life. The scar is a symbol of your strength."

Lindsay dropped her gaze as tears threatened.

"I'm thankful you lived." His thumb caressed her palm. "If you hadn't, I wouldn't be sitting here with you now. We wouldn't be having a baby together."

"Your life would be easier."

"My life would be empty." He swallowed. "I can't imagine my life without you."

She searched his hazel eyes. "Really? You aren't just saying that?"

"I mean every word." His gaze remained locked with hers.

What she saw in those hazel depths had her heart flip-flopping. "Maybe we *can* make this work."

Lindsay didn't realize she'd spoken aloud until Owen gripped her hands. "Trust me. There's no maybe about it."

"Well, isn't this cozy?"

Instead of releasing her hand at the sound of the unwelcome feminine voice, Owen held on.

For a second, Lindsay considered jerking back, but refused to give her mother the satisfaction.

Lindsay looked up and discovered it wasn't just her mother at their table, but also Leonard Swarts.

Though her mother wore a V-neck sweater with her dark pants and heels tonight, this top didn't show off as excessive an amount of cleavage as her sweaters had in the past.

Len, appearing comfortable in jeans, a gray sweater and cowboy boots, offered them a warm smile.

"We were waiting for a table to open up when your mother spotted you." Though retired, Len had a lawman's face, with an expression that gave nothing away.

Lindsay caught Owen's sideways glance. It was up to her, she realized. "Won't you join us?"

"We wouldn't want to intrud—" Len began, but Anita had already pulled out a chair and sat down.

"Are you two dating again?" Anita demanded as the waitress hurried over.

"Darlin'." Len placed a hand over Anita's and gave it a pat.

"How 'bout we order and exchange a few pleasantries before you begin the interrogation?"

To Lindsay's surprise, her mother, who didn't like anyone calling her out, blushed. Perhaps it was the way Len had phrased the question. Or maybe it was the word *darlin'* said with such obvious affection.

"Of course." Anita looked at their glasses of iced tea, then back to the pizza. "Chianti would do a better job of enhancing the flavor of the pepperoni."

"Probably." Owen answered before Lindsay had a chance to respond. "Tea just sounded better to both of us."

"Well, we're going to imbibe." Anita smiled coquettishly at Len. "The usual?"

The usual? Her mother and her new boyfriend had a *usual*?

"Great minds think alike." Len turned to the waitress with the same air of quiet command and kindness Lindsay remembered him showing when he'd arrived at their house after the Bernie episode. "This little lady and I will have a medium barbecue chicken pizza and a Guinness for each of us."

"Thank you, sir." The waitress, a pretty blonde with pink-tipped hair, hurried off.

Owen cocked his head. "Guinness with pizza?"

"Try it sometime," Len urged. "The dark roasted characteristic of an Irish stout is fantastic with chicken and the sweetness of the barbecue sauce."

Lindsay decided appearances really could be deceiving. She'd never pegged the tall, broad-shouldered sheriff with the bushy silver mustache as a chicken-pizza man, much less one into food and drink pairings.

Anita lifted her hands, spreading her fingers. "I was skeptical. Frankly, I couldn't see that particular combination working."

"Once I got Muffy to try it"—the older man shot her a wink —"she was hooked."

When the two exchanged a smile, Lindsay felt as if she'd stepped into an old *Twilight Zone* episode.

Owen's lips twitched. "Muffy?"

Anita straightened in her chair. The look she shot him was ice. "My maiden name was Muff."

"It's a pet name." Affection wove through Len's words like a pretty ribbon.

"I love it." Anita stroked his arm, then brushed a kiss across his cheek.

Owen rubbed his chin and studied Lindsay for so long her cheeks began to burn. "I should come up with one for you, Lin."

Before she could respond, the waitress returned with extra plates and two Guinness-branded glasses, each filled with the deep reddish-brown stout boasting a white foamy head.

Lindsay gestured to the half-eaten pizza in the center of the table. "There are extra slices of pepperoni if you'd like to munch while you wait."

The horrified look that appeared on her mother's face told Lindsay a person didn't pair pepperoni and Guinness. At least, not in Anita Fishback's well-ordered world. "Pepperoni needs the bitterness of an India Pale Ale to offset the saltiness of the meat."

Len smiled approvingly. "Your mother has become somewhat of an expert in such matters."

"Thanks to your tutelage." Anita circled a hand in the semblance of a bow.

Lindsay could only stare.

"I appreciate the offer, Owen, but I think I'll save my appetite for our pizza. I've been looking forward to it all day." Len glanced at Anita.

"Yes, ah, thanks for offering and for, ah, letting us share your table." Anita might have needed a nudge from Len, but she sounded surprisingly sincere.

Lindsay relaxed against the back of the chair. Perhaps sharing a meal with her mother wouldn't be so difficult.

Then Anita's gaze fixed on her. "Did you happen to read the Open Door today?"

Something in her mother's assessing gaze had unease traveling up Lindsay's spine. She tried to imagine what could have been in the e-newsletter. Did it involve Cassie? Or one of her children?

God, she hoped not. Cassie and the boys had been doing so well lately. Cassie had embraced the added responsibilities Ryder had given her at the Daily Grind, and the boys had both made the honor roll last quarter.

Surely the news didn't involve her niece. Dakota was back in Good Hope for the semester, hoping to earn enough money to return to college in the spring. Of course, Lindsay reminded herself, gossip didn't have to be bad. Perhaps one of the many scholarships her niece had applied for had come through.

Realizing her mother was still waiting for a response, Lindsay smiled.

"I saw the newsletter in my in-box, but time got away from me this morning. I haven't had a chance to open it." Like most Good Hope citizens, Lindsay enjoyed reading the feature stories and pursuing the advertisements and sales. And she always scanned the gossip section. "Good news for someone, I hope."

"That depends."

Her mother's cryptic comment had Lindsay glancing at Owen. Surely he'd have told her if he'd seen some good news about one of her family or friends. "Did you read it today?"

Owen shook his head. "I don't usually get around to it until right before bed."

Lindsay turned back to her mother and found Anita staring intently at her, eyes sharp and assessing. Something in the newsletter had captured her mother's attention and piqued her curiosity. It had to have been in the gossip section. Anita would never be this excited over a feature article.

Because it was apparent—at least to Lindsay—that her mother

expected her to press for details, Lindsay simply lifted her glass of iced tea to her lips.

"Well, don't keep us all in suspense, Muffy." Len's tone held a teasing edge. "Tell us what's got you so fired up."

Lindsay doubted the ex-lawman read the gossip section and cared even less what Katie Ruth had written. But it spoke to his affection for Anita that he played along so amiably.

Anita leaned slightly forward, as if about to impart news of great importance rather than simply spreading a bit of gossip. "Katie Ruth said a certain young woman she knew from high school is pregnant."

Lindsay's mind somersaulted. *She'd* gone to school with Katie Ruth. Then she reminded herself that so had any number of young women. Including Eliza, who hadn't yet publicly announced her pregnancy. "Did she give any clues? It could be anyone. I can think of several pregnant women in Good Hope. Ami, for one."

"Ami Cross being pregnant is old news." Anita brushed that possibility away with a quick flick of her wrist, then narrowed her gaze on her daughter.

A chill traveled up Lindsay's spine. Had her mother found out about the baby? But how? Owen wouldn't have said anything, and she trusted Ami and Eliza implicitly. Had someone seen her at the pharmacy picking up the prenatal vitamins? Or leaving Dr. Swanson's office that first time with baby-related samples?

Or, and this seemed more likely, was her mother simply on a fishing expedition? If Anita suspected Katie Ruth had been referring to Lindsay, wouldn't her mother simply ask her if she was pregnant?

As thoughts swirled and worry tried to take hold, it hit Lindsay just how profoundly weary she was of the subterfuge and evasions. She wouldn't be able to hide her pregnancy for much longer. The truth was, she didn't want to hide it.

She wanted to enjoy every moment of the experience. She

206 | CINDY KIRK

wanted to go to Swoon, the cute boutique in town that had just started carrying maternity clothes, and shop with Eliza and Ami. She wanted to compile lists of names and sit with Owen in Muddy Boots and come up with their top five without worrying about being overheard.

Though a pizza parlor hardly seemed the place for any momentous announcement, Lindsay knew relaying the news in her mother's living room would be too reminiscent of the Cassie fiasco. No. It was best to do it now.

Lindsey set down her tumbler of tea. She met her mother's gaze head on. "I'm pregnant."

"I think Fin's pregnant."

She and Anita spoke at the same instant.

Her always composed mother's hands fluttered in the air. She cleared her throat. "What did you say?"

Len, sweetheart that he was, didn't make Lindsay repeat the announcement. A broad smile lifted his mouth, the edges of his lips disappearing into his mustache.

"Well, I'll be." Len cast a glance at Anita. "This is wonderful news. Congratulations. When's the baby due?"

"The end of March." Owen spoke when Lindsay's tongue decided to go on strike.

"I take it you're the daddy." Len's tone remained jovial.

"I am." There was pride in Owen's voice, but also a warning directed at Anita.

Like Lindsay, her mother seemed to be having difficulty finding her voice.

"You're a lucky man, Owen." A shadow passed briefly over Len's rugged features. "My wife and I weren't able to have children. Last weekend, Anita and I watched Axl while Cassie was working. Little boys are a lot of fun."

"We're having a girl," Owen told the older man.

Len turned to Anita. "Looks like we'll have us a girl to spoil in the spring."

"Yes." Anita reached over and chugged a long drink of Guinness. "It appears so."

Lindsay braced herself when her mother set down her glass. While she believed Len's presence could be a mitigating factor, Anita Fishback was a woman who never shied from saying exactly what was on her mind.

"Katie Ruth knows?" Anita asked.

A reprieve came in the form of the waitress returning with a piping-hot barbecue chicken pizza. Obviously thinking ahead, in case they needed to make a quick escape, Owen asked for the rest of their pizza to be boxed up.

"I don't believe so," Lindsay told her. "The only ones I've told are Eliza and Ami. And, of course, Owen."

"Perhaps Katie Ruth *was* referring to Fin."

Lindsay blinked. She'd just told her mother she was pregnant, and Anita wanted to speculate on who else might be pregnant?

The comment must have hit her mother as odd, too, because she shook her layered mane of auburn hair as if clearing her head. "That's not important. What's important is you. How are you feeling?"

"Ah, fine. Actually, I'm great." Lindsay felt as if she was picking her way through a minefield. The tension of waiting was almost worse than the explosion to come. "Why are you being so nice about this?"

"That's an odd question." Her mother raised a perfectly tweezed dark brow. "Did you expect me to throw my hands up in the air? Rant and rave simply because my unmarried daughter is pregnant?"

Lindsay had to hand it to her mother. Anita's bluntness was a finely tuned blade.

"Yes," Lindsay said. "That's exactly what I expected."

Was that pain that sparked in her mother's hazel eyes?

Anita appeared to be gathering her thoughts when Len took

her hand and gave her an encouraging smile. "Time to speak from the heart, Muffy."

When Anita shifted her gaze from him back to Lindsay, a sheen glimmered in her hazel depths. "I don't know if you're aware, but I recently participated in a family counseling session with Cassie and Dr. Gallagher."

If Anita had announced she'd sold her business and was moving to Tahiti, Lindsay couldn't have been more surprised.

"Really?" was the best she could manage.

Anita nodded. Her fingers tightened around Len's. "Cassie is determined to get her life back on track. She's accepted responsibility for her choices and actions. It's time I do the same."

When Anita didn't immediately elaborate, Lindsay narrowed her gaze. "What exactly does that mean?"

"I wasn't there for Cassie after Richard died." Anita expelled a ragged breath. "She was Daddy's girl. You and I both accepted that theirs was a special bond. His heart attack and death rocked her world."

Lindsay slowly nodded.

"My world was thrown upside down, too. Richard was my rock. Then, one day—without warning—he was gone, and I was left with two grieving girls and a world that no longer made sense." Anita's chuckle held a harsh edge. "There's a reason they say to hold off making big decisions for at least a year after a loved one's death. Of course, I didn't listen."

"Don't be so hard on yourself." Understanding filled Len's tone. "I made plenty of mistakes myself that first year after Margaret died."

"I should never have brought Bernie into our lives. I was lonely. I didn't love him, not the way a woman should love her husband. I realize that now."

"Without love, a marriage is doomed to fail." Len's eyes took on a distant look as he no doubt thought of his beloved wife who'd passed on several years earlier.

"Cassie saw the marriage as a betrayal of her father and withdrew into herself. Worse, we all bore the brunt of Bernie's temper and mood swings during the years we were married." Tears, actual tears, glistened in Anita's eyes.

Lindsay couldn't recall ever seeing her mother cry. Even at her husband's funeral, she'd remained stoic.

"I should have kicked him out long before he destroyed Cassie's sense of self-worth and struck you." Anita reached across the table and surprised Lindsay by clasping her cold hand. "I should have supported my daughters when they needed me most."

Lindsay didn't know what to think. This was a side of her mother she barely remembered. "What are you saying?"

Anita met and held Lindsay's gaze. "I'll be here for you."

CHAPTER TWENTY-TWO

Owen unlocked his front door and pushed it open. Even after all the sorrows the single-story Craftsman-style house had witnessed within its walls, coming home still comforted him.

Each time he opened his red front door, he thought of Mindy and how she'd begged him to change the color to hot pink. She'd insisted that shade would look perfectly lovely with the dark gray exterior. She might have been right.

If he could go back, he'd paint the door pink just to see her smile.

"You lured me here."

Owen flipped on the lights and stepped back to let Lindsay enter. He inclined his head, not certain he'd heard correctly. "What did you say?"

"You lured me with your promise of Chunky Monkey."

"I suppose I did." Owen chuckled, then sobered. "I don't think either of us was ready to call it a night. While it was nice having Len and your mother join us, it was also—"

"Stressful," Lindsay supplied. "And a little bit weird."

He nodded. "On that note of agreement, follow me to the kitchen."

Once there, Owen moved to the refrigerator. By the time he pulled the carton out of the freezer's cavernous depths, Lindsay was sitting at the counter on one of the stools, two large spoons in her hand.

"No bowls?" He took a seat beside her and removed the ice cream lid.

She handed him a spoon. "This is an eat-straight-out-of-the-carton kind of night."

He bowed to her wishes and waited for her to take the first spoonful before dipping into the rich and creamy depths. "The evening went fairly well considering the bombshell we dropped on your mother. I was surprised how well she took the news, though I think the second glass of Guinness helped."

"It was creepy." Lindsay spoke around a spoonful of banana ice cream and chunks of fudge. "It was as if aliens had taken possession of my mother's body and replaced her with a robot. She didn't yell. Not once. And she was nice to you."

"I'm a nice guy."

"You've always been nice." Lindsay wagged a spoon at him. "That never mattered before."

"True." Owen brought the spoon to his mouth. "Do you think the change is because of Len? He appears to be a steadying influence."

"Steve was a good influence, too, but him being there wouldn't have stopped her from being nasty if the situation arose."

"At least now we don't have to keep the baby a secret." Owen had found it increasingly difficult as the weeks passed to keep his mouth shut. All the secrecy made it feel as if they were ashamed of the baby.

"I agree. It's a relief to have everything out in the open." Lindsay's gaze turned thoughtful as she sat back, her empty spoon poised over the carton.

She looked so pretty and so at home sitting in his kitchen that it seemed natural to lean over and kiss her.

Her spoon clattered on the counter as his lips continued their onslaught. When her arms looped around his neck, he deepened the kiss.

He'd missed this, he realized, missed this closeness with her. But as the heat rose between them, kissing was no longer enough. He wanted to run his hands across her smooth skin and stroke those sensitive places that never failed to arouse. He wanted to be as close to her as physically possible.

"Stay with me tonight," he murmured between kisses. "Let me make love to you. I want you, Lindsay. More than I've ever wanted any other woman."

The momentary stiffness he'd sensed dissolved, and she relaxed in his arms. The eyes that met his were intense and very blue. "I want you, too, Owen."

Giving her one last swift kiss, he hopped off the stool and made quick work of putting away the ice cream.

"Hey, did I say I was done with that?" Her tone turned teasing as she stood. "Maybe I had plans for that ice cream."

Owen paused, one hand on the freezer door. His mind raced with possibilities. Plans? Yes, he liked the sound of that. "What kind of plans?"

She laughed, a delightful sound. "Go ahead and put it away for now. I think we'll be busy enough without it."

Owen liked the sound of that even more.

LINDSAY'S HEART tripped over itself when Owen shut the freezer door. Feeling like a racehorse in the starting gate, she quivered inside, but remained absolutely still, one hand resting lightly on the center counter.

She knew getting physically involved with Owen again, allowing that level of intimacy, would make it difficult to maintain the needed distance between them.

Still, she yearned for his touch and the closeness and comfort she felt in his arms. He'd said he couldn't imagine life without her...

When he drew her gently into his arms, there was something in his eyes she hadn't seen before. Something that looked a lot like love.

Was it only wishful thinking, or had he fallen in love with her, the way she had with him?

She didn't have a chance to do more than think the question when his fingers slid into her hair and he lowered his head to kiss her.

He tasted like chocolate fudge. Lindsay poured her heart into the kiss, wanting him to know more than any words she could say that she believed they could make this relationship work.

She couldn't have said how long they stood in the kitchen kissing, warm lips pressed together, hands offering gentle caresses. All Lindsay knew was there wasn't anywhere else she'd rather be than here, with him.

When the kisses grew urgent and fire bubbled in her blood, Lindsay stumbled down the hall with him. The kisses didn't stop during the short journey, and she let out a breathless laugh when they finally made it to the bedroom.

This was her first time in his room. They'd always made love before at her apartment. She scanned the room, taking in the mission-style bed, with a duvet in shades of gray, and matching bedside table and dresser. All very masculine.

For a second, Lindsay froze. Did she really want to open her heart to him again? Then he was kissing her, and she realized it was a moot point. She'd already given Owen her heart.

Somehow, miraculously, they made it all the way to the bed with their clothing intact. She stood, the backs of her knees pressed against the mattress, his mouth melded to hers.

Her hands moved up, and she curled her fingers in the fabric of his shirt. She could feel the heat of his body beneath her hands, the steady thud of his heart.

Everything faded except the need to feel more of him, taste more of him, touch more of him. She started with the top button of his shirt, slipping it free before moving to the next.

He chuckled softly against her mouth as he caught on to her plan. "You want to see me naked."

The good humor in his voice had her lips curving upward as the last button popped open.

With his gaze still fixed on her face, Owen shrugged out of the shirt and flung it to the floor. His pants quickly followed.

Soon, he stood before her clad only in a pair of gray boxers. The moon shone through the bedroom window, bathing his lean, muscular body in a golden glow. He smelled of soap and some indefinable male scent that had desire surging low in her belly.

"One of us is overdressed." Owen's hazel eyes glittered in the dim light.

"You're right." Lindsay smiled. "Those boxers definitely need to go."

He laughed aloud, the sound so genuine and warm that any tension lingering in the room disappeared. "I was speaking of you."

Anticipation had her heart fluttering as she reached for the hem of her top, her fingers clumsy as she tugged it upward.

"Let me help."

With his assistance, the tunic slid easily over her head. Seconds later, leggings and underwear were removed with the same efficiency. Owen had seen her naked before, but suddenly self-conscious, Lindsay moved her hands to cover the belly that was no longer flat but rounded.

His gaze focused on the small mound. "Let me see."

Swallowing hard, Lindsay slowly moved her hands aside.

The emotion that flared in his eyes surprised her. She didn't know what to think when he dropped to his knees before her.

One hand gently stroked the swell before he pressed a kiss right below her navel.

She was still reeling from the sweet gesture when he gently pushed her back on the bed, then moved to lie beside her, his boxers remaining behind on the floor.

"You're so beautiful." He nuzzled the sensitive spot behind her ear.

He made love to her as much with the words he murmured as with his mouth and fingers. Prickles of pleasure danced across her bare skin as he stroked, caressed and kissed his way up and down her body.

When his hand slipped between her legs, she opened to him, her entire body quivering with need, with love. For him. Only for him.

When he entered her, filling her, hard and firm, she moaned with pleasure. Could something that felt this good be wrong? Lindsay fought the orgasm building inside her, not wanting this to be over so quickly.

As need became want, she kissed him with a ferocity that reflected the depth of her feelings for him. Tonight, she was a tangled mass of desires that centered around one man—this man —the only man she would ever love.

Owen pumped his hips forward and back, again and again, until holding on proved impossible. Lindsay surged against the pleasure swelling like the tide inside her until she could hold on no more.

The orgasm hit her with breathtaking speed.

"Owen," she cried out as her nails dug into his back and her body convulsed around him. She shuddered over and over again.

He continued to pump, drawing every last ounce of pleasure from her before taking his own release. When he rolled off of her, she felt bereft. Until he tugged her close and kissed her.

Lindsay let her eyes drift shut. As she lingered on the edge of sleep, his warm body pressed against hers, her lips curved.

All her dreams were coming true.

❧

OWEN WOKE the next morning with Lindsay's hand flat against his chest. It took him a second to remember what had happened. The dinner at Bayside Pizza. Sharing a carton of ice cream in his kitchen. Endless kisses.

He'd wanted Lindsay last night in a way he couldn't recall wanting any woman. There was something about her that drew him to her. Certainly, she was attractive, with a pretty face, long blond hair and blue eyes. But she was also funny and smart and kind.

Not to mention incredibly sexy. Simply watching her eat ice cream had had his body throbbing with need.

Last night's lovemaking had gone beyond the physical. The closeness and connection he felt for her was more than he'd bargained for, more than he wanted. If he was being honest with himself, he'd admit he was in imminent danger of falling in love with her.

The realization had him jerking upright in bed.

Lindsay opened her eyes. A smile hovered at the corners of her lips as she pushed herself up to her elbows, blinking the sleep from her eyes. "Good morning."

Though Owen wanted nothing more than to make love with her again, it couldn't happen. Not until he got his feelings under better control.

"I'm sorry I woke you." Owen made a vague gesture with his hand. "I need to get dressed. There are some things at the garage I need to tend to this morning."

Lindsay inhaled sharply. "What time is it?"

Owen glanced at the clock. "Nine."

Lindsay's eyes widened. She flung off the covers. "I told Shirley I'd be in at ten."

For a second, Owen was confused, until he remembered she'd agreed to help out her former boss. "You have plenty of time."

"Not really." She slipped around him and stood, her bare body even more glorious in the morning light. With quick, efficient moves, she gathered up her clothes. "Mind if I use your bathroom to freshen up?"

"It's all yours." Owen rose to his feet, feeling oddly put out at what almost felt like a casual dismissal of what they'd shared last night.

Which was absolutely crazy since he hadn't wanted her to read more into what had happened. Still, a little civility seemed indicated.

"I'll make coffee," he called out, just before the bathroom door shut behind her.

Owen took a quick shower in the other bathroom, then dressed. He had the Keurig brewing when he heard Lindsay's footsteps.

"The coffee is almost—" His smile faded when he saw the look on her face. "What's wrong?"

She swallowed convulsively, eyes large in a pale face. "I'm bleeding."

Owen's heart gave a solid thump. "Very much?"

What did he know about such things? But it seemed more blood would be worse than a trace.

"Just a little, on the tissue." She moistened her lips. "It was brown, but it was blood. Do you think color makes a difference?"

"I think brown is definitely better than bright red." Owen forced a confident tone.

Though his insides quivered, Owen didn't have the same sense of foreboding he'd experienced when he'd called the doctor about Mindy's headaches. Still, the fear was there.

This is what happens when you allow yourself to love, a cynical voice in his head whispered.

While he couldn't help but love the baby and wouldn't change that for the world, concern for Lindsay tugged at his heart just as strongly.

"Why don't you give Dr. Swanson a call?" He tossed the suggestion out there. "I'm sure it isn't anything to worry about, but you'll feel better talking with her."

"You're right. It's after nine. She should be in her office now."

Lindsay's wild-eyed glance around the room had his heart lurching. He moved to her and put steadying hands on her shoulders.

"It will be okay." His gaze locked with hers. "Tell me what you need."

"My purse. My phone with her number is in my bag. I don't know where it is."

"I'll get it." Owen covered the short distance to the living room, Lindsay on his heels. The large bag sat on a side table. He handed it to her.

With hands that visibly shook, she fumbled through the cavernous interior, tossing out the deck of relationship cards and a pad of tissues in frustration. "I can't find my phone."

He stepped close. "Let me—"

"I got it." After a few taps on the screen, she pressed the phone against her ear. She glanced up. "I'm on hold."

Owen swallowed a curse.

"I can't stop shaking." She held out a hand.

Owen covered the distance between them. Wrapping his arms around her trembling body, he held her close until the shaking eased.

"Don't go." She reached out when he stepped back.

"I'm not going anywhere." He captured her hand and brought it to his lips, keeping his eyes firmly on her.

"Miss Lohmeier." A voice sounded on the other end. A real voice. Not a recording.

"Yes, this is Lindsay Lohmeier. I'm a patient of Dr. Swanson.

I'm pregnant, and I've had some bleeding." The words caught on a sob, but Lindsay quickly regained control.

As she answered the endless stream of questions, her voice steadied. But Owen heard the fear. He understood the worry that had her in a stranglehold, because he felt the same way.

Please be okay. Please be okay. Owen prayed the words over and over as the conversation continued.

By the time she clicked off and set down her phone, healthy color had returned to Lindsay's cheeks. Owen took that as a positive sign. Still, his heart continued an irregular rhythm.

Lindsay twisted her hands together. "That was Dr. Swanson's nurse. She, ah, she asked if I'd had sexual intercourse prior to the spotting."

Owen inhaled sharply. Had he been too rough? Too aggressive? If he'd done anything to hurt Lindsay or their baby, he'd never forgive himself.

"I told her yes." Lindsay glanced at her entwined hands before pulling them apart. "She said in the second trimester a little spotting after intercourse isn't unusual. It has something to do with the cervix."

"Do they need to check you?" Owen placed a hand on her arm. "I can take you right now."

"I asked, and the nurse said it isn't necessary. This is, apparently, no big deal." As if sensing he wasn't entirely convinced, Lindsay offered a smile. "She made sure to tell me this doesn't mean we need to refrain from having sex."

Some of his tension eased, but Owen didn't fully relax. "I could have hurt you and our baby."

"We're both fine." Lindsay spoke with a certainty he found reassuring. "In fact, while I was speaking with the nurse, I felt our little girl move. It was as if she wanted us to know she's okay."

Pulling her tight against him, he buried his face in her neck. "If anything had happened to either one of you…"

Owen didn't finish the thought, *couldn't* finish the thought.

She stroked his hair, soothing him with the gentle touch. "I feel the same about you."

Love rose up inside him and spilled out. He'd vowed to never again put himself in a position to care so deeply. Despite that promise, his heart had been stolen by this blue-eyed blonde who had a way of getting under his defenses.

There was no denying he'd fallen in love with her. Now, he had to figure out what he was going to do about it.

CHAPTER TWENTY-THREE

"Promise you'll take care of yourself." Owen's gaze searched Lindsay's face. "If you feel the slightest bit funky, tell Shirley you're leaving."

"I promise."

Owen didn't like to see her leave this morning, didn't like it at all. "When you get tired, you sit down and take a break."

Her hand rose to cup his cheek. "The baby and I are fine."

He frowned. "I'd feel better if I was there."

"I didn't realize you have experience in floral design."

"What?" Startled, Owen had difficulty processing the comment.

"Just teasing." Emotion suddenly darkened her blue eyes. "What would I do without you?"

Unable to keep his hands to himself, Owen slid them up then down her arms. "I'm not going anywhere, so you won't ever find out."

He didn't understand why she insisted on going into the Enchanted Florist to help a woman who'd fired her. This morning of all mornings. It made no sense. Despite what the doctor said, she should be resting.

Lindsay's gaze shifted to the front door.

Owen thought he heard her sigh.

"I'll bring you breakfast in bed if you stay." It was a Hail Mary attempt, but it could work. They'd shared fruit and the coffee cake he'd picked up yesterday at the Daily Grind, but she was eating for two and—

"Naked?"

He blinked. "Pardon?"

Lindsay inclined her head, her gaze speculative. "Would you be naked when you brought me breakfast in bed?"

The devilish twinkle in her eyes had him grinning. "If that's what it takes to get you to stay."

Her laughter filled the room. "Your offer is oh-so-tempting, but I promised Shirley I'd be there. Besides, I'm sure you have lots of work waiting for you at the garage."

Lindsay grabbed her bag and pulled out her keys.

Owen graciously conceded defeat. "What time will you be finished there?"

"Definitely by one."

"I'll stop by then and take you to lunch." When he saw her indecision, he sweetened the deal. "You pick the place."

Lindsay hesitated. "Don't you have to work?"

"I have an in with the boss. Besides..." Owen leaned close and whispered, "You and I, Miss Lohmeier, have important things to discuss."

Her smile wavered. "We do?"

"We need to pick a name for our little one."

She blinked, and relief flooded her face. "We have plenty of—"

"What do you think of Odessa?"

"What? Odessa?" Her brows slammed together. "No."

"Okay." Owen swiped the air with a finger. "Consider that one crossed off the list."

Her eyes widened. "You have a list?"

"Don't you?"

The fact that he was teasing appeared to finally register. She gave his arm a playful punch. "You rascal. Okay, lunch at one. Don't forget to bring your list."

AFTER LINDSAY LEFT, Owen decided he had to make a stop before heading to the garage. He had too much on his mind to work right now, anyway.

"I miss you, kiddo." Owen's voice was thick as he scooped up loose dirt at the base of the headstone and let it sift through his fingers. "You'd be an awesome big sister. Lindsay, well, she'd be a fabulous stepmom. I-I just know if you were here, things would be different.

"The baby is a little girl," Owen continued, blinking rapidly. "This afternoon, Lindsay and I are going to talk about names. I told her we should call her Odessa…"

Despite the threatening tears, Owen chuckled, knowing his daughter would get the joke.

His smile faded as his gaze settled on the headstone made of rose-colored granite. Mindy's monument was an angel holding a rose with the wing draped over the top of the headstone. A picture of Mindy in her flower-girl dress smiled back at him.

"Sometimes, I don't think I can make it through the day. Being without you hurts so much." The familiar tightness wrapped around his chest and squeezed out a few tears.

For the first few months after Mindy's death, he'd come to the cemetery every day to talk to her. Guilt sluiced through him as he realized his last visit had been nearly two weeks ago.

Owen gently brushed the leaves from the top of the stone and had to smile. How many times had he picked leaves and grass from Mindy's hair? Though his daughter loved all things pink and frilly, she'd also liked to play hard and hadn't been afraid to get dirty.

"You were the best daughter." Tears slipped down his cheeks. "I was lucky to be your dad."

Lost in the memories, Owen wasn't sure how long he'd stood there when the sound of a man clearing his throat had him swiping away the tears and whirling.

"I hope I'm not intruding."

The minister stood a couple of feet away. Dan lifted the bouquet of pink rosebuds. "I was looking over some paperwork for Mindy's Closet and felt called to visit her today."

Stepping around him, Dan laid the roses at the foot of the monument. "Mindy was an amazing child. I have no doubt she's keeping everyone in heaven entertained."

It was the belief that Mindy was now happy and no longer in pain that kept Owen sane.

"Have you ever lost someone close to you?" In all the times he and Dan had spoken, Owen had never asked the question. He wasn't sure why he asked it now.

"A friend in seminary. But no one as close as a daughter."

"It's like someone reaches inside your chest and rips out your heart." Owen gave a humorless chuckle. "But not just one time. Day after day after day. I can't do it again. I won't do it again."

"Hopefully, you won't have to for a long, long time." Dan hesitated. "Still, loss is a part of life."

"Stop, Dan. Just stop." Anger mingled with pain, so tightly woven that Owen couldn't tell where one ended and the other began. "Lindsay's pregnant."

Surprise skittered across Dan's face.

"The baby is a girl." Owen gestured to the monument. "I was just telling Mindy the news."

"You and Lindsay are together."

Owen heard the question in the statement, and he resented the hell out of it. "Didn't I just say we're having a baby?"

Ignoring the sarcasm, Dan studied him for a long moment. "You seem upset."

"I want to marry Lindsay." He clenched his jaw so tightly a muscle jumped. "She won't marry me."

Dan took a seat on an ornate iron bench near the grave, an indication he wasn't going anywhere. "That surprises me."

"Lindsay wants love."

"She wants you to love her, and you don't."

Owen ignored the statement. His gaze returned to the monument, to Mindy's gap-toothed grin, and his heart shattered all over again.

"I won't put myself in the position to lose someone I love again," he murmured.

The problem was, Owen knew he was already there.

"If Lindsay is having your baby, you have an obligation to her."

"She won't marry me." It took every ounce of inner strength for Owen not to shout. "If you're concerned I'm going to abandon her and my child, I'm telling you straight up that's not happening."

"I'm glad to hear it."

"It probably would have been best if she'd married you." Owen dropped down on the bench, overcome with weariness.

"Lindsay knows her own mind. She wanted you, not me." Dan's gaze searched his face. "I believe this will all work out as Mindy hoped."

Owen scowled. "What do you mean?"

"Mindy and I had several conversations about death. She had a strong faith." Dan met Owen's gaze. "There was only one thing that worried her."

"Why am I only hearing about this now?" The belligerence returned, but Owen didn't care. If his daughter had been worried about something, he should have been told. He would have moved heaven and earth to ease her fears.

"She was worried about you." Dan's expression softened. "Mindy knew you'd miss her, and she didn't want you to be sad. I assured her you would eventually find joy again. I think she'd be happy knowing you have Lindsay and a new baby coming."

"Mindy always thought of others first."

"Isn't that what love is?" Dan placed a hand on Owen's shoulder. "Putting the needs of others before our own needs and fears?"

Owen nodded slowly, his thoughts turning to Lindsay.

She'd told him what she needed.

The next step was up to him.

LINDSAY LEANED back on the park bench and let the sun warm her face. It would have been a shame to eat inside on such a beautiful day. When she texted Owen that the park sounded like the perfect place for their discussion, he'd met her promptly at one, brown-bag lunches from Muddy Boots in hand.

Owen gave her shoulder a bump with his. "You look relaxed and happy."

"Getting a sack lunch from Muddy Boots was the best idea ever." She gazed down at the Honeycrisp apple in her hand and took a bite. "The turkey and gouda panini was spectacular. Ami mentioned a few weeks ago the sandwich was a big hit, but this was my first time trying one."

"I'm not big on turkey, but I agree it had a really good flavor." He paused. "I swear I tasted brown sugar."

"Your taste buds are on target. There's honey mustard, onions, balsamic vinegar and brown sugar. Oh, and cranberry butter."

"Whatever the ingredients, it was darn good." Owen slanted a sideways glance. "You haven't said much about your morning."

She gave a dismissive laugh. "We were too busy chowing down on the sandwiches."

"We're done now." He made a go-ahead motion with one hand. "How's life at the floral shop?"

"Before she left, Shirley told the girls to divvy the work into thirds." Lindsay made a face. "They didn't. I ended up doing mostly cleanup stuff."

"That had to be disappointing."

She shrugged. "Tell me about your morning."

"I went to the cemetery."

Lindsay slowly lowered her half-eaten apple.

"I ran into Dan there."

"Was there a funeral?"

"What? No. He was bringing flowers to Mindy's grave." Owen met her gaze. "I told him about the baby."

Lindsay closed her eyes.

"It just came out."

"It's okay." She gave a weak smile. "My mom. Now the minister who was once my fiancé."

He leaned over and kissed her. "All downhill from here."

"How did Dan take the news?"

"He said Mindy wanted me to be happy. Dan thinks she'd be happy knowing you and I are together and having a baby."

"That was nice of him to say."

"I believe it, too." Owen slipped a lock of hair behind her ear. "Speaking of the baby, I think it's time our girl had a name."

Our girl. Lindsay liked the sound of that, liked it a lot. "What do you think of gender-neutral names?"

"Gender neutral?"

"You know, a name that can work for a boy or girl."

His brows pulled together in puzzlement. "I thought that's why we found out the sex, so we could pick a girl name."

Lindsay wondered if all couples having a baby chose the name together. Probably. Unless one of the partners wasn't involved or just didn't care. Not Owen, she thought. He was fully involved, and she loved him for it. "I'm glad you want to do this."

"Do what?"

"Argue about names."

"Are we arguing?"

"Not yet." She grinned. "But we may be, once we compare lists."

During her break at the Enchanted Florist, Lindsay had written down several favorite names. She reached into her purse for the paper and wasn't surprised to see Owen pulling one from his pocket.

"Let's see how many we match." The eagerness in her voice surprised her.

"Yes. Let's."

A minute later, they both sat back. Lindsay rolled her eyes. "What are the odds? Not a single name in common."

"I can't believe you listed Riley. I played football with a Riley."

"I didn't even think of it being gender neutral," she admitted. "And the flower names on your list definitely have to go. The Bloom family has those names sewed up in this town."

"Understood." Owen pushed to his feet. "Once we come up with more names, we'll do this again. And hey, maybe there'll be several we both like."

Lindsay frowned, disappointed. "You're leaving?"

"You're not getting rid of me that easily." He smiled. "Since you have the afternoon free, I thought we could look at furniture for the nursery."

Lindsay's heart simply melted. Reluctantly, she shook her head. "I'm not sure I'll still be in my apartment when the baby comes."

"Then we'll do the nursery in my house first. Hopefully, I'll convince you we belong together, so we only have to do one nursery. But"—he lifted a hand as if to ward off her protest—"if not, once we finish with mine, we'll start on yours."

Although an afternoon of shopping for baby furniture with Owen sounded like heaven, Lindsay stifled a sigh. "I'd love to, but I don't have the money right now."

"My baby. My house." He pulled her to her feet. "My money. Today's shopping spree is on me."

Instead of stepping away, Lindsay looped her arms around his neck and gazed up at him. "You're a pretty good guy."

He tapped her nose with his finger. "Remember that when I present you with my next list of names."

CHAPTER TWENTY-FOUR

Anticipation had Owen taking the steps to Lindsay's apartment two at a time. Though they didn't have plans for tonight, he hoped to tempt her with dinner or a movie. Maybe both.

He knocked on her door and waited. When he received no response, he knocked again.

"Just a minute." Lindsay's voice sounded from inside the apartment.

A moment later, she opened the door. She wore yoga pants and an oversized faded tee and had pulled her hair back in a ponytail. Lines of fatigue edged her eyes. "Owen. This is a nice surprise."

He smiled and leaned over to kiss her. "You texted you were having a bad day. I came to see if I could cheer you up. Maybe take you out for dinner? Or we could catch a movie?"

She stepped back and motioned him inside. "It's sweet of you to stop by, but as you can see, I'm right in the middle of something."

Lindsay gestured toward the kitchen where a long, folding table had been taken over by buckets of flowers.

He cocked his head. "Are you doing a little moonlighting for Shirley?"

Lindsay gave a self-conscious-sounding laugh. "Actually, going back to the Enchanted Florist was a bad move. Today, I'd had enough. The girls were—"

She paused as if trying to find the words, then gave up. "It just didn't work out."

"What's with all this, then?"

"A last-minute wedding job for a bride in Egg Harbor." Lindsay moved behind the long table that swallowed up all the space in the tiny kitchen. "The friends who offered to make up the bouquets for her wedding tomorrow backed out at the last minute."

"And you stepped in."

"I was happy to get the business." Lindsay shifted from one foot to the other. "I don't want to be rude, Owen, but I really need to get back to this."

"I'd like to help." Owen stepped close, not bothering to hide his eagerness. This was the perfect opportunity to show Lindsay he meant what he said about supporting her. "You tell me what to do, and I'll do it. I'm a wiz at following directions."

"Okay." She smiled hesitantly. "Let's get to it."

Over the next hour, Owen cut stems, removed leaves and tied ribbon around finished bouquets. They quickly fell into a relaxed rhythm.

While she arranged big burgundy carnations, tiny white carnations, baby's breath and some glossy, waxy foliage called salal into amazing bouquets, he learned more about her week.

"Working at the Enchanted Florist wasn't a good fit anymore." With well-practiced expertise, she tied a shiny burgundy ribbon into a knot around the stems before fashioning the strands into a beautiful bow. "While the extra cash was nice, not having to work there will give me more time to focus on growing my business. Especially now that the seller's permit came through."

Lindsay handed him the finished bouquet, and he put it in the bucket beside several others. "That's the last one."

"Do you need me to put the buckets in the refrigerator?"

"I'm keeping the temperature in the apartment on the cool side. Since the wedding is tomorrow, they'll be fine."

"Why not just put them in the refrigerator?"

"Flowers and fruits and vegetables don't mix." Lindsay tossed the last of the stems into a waste can she'd designated for green waste. "Fresh produce emits chemicals that can wilt, or even kill, flowers."

"I learned something new today." Owen flashed a smile and received an answering one in return. "How about I take these garbage sacks down to the dumpster?"

"That'd be lovely." Lindsay stepped close and kissed him lightly on the mouth. "Thank you. You've been a great help."

Owen found himself whistling as he descended the stairs. As a result of working side by side with Lindsay this evening, he understood her profession in a way he never had before. She had talent. That was evident by the way she'd taken what she'd told him were inexpensive flowers and fashioned them into something beautiful.

This bride, whoever she was, had hit the jackpot.

Lindsay had been available to step in and help the bride because Shirley had disappointed her.

Such was life, he thought.

He opened the lid of the dumpster and discarded any lingering philosophical thoughts along with the trash.

Lindsay would get good publicity from this wedding, which would hopefully lead to more business.

Now that her work was done for the day, she was tired and in need of serious pampering. That's where he excelled.

Owen couldn't wait to begin.

$\sim$

"Besides the obvious, what exactly goes on at a gender-reveal barbecue?" Owen asked the next evening, his head tilted back to take in Eliza's impressive home.

Lindsay laced her fingers with his as they ambled down the stone walkway leading to the back of Eliza and Kyle's three-story Victorian.

Even if the invitations hadn't specified the backyard, the bursts of laughter floating on the air would have told them where to go.

Lindsay felt her spirits lift as the noise grew louder. "We're going to eat, be merry and find out whether Baby Kendrick is a girl or a boy."

Owen's voice lowered. "Do you know?"

Lindsay shook her head. "I asked, but Eliza wants the big splash."

"Is it true Kyle's parents flew in just for the party?" Owen glanced at Lindsay, then added, "I heard some customers talking at the shop."

"His parents and sister," Lindsay confirmed. "Since they have a private jet, flying from Kentucky at the last minute wasn't a big deal."

"Is the nice weather the only reason Eliza got this together so quickly?"

Lindsay realized just how much she enjoyed talking with Owen about the day-to-day. Their conversations didn't have to revolve around important news and events to feed her soul. Simply being together was enough.

"The forecast played a part, as did knowing the rest of the month is crazy busy. Next weekend is Hadley and David's wedding. Then we're into the Harvest Festival and homecoming." Lindsay gave his hand a swing. "The bottom line is, they're over the moon about this baby and want to share their joy."

"With a few hundred of their closest friends." They'd reached the back of the house, and Owen appeared startled by the sheer number of people milling around the large tables filled with food. "What's on the menu?"

Lindsay glanced toward the grills manned by Jeremy and Ethan. "There will be burgers, because that's expected. As well as grilled salmon collars and sambal chicken skewers."

"What kind of skewers?"

"Sambal." Lindsay considered how to best explain. "The chicken has a spicy, sticky glaze with an Asian flare. They're very tasty."

"I might have to give one a try."

"Trust me, you'll love 'em." Lindsay slid her gaze to the long, rectangular tables covered in cloths with pink, white and blue stripes. Along with the expected potato salad and coleslaw, there were pretty bowls and plates with more unusual side dishes, such as spicy peach and avocado salad and sliced tomatoes with corn and feta. "Eliza never does anything halfway. They're seriously excited about this baby."

Owen pulled Lindsay to the side and lowered his voice. "I hope you know I'm equally excited about our baby. Once you give me the go-ahead, I'll be shouting the news from the rooftops."

"When Eliza announced this party, I didn't want to steal any of her thunder by publicly announcing my pregnancy." She looked into his soft, hazel eyes, and emotion swamped her. "Thank you for understanding."

He smiled. "Just remember that when you see everyone congratulating Kyle and Eliza tonight, very soon everyone will be just as happy for you and me."

~

LATER, after Lindsay had enjoyed both the salmon and a hearty helping of the peach and avocado salad, Jeremy sauntered over to where she stood talking with Eliza and Kyle.

For tonight's festivities, Eliza had eschewed her trademark

black and given a nod to fall in a wrap dress the color of golden pumpkin seeds. Her husband had kept it casual, wearing khakis and a hunter green Henley.

Jeremy sauntered over and gave his brother a punch in the shoulder before brushing a kiss across Eliza's cheek. He'd let his hair grow long again. Golden waves now brushed his collar, curling up in little tufts.

When Eliza narrowed her gaze, Jeremy held up a hand. "The grills are covered. Steve and Max are now in charge. They're fully trustworthy. Most of the time, anyway."

Jeremy flashed her a devilish smile.

"I wasn't worried." Eliza placed a hand on the arm of the man who everyone knew was one of her dearest friends. "You've been a great help today. Thank you."

"I don't ask much." Jeremy grinned. "Just name the kid after me."

Kyle chuckled. "Good try, but not happening."

Lindsay's gaze darted from Kyle to Eliza. "Is the baby a boy?"

"Jeremy is fishing for information." Eliza shook her head, her smile indulgent. "Typical Rakes move."

"Can't blame a guy for trying." Jeremy rubbed his chin. "Though Jeremina also has a nice ring."

Lindsay laughed along with the rest of them, the silly banter reminding her that she and Owen needed to revisit the name discussion.

"Fin and I are happy for you guys." Jeremy shifted his gaze to Lindsay. "It's also nice to see you and Owen back together."

"He's a good guy." Lindsay glanced around. "Where's your wife?"

"Actually, Fin is with your *good guy*, finalizing details for the opening of Mindy's Closet."

"How are the plans coming?" Lindsay realized she hadn't heard an update since Owen had first given the project his blessing.

"Fin is hoping to open the doors next Saturday."

"Next Saturday is the farmers' market and Craft Beer Festival in the square." Eliza jumped into the conversation, her tone clearly conveying her displeasure. "I'm not sure it's a good idea to have any activity drawing attention away—"

"Mindy's Closet isn't an activity, it's clothing for children in need," Fin responded, obviously overhearing the last bit of the conversation as she and Owen strolled up.

Like Eliza, the always stylish Delphinium had embraced fall colors with formfitting black pants and a leopard-print button-back top.

Lindsay glanced down at her simple olive-colored tunic with underlying lace and leggings and immediately felt underdressed.

Owen slipped to her side. As if understanding her distress, he leaned close and whispered, "You look beautiful."

The strange thing was, though Lindsay knew it wasn't true, the compliment made her feel better.

"With winter just around the corner, there are many children who will need warm winter coats. They'll also need scarves and gloves and boots." Fin's voice burned with a passion that surprised Lindsay.

The only other time she'd seen Ami's sister so fired up was when she and Jeremy were performing on the community theater stage.

"Mindy's Closet is a needed service here in Good Hope." Owen spoke softly, but with equal fervor. Fin and Pastor Dan might be spearheading the project, but because this project carried his daughter's name, Owen's words carried weight. His gaze never left Eliza's face. "Fin and I discussed other possible opening dates, but we don't think we can wait. This is Wisconsin. We're fortunate we don't already have snow on the ground."

"I don't think it will affect any of the activities planned by the Cherries," Lindsay added. "In fact, some people may come out for Mindy's Closet and end up enjoying the festivities. A win-win."

"Okaaay." Eliza gave a melodramatic sigh, as if she was making a huge concession, but her smile gave her away. "You've convinced me."

"We'd have done it without your approval," Fin said with a cheeky smile.

Jeremy slung an arm around his wife's shoulders. "Shhh, give her the illusion of power."

Eliza, who might have bristled at that in the past, was laughing as Katherine hurried up.

"Everything is in readiness for the big reveal," the older woman informed Eliza.

"Is this one of those cake deals?" Jeremy asked. "Where the inside is pink or blue?"

"There will be cake, with a pink or blue center, but that will come after the reveal." Eliza glanced over to a small round table.

The reserved sign had been replaced with a fortune-teller's ball. Gladys stood beside the table, dressed as her alter ego, Madame Gitana.

"Why is she dressed like that?" Eliza demanded. "All she was asked to do is pluck the sorcerer's hat off the table to reveal a pink or blue onesie."

Katherine clucked and patted Eliza's hand. "Oh, honey, Gladys would never do anything so mundane."

CHAPTER TWENTY-FIVE

Even without the jet-black hair striped boldly with silver and the scarf adorned with gold coins, Gladys's commanding presence drew the eye. Chandelier earrings boasting an assortment of purple stones dangled from her ears. A half-dozen gold bracelets etched with symbols Lindsay couldn't decipher encircled the woman's bony wrists.

"I don't want her going rogue." Eliza's brows slammed together, reminding Lindsay of two dark storm clouds colliding. "I need to speak with her before we get started."

"Leave her be." Katherine patted Eliza's shoulder. "It will be magnificent. Trust me."

"I trust you," Eliza told her cousin, then inclined her head in Gladys's direction. "It's *her* I don't trust."

Katherine laughed as if Eliza had said something uproariously funny.

Eliza had taken only one step when Ami and Beck, along with their daughter, stepped from the crowd.

Ami gestured with one hand. "I didn't know Madame Gitana would be here today."

Eliza huffed out a breath. "Gladys was assigned one task.

When cued, she was supposed to lift the tall pointed hat off the table to reveal a pink or blue onesie beneath. But Katherine informed me that task is too mundane for Gladys."

"I agree with Katherine." Beck's soft Southern drawl might have become less pronounced over the past few years, but it was evident this afternoon.

Eliza's gaze narrowed on Beck. "Why do you agree?"

Beck didn't hesitate. "Gladys has never been a woman who does ordinary."

"He's right." Ami lowered her voice. "What were you thinking, Eliza? You know Gladys's proclivity for the dramatic."

"That isn't always a bad thing," Lindsay offered. "Mundane can be boring."

"I see your point." Eliza tapped a finger against her red lips. "A little drama might add a nice touch of spice to the reveal."

"Madame Gitana told me I was having a boy before I even knew I was pregnant," Ami reminded Eliza and Kyle. "We won't know until this spring if that prediction is accurate, so I'm eager to hear what she tells you."

Eliza's lips lifted in a wry smile. "The fact that the onesie is under the hat, which I'm certain she's already seen, makes this prediction a slam dunk."

"Oh, no, dear, Gladys hasn't peeked. I made sure of it." Katherine swiped a cross over her breast. "There will be no skull-duggery on my watch."

"It's show time, E." Kyle took his wife's hand and brought it to his lips for a kiss.

Kyle's parents, Scott and Erin, stood with his sister near the wooden table, chatting with Eliza's parents, who'd arrived in Good Hope that morning. Jeremy's parents had arrived last night from Florida.

Though Ed and Cheryl Rakes held back, obviously not wanting to intrude, Kyle motioned them forward. Most in atten-dance were by now aware that Ed was Kyle's biological father. It spoke to the kind of man Scott Kendrick was that he not only made room for Ed and Cheryl, but welcomed them warmly.

"I want you two up close for this." Eliza took Lindsay's and Ami's arms and led them to the front, with Beck and Owen following behind.

Lindsay stood next to Ethan. "Ready for the big reveal?"

Ethan's gray eyes twinkled. "Ten says it's a boy."

Lindsay bumped her fist against his. "You've got a bet."

Donald Shaw shot Lindsay and his son a censuring glance.

Accustomed to such looks from her own mother, Lindsay only smiled.

Lolo appeared and held out her arms for Sarah Rose. Seconds later, the toddler's chubby fingers were wrapped around the beads of Lolo's brightly colored necklace.

Lindsay studied Kyle's sister. Curls that had been long and crazy wild when she'd arrived in Good Hope last spring now barely brushed her shoulders. "I love your hair."

With her free hand, Lolo patted her head. "Marigold cut it yesterday. I don't trust anyone but her."

It struck Lindsay she hadn't seen Marigold or Cade. She turned to Ami. "Is Marigold here?"

Ami shook her head. "She was completely booked today and didn't feel right about canceling."

As Saturdays tended to be a big day for hairstylists, Lindsay didn't doubt that in the least. But something in Ami's green eyes told her that wasn't the entire story.

"She's happy for Eliza and Kyle," Ami insisted, appearing relieved when Hadley and David strode up. "Hey, you two. Where have you been?"

Hadley rested a hand on her daughter's shoulder. "Rock-climbing class at the Y."

David rocked back on his heels. "Looks like Madame Gitana is getting ready to free that third eye."

Hadley jabbed him in the ribs. "When she did that reading for me, it was spot-on."

"The jury is still out if her baby-boy prediction is accurate." Ami's hand dropped to her baby bump.

"If I were you, I'd start coming up with boy names." Hadley lifted her hands. "I was as much a doubter as anyone, but she—"

"Is K.T. here?" The question from Lolo drew Lindsay's attention.

"'Fraid not. He's at the high school working on a homecoming display."

Lolo and Lindsay's nephew had formed a friendship based on their mutual love of art. "Will you be in town for David and Hadley's wedding next week?"

The girl's gaze shifted to Hadley. "You're getting married?"

"The wedding is next week." Brynn clapped Sarah Rose's cowboy boots together, making the toddler chortle. "You should come. I'm the flower girl."

Beside Lindsay, Owen tensed.

Lolo scuffed the toe of her shoe in the grass, the gesture making her look much younger than thirteen. "I don't know if we're invited."

David glanced at Hadley and received a little nod. "We'd love to have you attend."

"K.T. will be there," Lindsay informed Lolo, which had been the whole point in mentioning the event in the first place.

A spark flared in Lolo's eyes.

"I'm going to ask—" The girl stopped and inhaled sharply. "Madame Gitana is ready to speak."

OWEN WATCHED Gladys hold up the purple ball that had been resting on the obsidian stand. "I thought crystal balls were supposed to be clear."

"Not necessarily." David's voice remained low. "Gladys told me the ball is merely a tool for freeing her third eye."

"Third eye?" Owen scoffed. "Seriously?"

"She was amazingly accurate with some things she knew about me," Hadley told him. "I'm a believer."

"Since Eliza and Kyle already know the sex, we'll be able to assess the accuracy of Gladys's prediction." David brought Hadley's hand to his lips. "We may have to give her predictive talents a shot when we decide to add to our family."

Brynn's gaze swiveled to her father, proving that simply because her eyes had been glued on Gladys didn't mean she hadn't been listening. "I want a baby sister or brother."

Babies, Owen realized, were a hot topic among their friends. Considering most of them were in their thirties, it was to be expected.

"After the wedding, we'll talk babies." David's expression softened when disappointment flooded his daughter's face. "We won't make you wait too long."

Brynn met his gaze. "Promise?"

David slung an arm around Hadley's shoulders. "Let's just say I'll do my best."

Owen covered his laugh with a cough. Out of the corner of his eye, he saw Gladys, who'd been staring unblinkingly at the ball for nearly two minutes, place it back on the stand.

Once she had everyone's attention, Gladys flung out both arms in a gesture worthy of any stage thespian. "In the spring, Kyle and Eliza will welcome a baby girl."

Without missing a beat, the older woman grasped the pointed tip of the sorcerer's cap. "For the naysayers among you—and you know who you are—this will confirm my vision."

In one fluid movement, Gladys lifted the hat to reveal a bright pink onesie.

A cheer rose from the crowd. Everyone clapped, including Owen. It had been quite a show.

Kyle enfolded Eliza in his arms and kissed her before they separated, grinning, to accept pats on the back and handshakes from family and friends.

Lindsay gave Eliza a hug. "I'm so happy for you."

"Our daughters will be besties," Eliza whispered before releasing Lindsay.

By the time the lights came on and Lindsay mentioned she was ready to leave, the barbecue had turned into a full-fledged party.

Owen caught Lindsay enviously eyeing Eliza chattering happily with her in-laws, Kyle at her side, while friends continued to come up and offer their congratulations.

"This gender reveal ended up being a big deal," Owen commented.

"Eliza never does anything by half measures." Lindsay took his arm as they strolled around the house. "Next Saturday will be David and Hadley's wedding. That will be fun, too."

As they reached the front, Lindsay's gaze strayed. "I love porch swings."

Owen took her hand and gave it a tug. "Let's check this one out."

As they climbed the steps side by side, Lindsay gestured with her free hand. "In the South, they painted porch ceilings blue to ward off troubled spirits or ghosts."

"I'm not a big believer in ghosts, troubled or otherwise," Owen admitted. "But I like the color."

"Eliza's grandmother did, too." Lindsay took a seat on the swing. "When the ceiling needed repainting, Eliza considered going with white, but decided to stay with blue because of her grandmother. They were very close."

"I've left Mindy's room untouched." With great effort, Owen kept his tone even. "Fin asked me again tonight if there's anything of Mindy's I want to donate."

Lindsay patted the spot beside her. "What did you tell her?"

"That I'm not ready to part with any of her things." Owen

dropped down next to Lindsay, but kept his eyes focused straight ahead. "Do you think I should?"

"Not until you're ready." Lindsay closed her hand around his.

Owen nodded and slipped an arm around her shoulders. "I saw you speaking with Madame Gitana after the reveal. Looked like a rather intense conversation."

Bright patches of pink dotted Lindsay's cheeks. "We were talking babies."

Owen raised a brow. "Did you tell her about ours?"

"She already knew."

"Eliza must have told her."

Lindsay shook her head. "Eliza wouldn't tell anyone without my permission. Gladys also knew we're having a girl."

"Maybe the woman really does have a third eye." Owen chuckled as if he'd made a joke.

"She mentioned Mindy."

Owen inclined his head.

"She told me"—Lindsay cleared her throat—"that Mindy loves rose petals."

The tension that had gripped Owen eased. "Everyone in Good Hope knows pink roses were Mindy's favorite flower."

"Gladys said that, just like coins, finding rose petals can be a sign that a loved one is watching over you." Lindsay spoke quickly, as if afraid he'd interrupt. "Apparently, petals can seem to point you in the right direction."

"I don't believe in this kind of stuff." Owen's voice sounded harsh and unyielding, even to his own ears. He took a breath and let it out slowly. "I wish Gladys *had* seen Mindy and that my daughter might try to communicate with me. But I learned long ago that wishing for something doesn't make it so."

They continued to swing back and forth in silence, the darkness closing in around them.

Petals can point you in the right direction.

The words kept circling in Owen's head. What was the right

direction? He'd thought he and Lindsay were moving in the right direction, but now he feared he'd taken a wrong turn.

Sleeping with Lindsay had been a mistake. It had brought all those feelings for her that he'd suppressed to the surface.

Owen would be there for her and their daughter, but the pain he'd felt at the cemetery had been a potent reminder. He couldn't survive losing someone he loved again.

CHAPTER TWENTY-SIX

"I love the energy." Lindsay breathed deep, as if attempting to inhale the festive atmosphere in the town square.

Owen had stopped by her booth and asked if she wanted to walk with him to the church for the opening of Mindy's Closet. While part of him wanted her at his side, another part wished he was alone.

All around them, residents of Good Hope shopped at stands of fresh vegetables and fruits. With Halloween fast approaching, there was an abundance of pumpkins, gourds and cornstalks.

Even in inclement weather, the farmers' market was a draw. Today, with sunshine and unseasonably warm temperatures hovering near fifty, tourists and year-round residents flooded the town square.

The laughter and conversation scraped against Owen's raw nerves. As Lindsay finished giving Izzie last-minute instructions, Owen made sure not to let his irritation show.

"Your booth looks nice." He'd spent last evening helping Lindsay put together a collage of her fall collection—bouquets featuring sunflowers and pumpkins that sprouted mums in autumn hues. There was even a centerpiece with cattails and pheasant feathers.

"I wish I could set out the arrangements. But forty-eight is too cold for fresh flowers." Lindsay's lips lifted in a rueful smile. "Still, a lot of people are entering the drawing, so that's a positive."

Lindsay had decided that everyone who subscribed to her mailing list by dropping a business card or piece of paper with their name and email address into the glass bowl would be entered to win one of the arrangements.

She heaved a sigh. "I wish I'd had more time to push the wedding business."

"When I walked up, there was a woman and her daughter flipping through the book." Owen pointed to the table where, even now, two young women were intently studying the pictures. "The blonde already put a coupon in her purse."

Last night, Lindsay had showed him the book she'd compiled. It contained photos of past wedding bouquets and arrangements, along with a price sheet and a coupon for twenty-five percent off for any wedding floral arrangements booked by the end of the year.

Owen was amazed at all she'd accomplished in such a short time. Earlier this week, she'd approached her nephew, as well as local artist Izzie Deshler, with a proposed business arrangement.

In order to compete with the Enchanted Florist, Lindsay had decided she needed to offer more than floral arrangements. Joining forces with local artists was a first step.

Which was why the three were sharing time in today's booth. In a nod to the season, there were gourds painted with quirky scarecrows and black cats, as well as elegant ones with hand-carved autumn leaves. Orange pumpkins sported scary or funny faces, while white pumpkins were festooned with sequins and fur.

"The pumpkins and gourds are a big hit." Owen shook his head. "On my way to your booth, I ran into Cory White. He had three of your pumpkins in his arms."

"What can I say? Izzie and K.T. are übertalented." Lindsay's eyes sparkled as if she found as much pleasure in their success as her own. "Eliza is cool with us adding unique art to my corner of her store. Though she's not charging me rent, once I'm on my feet, I'll pay her for use of the space."

"What about the wedding stuff?"

"I have exciting news on that front." Lindsay's face lit up. "You know Piper Ambrose."

"Of course." He smiled, finding her excitement contagious.

"She and I reached an agreement this morning. I'm going to base my wedding business out of her store. Piper wants to make Swoon a one-stop shop for brides. Bringing my business under her roof is a first step."

"You'll work for her?"

"I'll be an independent contractor and pay rent on the space I utilize. She wanted a percentage of my profits, but I told her that was a deal-breaker."

Owen's head spun at the thought of how many irons Lindsay now had in the fire. He wondered when she planned to sleep, or take care of herself and their child. "Don't forget you're having a baby."

Lindsay's feet came to an abrupt stop. She narrowed her gaze and studied him with unblinking, blue eyes. "What's that supposed to mean?"

"Just be careful not to overcommit." Owen recalled those first couple of years after Mindy's birth when sleep became a luxury. A baby's schedule was exhausting. "I have to hand it to Tessa. Though she still carried a full load at school, she made sure not to take on any unnecessary, additional projects."

Lindsay stiffened, and her eyes turned cool. "Good for her. But unlike your ex-wife, I have to support myself."

"I didn't mean—"

"Baby stuff is expensive."

"I'll take care—"

"No." Lindsay spoke the word through gritted teeth. "While I appreciate you doing your part, I have to be able to do my part, too."

"You don't have to—"

"We're not married, Owen," she snapped. Closing her eyes for a second, she inhaled deeply. "I'm sorry. There's no need for rudeness."

He met her troubled gaze and wondered how to make her see that a baby—their baby—would need time more than stuff. If she'd only let him shoulder more of the load. "We *could* marry. My offer is still on the table."

Lindsay shook her head. "I—"

"Why are you standing here?" Fin called to Owen as she hurried over. She gestured to the side entrance of the church where a large crowd gathered. "I need you up front. We're ready to begin."

"My fault." Lindsay lifted a hand. "I distracted him by talking about my new business."

"Which is going to be a smashing success." Fin spoke as if that was a given. "I want to hear all about it. But not now."

With a resigned sigh, Owen followed Fin to the front of the crowd where Dan stood. Along the way, Lindsay broke off to speak with Eliza and Ami.

Owen hoped Lindsay wasn't angry with him. But darn it, he'd built a business from the ground floor. He knew the time involved. The last thing he wanted was for her to bite off too much, too fast. He still regretted spending so many hours away from his wife and daughter in those early years.

When he saw the white sign fastened to the side of the church, Owen forgot all about Lindsay.

The hot pink lettering read "Mindy's Closet." Izzie—he recognized her work—had dotted the "i" in Mindy's name with a sparkly pink flower.

Owen was thankful the minister and Fin were slated to speak

first. At the moment, he didn't think he'd be able to choke out a single word.

He took a steadying breath while Dan spoke about Good Hope's neighbors-helping-neighbors mentality. The minister gestured widely with one hand to those assembled and said how proud he was to live in a community where, once a need was identified, the citizens rose to meet that need.

"Fin Rakes would like to say a few words about why this particular project holds a special place in her heart." The minister handed Fin the microphone.

Standing tall, and looking every inch the PR executive she'd once been, Fin surveyed her audience. As if understanding an expensive, tailored suit would have been out of place in a group composed primarily of citizens who'd fallen on hard times, she'd dressed simply. Under a long, open-front cardigan that fell to her knees, Fin wore a skirt the color of merlot with a tan sweater and boots.

"The pastor did an excellent job giving you the background on this project. I'm here to put a face to the effort." As she continued to speak, the brightness in Fin's smile dimmed.

Owen clenched and unclenched his hands, knowing what was coming.

"I want to take a few minutes to tell you about Mindy Vaughn." Fin glanced at Owen for the briefest of seconds. "I became acquainted with eight-year-old Mindy when I was back in Good Hope for a visit. Under the program Your Wish Fulfilled, Mindy—who suffered from an inoperable brain tumor—had requested an early Christmas. I had the privilege of helping make that happen at Rakes Farm."

Jeremy stood near the front. When Fin's voice faltered, he offered his wife an encouraging smile.

Fin cleared her throat. "I fell in love with Mindy. Despite her circumstance, she radiated joy. She loved life and she loved people—old, young, in-between, it didn't matter. Mindy was a good friend, a loving daughter and a caring citizen of Good Hope."

Off to the left, Brynn began to cry. Hadley tugged her close while her father stroked her hair.

Owen gritted his teeth.

"That's why, when we were thinking of what to name this project, Dan and I agreed we had to involve Mindy." Fin's lips trembled before she firmed them. "She was a girl who would offer a bright smile even when she was hurting and who would give you the clothes off her back. Mindy's Closet. The name fits."

Fin waited for the applause to die down, then motioned to Owen. "Owen Vaughn, Mindy's father, is here with us. We've asked him to say a few words."

Owen took the microphone from Fin. She'd assured him he didn't need to talk long, and he was holding her to that promise. "My daughter would be proud to have her name on something that represents the best of Good Hope. She would be exceedingly pleased with the pink lettering on the sign."

Laughter rumbled through the audience.

"Thank you for honoring my daughter in this way." Owen paused, not for effect, but to regain his composure. "It means a lot to me."

He thrust the microphone back into Fin's hand and stepped back to applause. His heart hammered as the doors behind him were flung open.

He moved to the side as the crowd surged forward.

Owen jerked at the touch on his arm, but relaxed when he saw it was Lindsay.

"That was lovely."

He shook his head. "I didn't say much."

"What you said was lovely and just enough."

He glanced in the direction of the door. "I suppose we should go in."

"I don't believe that's necessary."

Hope tap-danced across his heart. "You don't?"

"You did your part." Her hand stroked his arm. "Why don't we go for a short walk, breathe in the fresh air?"

He gave a little laugh. "Do I look that bad?"

"You look like you could use a walk." Lindsay slipped her arm through his. "With a friend."

~

THE FIRST THING Lindsay noticed when she stepped into First Christian for the wedding of David Chapin and Hadley Newhouse were the flowers.

Lindsay tightened her fingers around Owen's suit sleeve and inhaled the pungent scent of evergreen and the sweet smell of roses. "It looks and smells wonderful in here."

Owen said nothing.

Lindsay pretended not to notice. Ever since the opening of Mindy's Closet earlier this afternoon, Owen had been unusually quiet. His somber mood had continued when he picked her up for the wedding.

Lindsay studied the ends of the pews decorated with tulle and white roses interspersed with evergreen and baby's breath. It was a lovely arrangement. At the front of the church were two pedestals with huge bouquets of white roses.

Max, Ami's brother-in-law and one of the ushers, offered Lindsay his arm. He wore a gray tux with a deep royal blue tie. His normally unruly blond hair was perfectly groomed.

Lindsay slipped her hand into his. "You look very handsome tonight, Mr. Brody."

The accountant grinned. "I was about to say the same to you, Ms. Lohmeier. Except, I'd substitute lovely for handsome."

"The church is beautiful." Lindsay's gaze swept the interior that was already nearly full. "I didn't expect this many people. For some reason, I thought Hadley wanted small and intimate."

"I expected a crowd." Max lifted one shoulder in a shrug. "She and David have lots of friends in Good Hope."

Lindsay wondered briefly how it would be if she got married, then shoved the thought aside as of no consequence.

When Max stopped halfway down the aisle, she slid into the pew and Owen slipped in next to her. He'd barely settled into his seat at the end of the pew when he frowned at the floor.

"What's wrong?" she whispered.

When he didn't respond, she followed the direction of his gaze. She inhaled sharply. At his feet was a single pink rose petal. Undoubtedly from last night's rehearsal, although it seemed strange they'd use real petals for a rehearsal.

Lindsay remembered the pink ones Mindy had tossed at Fin's wedding and knew Owen must be making the same connection. She wrapped her hand around Owen's bicep and found the muscles rock hard. She longed to comfort and soothe, but didn't know what to say.

The music shifted.

Owen's gaze was now focused straight ahead.

Lindsay shifted in the pew to watch Lynn Chapin Bloom glide gracefully down the aisle. Resplendent in a silver lace jacket dress with a scalloped hem, David's mother continued to the front of the aisle.

Once she'd taken a seat in the first row, David appeared at the front. He looked incredibly handsome and more than a little nervous. No, Lindsay corrected, not nervous. *Eager.*

Shifting her attention to the back of the church, Lindsay saw David's sister, Greer, and Beck begin their trip down the aisle. Greer's dark hair was the perfect foil for her cocktail-length dress in royal blue.

The dress, a floral stretch lace over a smooth, soft, stretch jersey fabric, flattered Greer's trim figure. But Lindsay knew one of the big selling points for Hadley had been that the dress came in a maternity style for Ami.

Once the two were at the front, it was Clay and Ami's turn to make the trek as best man and matron of honor.

Lindsay hadn't believed the tension in Owen's arm could grow any tighter, but as David's brother and Ami neared the front, the muscles turned to granite.

Apparently, like her, Owen had attended enough weddings to know what—or rather, who—came next.

As Hadley and David had elected to forgo a ring bearer, Brynn walked the aisle alone. Her white lace dress sported a tulle skirt and a royal blue satin sash. She carried a satin basket filled with rose petals.

Lindsay hid a smile. She could almost hear the child counting in her head in order not to rush. With each step, Brynn flung white petals onto the aisle in front of her.

As the child passed their pew, Lindsay's gaze was once again drawn to the perfect petal at Owen's feet.

For a second, she considered asking if seeing the petal gave Owen comfort. The grim look on his face and tightly clenched jaw had Lindsay swallowing the question.

As soon as Brynn reached the front, the child rushed to her father.

David bent and gave his daughter a hug. Whatever he whispered in her ear had Brynn nodding and smiling before skipping to sit beside her grandmother.

The music changed again, and everyone rose to their feet.

Hadley stood at the back of the church. From her wedding-competition days, Lindsay recognized the dress as an off-the-shoulder mermaid lace. The beautiful baker wore no veil. Instead, Marigold had fashioned Hadley's hair into a braided-crown style and woven baby's breath through the blond strands.

Her bouquet held blue and white roses with baby's breath and greenery. The stems had been wrapped in lace ribbon that was tied in a bow. Lindsay could practically guarantee that Shirley, rather than one of the twins, had designed the gorgeous bouquet.

As Hadley's father had died years ago, it was Steve Bloom, David's stepfather, who offered his arm to Hadley.

The bride paused for an instant, her gaze searching the front of the church. When she found her groom, Hadley let her lips curve in a slow smile.

Lindsay's heart swelled at the look in David's eyes. It was all there. The promise. The trust. Most of all, the love.

Blinking rapidly, Lindsay cleared the tears that wanted to fall.

This wedding had come at just the right time, Lindsay thought as she watched Hadley walk down the aisle to join her life with the man she loved. It was a reminder to hold fast to what you knew was right.

Hadley hadn't settled for less than she deserved.

Neither would she.

CHAPTER TWENTY-SEVEN

"Are you positive you don't want to dance?" Concern filled Lindsay's blue eyes even as her lips lifted in an enticing smile. "Not even to a slow song that simply involves swaying to the music?"

"You go ahead." Owen had hoped the ache that had taken up residence in his chest during the wedding ceremony would ease soon after they left the church. But he couldn't get the image of Mindy walking down the church aisle for the last time out of his head. "I'm sure there are any number of men here who'd be happy to dance with you."

The hurt that flashed in her eyes had Owen wishing he'd chosen his words more carefully.

He didn't know how he'd have made it through the ceremony without her. As if sensing his distress, she'd carried the conversation on the short drive to Rakes Farm where the reception was being held.

Once inside the barn, she'd been his ray of sunshine in a world gone suddenly dark. He wished he could give her the one thing she'd asked for this evening, but he'd never felt less like dancing.

Lindsay studied him for a long moment, then her expression softened. "You need some time alone."

Owen nodded. The wedding had opened his eyes. There was no way he could marry Lindsay. Not unless he wanted to fall even more deeply in love with her than he was now.

"I won't be long."

He blinked, then watched in startled surprise as she strode several feet and tapped Ethan on the shoulder. The man turned, drink in hand.

They looked as if they belonged together. Her so blond and pretty in her cherry-red dress. Ethan with his dark suit and hundred-dollar haircut.

The green knife of jealousy twisted in Owen's belly, but he forced a smile when Ethan glanced his way. It was as if the guy was asking his permission. Owen's slight nod resulted in Ethan offering his arm to Lindsay and leading her onto the dance floor.

"They make a nice-looking couple."

Owen turned to find Ruby, margarita glass in hand, smiling up at him.

Jeremy's grandmother might be in her eighties, but the woman had more pep than he did tonight. Only moments before, she'd been shimmying on the dance floor with her grandson.

Before that, she'd been working the margarita machine, which appeared to be a particular favorite among her and her cohorts. Out of the corner of his eye, Owen spotted Gladys and Katherine near the cake table, margaritas in hand.

For not the first time that evening, Owen had the feeling he was under observation. The crazy thought was dispelled when schoolteacher Etta Hawley, who stood nearby, waved wildly and hurried over to greet the two women.

"Don't you think?" Ruby pressed.

Owen hadn't heard what she'd said before that. He offered a polite smile, hoping that would satisfy her.

The older woman, champagne-colored hair the same shade as her dress, tapped his leg with her ornate cane. "Are you listening to me, boy?"

Owen reined in his irritation. The anger gnawing at him wasn't directed at her, but at himself. How could he have let himself fall in love with Lindsay?

"Why is she with Ethan?" Ruby demanded.

"I didn't feel like dancing." Owen watched Lindsay smile up at her partner. Would they eventually end up together?

Breathing became difficult as he imagined Ethan kissing Lindsay, touching her…

"It's past time to let her know how you feel."

Owen jerked his attention back to the older woman.

"You love Lindsay. I see it every time you look at her." Ruby patted his arm. "Tell her how you feel."

Forcing a cough, Owen offered an apologetic look. He gestured toward the bar. "If you'll excuse me, I need to get something to drink."

Under Ruby's watchful gaze, Owen strolled to the bar and ordered a club soda with lime. He stationed himself behind a large plant draped in lights. Sipping his drink, he contemplated his next step.

There was only one option. He would give her what she'd said she wanted.

"Hey, you."

He whirled, and there she was, cheeks flushed from dancing and looking as pretty as a strawberry parfait.

"I've been looking all over for you."

"I grabbed something to drink." Owen lifted his glass. "Club soda. Let me get one for you."

He turned toward the bar but was stopped by her hand on his arm.

"Owen." The way she said his name wrapped around his heart like a caress. "I know seeing Brynn walk down that aisle was difficult for you."

They'd avoided talking about Mindy on the drive to the farm. He wondered why Lindsay felt the need to bring her up now.

Owen was spared the need to respond when a joyous peal of laughter rent the air. He turned and saw Hadley laughing, with David's arm looped around her shoulders.

Lindsay smiled at the happy couple. "The two of them are so in love."

She'd given him the perfect opening, and Owen took it. "I've been doing a lot of thinking and…you were right."

"I like the sound of that." Her voice took on a teasing tone. "What was I right about this time?"

Before he could answer, she lifted the glass from his hand and took a long sip. "Thank you. I guess I was thirsty."

Owen ignored her red, moist lips and tamped down the surge of desire. He would give Lindsay what she'd told him she wanted, and she would be satisfied. So would he.

"When we first discussed your pregnancy, you said it was best if we simply remained friends. Once the baby was born, we would discuss how to share parenting duties."

A self-conscious-sounding laugh escaped her. "What are you saying, Owen?"

"I shouldn't have proposed." He gestured with his glass. "We definitely shouldn't have slept together. You were right about that, too. Sex muddies the waters."

"*Sex*."

Something in the way she said the word had him hesitating. And the look in her eyes…

Take it back. Take it back, the voice inside Owen's head urged. But he couldn't do that, not with his very survival at stake.

"It's what you want," he reminded her, his palms turning sweaty. "I'm giving you what you said you want."

Lindsay said nothing for a long moment. When she finally did speak, her voice was calm, though her eyes held a bleakness that tugged at his heart. "I-I appreciate your honesty."

"I didn't mean to mislead you." What did that even mean? And why did he feel like he was digging his own grave with every word?

She swallowed convulsively. "It's always best to be honest."

The tightness in his chest eased slightly. She understood. Of course she understood. Without him having to go into detail, she recognized the rightness of this course of action. "Good. I'm glad we got that settled. If you're still interested in dancing—"

"I'm not." Her voice cracked. "I want you to take me home."

His heart began to pound as he gestured to the now crowded dance floor. Owen licked suddenly dry lips. "The party is just getting started."

Lindsay's gaze shifted in time to see David sweep Hadley into an exaggerated dip that had the couple once again dissolving into laughter.

Instead of answering Owen, she turned and headed for the door.

~

LINDSAY BARELY SPOKE on the drive to her apartment. Owen's attempts to further clarify his position seemed to make matters only worse.

"I'll walk you to the door." When he reached for his door handle, Lindsay placed a hand on his arm.

This was the first she'd touched him since they left the barn. His heart leaped. Hopeful, he turned toward her.

"Stay in the truck." The words sliced like cold metal into him. Her face held lines of strain, while her eyes reflected controlled fury. "I can't believe I didn't see what you were doing."

Owen rubbed the back of his neck. "What are you talking about?"

"You're not over the pain of losing Mindy. I'm not even sure you're over Tessa." She bit her bottom lip. "I need to rethink this whole joint-custody thing. Your behavior makes me wonder if you're only pretending to love our daughter, the same way you pretended to care for me."

"How can you say that?" Startled, Owen stared incredulously. "How can you accuse me of not loving our child?"

"You've been courting me ever since you found out about the baby, saying you want to be there for me, kissing me, sleeping with me." She closed her eyes for a heartbeat. When they opened, they were ice. "As soon as we had *sex*, you pulled back and pushed me away, just like before. Maybe it's because Mindy's memories still overwhelm you, but do you think that will stop once the baby is here? I will not let my daughter feel second best or be pushed aside."

"Lindsay"—Owen heard the panic in his own voice—"you know me."

"I thought I knew you." Her voice was heavy with disappointment. "Now, I'm not sure."

"Please." He started to reach for her but pulled his hand back. "Don't throw our friendship away."

"I'll always be your friend." As Lindsay pushed open the passenger door, she sounded incredibly weary. "It may have to be from a distance, though. I won't make the mistake of letting you get too close a third time."

"I'm giving you all I can, Lin. I care about you and our child. I want to provide for you both, to take care of you both. So maybe I'm not some Prince Charming who believes life is like a movie. There's more to a relationship than roses and big, romantic gestures. We're having a baby, and I'm offering you support, security and respect. Doesn't that count for anything?"

By the time he finished, he was out of breath. He could tell by the set of her jaw that she wasn't swayed.

"What you're offering does count, Owen." Steely determination replaced the sadness in her eyes. "But I won't apologize for protecting my child. And I won't apologize for wanting the fairy tale."

She shut the door without waiting for a response.

He rolled down the window. "You're drawing a hard line in the sand, Lindsay. Think about our baby. Think about our future."

She didn't turn around, but the words tossed over her shoulder carried on the evening breeze. "As long as you're unable to make peace with your past, we don't have a future."

~

THE NEXT MORNING, Lindsay woke early from a fitful sleep. Instead of taking the direct route to the church, she strolled through the downtown area. This gave her the opportunity to see how the homecoming displays in the town square were holding up to the wind.

The frigid air had her not lingering long. Her thoughts kept returning to Owen. She told herself if he didn't return her love, it was his loss. A sentiment much easier to embrace in the light of day than last night.

By the time Lindsay reached the church's front steps, the service had already started. Standing in the back, she let her gaze sweep the room. She spotted Cassie halfway up the aisle.

When Lindsay reached her sister, she found Cassie and her daughter sharing a hymnal, while Axl stood on the seat of the pew. The older boys were nowhere in sight.

Lindsay tapped her sister on the shoulder, and Cassie responded by scooting closer to Dakota to make room.

Her niece, a pretty girl with dark hair and her grandmother's hazel eyes, wiggled her fingers in welcome and continued to sing.

There was no opportunity for Lindsay to speak with her sister and niece. Knowing his congregation preferred a faster-paced experience, Dan kept the service moving forward like a well-oiled machine.

Lindsay had hoped to relax and let her mind drift during the sermon. After only a minute, the word *acceptance* caught her attention.

"If we view ourselves as unworthy, we act in that manner. If we see ourselves as a victim, we tend to let others victimize us." Dan's gaze seemed to be directed directly at her.

Lindsay knew his ability to make you believe he was speaking only to you was one of the young minister's gifts.

"By our beliefs, we set ourselves up for success or failure." Dan spoke with a fervor that said these weren't simply words to him. "Many of these beliefs start in childhood. We don't leave them there. They come with us, many staying with us our entire lives."

She and Cassie exchanged quick glances.

Was her sister recalling Bernie's ugly words?

Was the fact her parents had doted on Cassie the reason Lindsay had always viewed herself as second best?

"These false beliefs beat you down. You feel lost and alone. But you aren't alone. God loves and accepts you as you are, with all your flaws and imperfections."

Cassie's gaze remained straight ahead.

Lindsay took her sister's hand and gave it a squeeze. They both had their demons.

After a moment, Cassie squeezed back.

"The good news is the slate has been wiped clean. Your sins have been erased permanently. No matter what you've done, you are forgiven." Dan's gaze swept the congregation. "You are worthy of love and respect. You should demand nothing less."

The minister's words had the ache in Lindsay's heart lessening. She felt more at peace than she had since learning she was pregnant.

The reality was, for Owen to love her—or anyone—he had to risk the possibility of future pain. It was clear that was something he wasn't ready to do. Not now, anyway. Perhaps never.

Lindsay felt sorry for him. Because she knew he would never find true happiness in the present until he took that step.

CHAPTER TWENTY-EIGHT

"Where are you headed in such a hurry?" Wayde wiped his hands on a grease rag as Owen strode through the garage.

"Be back later." Owen kept walking as if he was a man on a mission.

Which he was, if retrieving an item from his daughter's room qualified as a mission. It spoke to how low he'd sunk that a text from Fin on a Wednesday morning was a high point of his day.

When her message had come through, Owen had been staring at his computer screen saver. He couldn't seem to focus. He didn't trust himself to work on anyone's vehicle. Heck, he didn't even trust himself to order parts. His mind was too preoccupied with Lindsay.

He'd decided to give her a few days, maybe a week, before approaching her. Hopefully, they'd talk and things would get back to normal. The notion struck him as foolishly optimistic.

Lindsay had drawn her line in the sand.

As had he.

Once home, Owen went straight to Mindy's bedroom. Fin had assured him that they wouldn't be selling the personal item, merely putting it on display. The item would be used to open up dialogue with customers about Mindy and the store, as well as the work done by Your Wish Fulfilled.

Owen decided to take the stuffed octopus Tessa had given Mindy for her sixth birthday. Odessa was pink with blue and orange polka dots and long eyelashes. Tessa had brought the silly, stuffed creature back from a business trip to Vancouver.

With chagrin, he recalled saying something about it being a ridiculous gift when Tessa had proudly showed it to him. As if a switch had been flipped, the light in her eyes had been extinguished.

It had been a cheap shot. He'd been angry with her about the conference. He and Mindy hardly saw her, and when she did have free time, she'd chosen to spend it away from them. Or that's how it had seemed at the time.

Looking back, Owen realized the tighter he'd tried to hold on to Tessa, the more she'd pulled back. From him. From their daughter.

As his fingers stroked Odessa's soft tentacles, he reconsidered. The octopus had been in Mindy's arms when she passed away. He'd considered burying it with his daughter, but had changed his mind when Tessa hadn't shown up for Mindy's funeral.

Supposedly, his ex-wife had come down with some sort of virus. He remembered thinking how, once again, Tessa hadn't been there for their daughter. Or for him.

His gaze swept Mindy's room, searching for something small. A wooden box with engraved colored pictures of princesses caught his eye. He froze at the sight of pink rose petals scattered across the top of the box.

Gladys's words replayed in his head.

After a moment's hesitation, he scooped up the petals. Staring down at them in his open palm, he inhaled the sweet fragrance.

His gaze shifted back to the box. He'd made so many mistakes. *The petals will point you in the right direction.*

With trembling fingers, Owen opened the box. Colored strips of paper tumbled out.

He opened one that started with, "The five people I'm thankful for..."

In her childish penmanship, Mindy had written, "Jesus. Daddy. Mommy. Brynn. Fin."

Mommy jumped out at him. Though she'd rarely mentioned Tessa the last year of her life—at least to him—Mindy had never forgotten her mother. Or stopped loving her.

Owen swallowed hard against the lump in his throat and opened a sunny-yellow sheet. This one had a half-formed smiley face. Mindy had drawn in an upturned mouth and completed the sentence, "The best part of my day was...*being a flower girl and wearing a princess dress.*"

This, Owen realized, breathing past the sharp, stabbing pain in his chest, had been written the night of Fin and Jeremy's wedding. Written right before his daughter went to sleep...and never woke up.

With careful, deliberate movements, Owen returned the papers to the box, closed the lid and set it back on the bedside table.

In desperate need of fresh air, he'd reached the door before remembering why he'd come home.

Owen cast a wide glance around the room. Next to the bed, he spotted Mindy's sparkly, pink cowboy boots. There wasn't anything in the room that reflected his daughter better than the flashy boots she'd loved.

Fin had instructed him to leave the item with whoever was handling the shop when he arrived. Owen wasn't sure what to think when he spotted Gladys behind the counter.

Though he'd flooded his eyes with Visine before leaving the house, Gladys studied him with the intensity of a pawnbroker considering making an offer. Her expression softened at the sight of the boots in his hands.

"Fin told me to expect you." She took the boots and nodded approvingly. "These are perfect. I'll put them right beside her picture."

Behind the counter was a blown-up photo of Mindy, dressed in the flower-girl dress she'd worn that last night. She didn't look sick. She looked happy.

"Your child brought a lot of joy to this town."

Reaching into his pocket, Owen pulled out the petals and placed them on the counter. "I found these in her room. On top of her gratitude box."

Gladys lifted a brow. "Sounds like someone is sending you a message."

A message from beyond the grave?

"If Mindy had something to say to me, she'd send me a text."

Gladys dismissed the sarcasm with a wave of her bony, bejeweled hand.

"I've always believed life is best lived in the present." Gladys gestured to the photo of Mindy, and the bracelets on her right wrist clinked together. "That feeling was something your daughter and I shared."

Owen frowned. "How do you know that?"

"You said the petals were on her gratitude box. Gratitude is about appreciating our daily life. Instead of worrying about the future, Mindy joyously embraced the here and now." Gladys arranged the boots on the shelf next to Mindy's picture, then turned back to study him with unblinking, pale blue eyes. "It appears she's suggesting you do the same."

Though his knee-jerk reaction was to disagree, Owen kept his mouth shut. He didn't want to get into an argument with the older woman. Certainly not about rose petals. Gladys was a fixture on the Door County peninsula and one of those people who made Good Hope a special place to live. "I need to get back to the garage."

"Lindsay is volunteering here tomorrow morning," Gladys

called out as he reached the doorway. "She'd appreciate your company."

"Thanks for letting me know." Owen lifted a hand in a gesture of farewell and continued out the door.

Appreciate his company?

Owen shook his head. If he walked through that door tomorrow morning, Lindsay was as likely to kick his ass as welcome him with open arms.

For someone who professed to be psychic, Gladys had missed the mark, not only with Mindy's message, but this one as well.

~

INSTEAD OF HEADING IMMEDIATELY BACK to the garage, Owen detoured to Muddy Boots. Though the noon hour was normally busy, today was Wednesday. Outside, the day had more in common with winter than fall.

The second Owen stepped into the warmth of the diner and saw the crowd of unfamiliar faces, he realized a lot of people must have arrived early for the upcoming festivities.

He turned to leave when a hand on his coat sleeve stopped him.

Turning, Owen found himself face-to-face with Krew Slattery. He couldn't recall the last time Krew had made it back to Good Hope, but it had to have been eons ago. That time, Krew had been a boy.

A man stood in front of him now—six feet two inches and two hundred pounds of lean muscle. Dark, wavy hair brushed the collar of his coat, and it appeared he'd forgotten to shave that morning. Despite that fact, or maybe because of it, Owen noticed several women looking twice.

"Hey, man. Good to see you." Owen grinned and clasped his hand in a firm shake. "It's been a long time."

"Too long." Krew gestured toward the dining area. "I've got a table. Join me for lunch."

Owen hesitated for only a second. Considering Krew was the homecoming guest of honor, they probably wouldn't have another chance to catch up.

"Okay. Sure."

Krew threaded through the tables with the same skill he'd once woven through an opposing team's secondary. Though Owen knew his former brother-in-law had been able to come to Good Hope only because of an injury, from the ease with which he was moving, the man looked a hundred percent.

He assumed Krew had snagged one of the coveted two-tops near the window. But the table Krew stopped beside was a round one capable of seating five or six.

"Hello, Owen." Tessa gazed up at him through the bright blue eyes Mindy had inherited.

Krew gestured with a large hand that could grab a football from midair even when he was triple-teamed. "I hope you don't mind that I invited Owen to join us."

"I don't mind." Tessa hesitated only a second, then introduced her husband, Jared, a scholarly looking man with dark-rimmed glasses. "This is Lily."

The child in the high chair had dark hair like her mother and her father's brown eyes. She couldn't be more than a year old.

"It's nice to meet you." Owen supposed running into Tessa had to happen sometime. He just wished it hadn't happened today. Resigned, he pulled out a chair and sat down. "You arrived early."

"Jared has never been to Good Hope." Tessa's tone might be easy, but her eyes remained wary. "I thought this would be a good opportunity to show him where I grew up."

As he searched for something polite to say to that, Dakota approached the table and offered a bright smile. "I'm sorry for the delay. My name is Dakota, and I'll be taking care of you today. If you need anything, please let me know. Are you ready to order?"

Tessa slanted a glance at Owen. "We've had a chance to look at the menus, but you just got here."

"I can give you a few minutes—" Dakota began.

"Not necessary." Owen smiled at Lindsay's niece. "I eat here so much I have the menu memorized."

Dakota took their orders with an efficiency born of years of waitressing, then returned with their drinks.

Owen must not have been the only one who noticed Krew's intense scrutiny of the college girl each time she came anywhere near the table, because Tessa punched her brother in the arm. "She's too young for you."

"It's not like that. She reminds me of someone." Krew's dark brows pulled together. He turned to Owen. "What do you know about her?"

"Dakota is Cassie Lohmeier's daughter."

There was an odd look on Krew's face that Owen couldn't decipher. "This girl must be, what, eighteen?"

"Jailbait," Tessa warned and snatched a fry from her husband's plate.

Krew ignored his sister, his gaze riveted on Owen.

"Closer to twenty. She finished one year of college already. She's back in Good Hope for this semester trying to earn enough money to return to La Crosse for the second semester."

Krew opened his mouth as if he was about to say something, then shut it and picked up his glass of soda.

"I know this isn't a good time, but I'm not sure when would be better." Tessa cleared her throat. "I want to say again how sorry I am that I didn't make it back for Mindy's funeral. If there would have been any possible way I could have dragged myself onto a plane, I would have been here."

Tears shimmered in Tessa's eyes.

"He knows that, Tess." Her husband reached over and took her hand. "You were too sick to fly. He understands."

The look Jared shot him said that even if he didn't, he better say he did.

A man standing up for his woman. Owen respected Jared's loyalty.

"I know you'd have been here." Owen might have tightened his grip on the plastic tumbler of water, but his voice remained even. "It was a beautiful service. The church was packed. Mindy had a lot of friends. So many people loved her. They've started something at the church called Mindy's Closet in her honor."

He went on to explain how the clothing giveaway worked, and Tessa told her husband she wanted to stop by and see it before they left.

The time went by quickly. When they'd finished eating and were getting up to leave, Owen turned to Tessa. "I have some things of Mindy's I'd like to give you."

"Lily needs to nap." Tessa appeared uncertain. "Perhaps after—"

"If you want, I can take Lily to the motel and get her down." Jared met his wife's gaze. "You two probably have a lot to talk about. But if you'd like me to come, we'll make it work."

We'll make it work. Tessa and Jared appeared to be a team in a way she and Owen never had been.

"You can ride with me over to the house," Owen offered. "I can drop you off at the motel."

"Ah, sure, that'll be fine." As she rose, Tessa gave her brother an even stronger punch to the shoulder. "Quit staring at that girl. It's downright creepy."

It was so reminiscent of their interactions in high school—her scolding, her brother ignoring—that Owen had to laugh.

Some things never changed.

CHAPTER TWENTY-NINE

Owen kept the conversation light on the way to the house they'd once shared. They spoke of classmates and what they were doing now.

He learned that Tessa and her husband had opened a family-law practice in Des Moines. Jared had grown up in Iowa and had relatives in the area.

More important, according to Tess, running their own practice gave them the ability to flex their schedules around Lily's needs.

"The house hasn't changed much." Seconds after stepping into the living room, Tessa moved to a ceramic sparrow that Mindy had painted when she'd been not more than five or six. After setting it down, she picked up the deck of cards, turning them over in her hand. "These are different."

"They're relationship cards." For a second, Owen couldn't recall what the cards were doing in his house, until he remembered Lindsay tossing them out of her bag when she'd been digging through her purse.

"Are you in a relationship, Owen?"

He hesitated a fraction of a second, then nodded. "With Lindsay Lohmeier. We're having a baby girl this spring."

"Congratulations. I'm happy for you." She sounded surprisingly sincere. "You and I might not have been good together, but I believe separately we're both good people."

Tessa's gaze turned assessing, and he found himself reminded of the way Gladys had looked at him that morning.

"I like Jared," he said to fill the silence.

"I like him, too." Her lips curved. "He makes me happy."

Owen had seen the connection between them at lunch. "Weren't you scared to commit? I mean, after the failure of our marriage? The ink was barely dry on our divorce papers when you married the guy."

Her head jerked up, and she dropped the cards back to the table as if they'd turned red hot. "If you're intimating that I was involved with him before we split, you're wrong. I wouldn't have done that to you."

Owen *had* wondered. Knowing she'd remained faithful shouldn't have mattered, but it did.

"I made so many mistakes in our marriage and with Mindy."

The guilt and pain in her blue depths tore at his heart, but she wasn't the only one who'd made mistakes. "I should never have told you to stay away."

"You were worried about her. I put my career before my child. I knew it hurt Mindy terribly when I had to cancel our times together at the last minute, but at the time I was a junior associate and had little control over my sched—" She stopped herself and held up a hand. "No. No excuses."

She remained silent for so long, he was tempted to jump in. But he waited, sensing that getting the words out was important to her.

"There is no excuse for a mother staying away from her daughter, especially when that child is fighting for her life." Tessa's voice trembled with emotion. "I should have quit my job and been here for her."

It wasn't anything he hadn't thought, hadn't said to her. Back then, she hadn't wanted to listen.

"I was wrong to insist you stay away," he repeated.

"That isn't on you, Owen." Tessa blew out a breath. "Mindy was my daughter. My child needed me, and I wasn't there. I will regret that to my dying day."

Tessa's eyes dropped to the hands she was twisting and untwisting. "I'm sure she hated me."

"She never stopped loving you."

Her gaze jerked up. Hope flared, but was extinguished almost immediately. She shook her head. "I wasn't there when she needed me most."

True, Owen thought, but he was done playing judge and jury. "She missed you. But she always loved you."

Tears slipped down Tessa's cheeks. "You're just saying that to make me feel better."

"Why would I be that nice?"

The comment had her laughing and brushing away tears.

He gestured down the hall. "I want to show you something."

Tessa stood for a long moment in Mindy's bedroom doorway and took in the explosion of pink. Her lips curved. "It hasn't changed. It's the same as I remember."

"Her love for the color pink never wavered." Owen moved to the bed and picked up the octopus. "Mindy died in her sleep with Odessa in her arms. I believe the octopus was precious to her because it came from you."

Tessa stood there, biting her lower lip.

"I want you to have it." He pressed the colorful stuffed animal into her hands. "And something else."

Owen lifted the box from the dresser.

Tessa inclined her head. "A jewelry box?"

"It's a gratitude box. Mindy faithfully filled out slips of paper every night. I've only read two, so I can't guarantee what she may have written, but these are all things she was grateful for. If you read them all, I bet you'll see we raised a happy child."

"I can't take this. It should be yours. You were the one who was here for her." Tessa lifted her hands. "You raised her, not me."

"You were here for the first seven years of her life, Tess. You were in her heart. She'd be happy to know a part of her is with you."

"If you're sure." Tessa's fingers shook as they closed around the box. "I'll treasure this always."

"I'm sorry I wasn't a better husband." Owen blew out a breath. "I wasn't as supportive as you needed me to be."

"I'm sorry, well, for so many things, too. But I've come to see my mistakes led me to where I am now. I wouldn't be the wife I am to Jared if not for the hard lessons I learned about being honest about my feelings and my needs. I'd venture you wouldn't be the man you are for Lindsay if you hadn't learned from the mistakes in our marriage."

Owen rocked back on his heels. "I don't know about that."

"Think about it. If your mother hadn't left you in that fire station in Minnesota, your parents wouldn't have adopted you. You wouldn't have eventually moved to Door County with them. We wouldn't have met, and Mindy wouldn't have been born." Tessa paused. "If I hadn't married you, I might never have achieved my dream of being something more than the town drunk's daughter. Your parents were so encouraging to me."

"Yes, they were. To you." He couldn't quite keep the bitterness from his voice.

Puzzlement filled her eyes. "To you, too."

He made a scoffing sound. "They wanted me to be a doctor or lawyer. Or, follow in their footsteps and be a college professor."

Instead of denying it, she chuckled. "They're academics, Owen. Higher education is what they know, what they understand. But they're immensely proud of you and what you've accomplished. Take my word on that."

He inclined his head. It almost sounded as if she'd been in contact with his parents. "When did you last speak with them?"

"Last week. You?"

"Three months ago." He shoved his hands into his pockets. "After Mindy, after she passed, they were checking in all the time. I finally told them I needed space, and they backed off."

She touched his arm. "I'd say three months is enough space. Call them, Owen. They love you. They're grieving, too. Don't make them lose a son as well as a granddaughter."

"I'll call them." Then Owen did what this morning he'd never imagined doing. He wrapped his arms around Tess and hugged her.

When he released her, it felt like closure. "Have a happy life, Tessa."

She touched his cheek with the tips of her fingers. "You, too."

Perspective, Owen thought when he dropped Tessa off at the Sweet Dreams motel, was a funny thing. All these years, he'd been counting his heartaches instead of his blessings. And recently, he'd worried about what might happen in the future rather than joyously embracing the here and now.

There was still time, he told himself, to make things right. He had to think positively.

Once back in his truck, he pulled out his phone. Wayde answered on the first ring.

"I won't be back in today," he informed his shop foreman. "I've got some important shopping to do in Sturgeon Bay."

"That's right. The auction is this afternoon." Wayde's voice boomed through the line. "We could use another four-post hoist with jacking beam."

Wayde obviously inferred Owen planned to attend the auction of an automotive shop that was going out of business. The truth was, he had a far more personal destination in mind—a certain prominent jewelry store on Madison Avenue.

~

LINDSAY ARRIVED EARLY for her morning shift at Mindy's Closet. She stopped by the church office to pick up the key and was relieved to find Dan alone.

The minister looked up from where he was shuffling through some papers on his secretary's desk. A smile blossomed on his lips, and Lindsay was struck anew by what a nice guy he was and how her life would have been so much easier if she'd just been able to love him.

"Lindsay. This is an unexpected pleasure."

She returned his smile. "I've got the first shift of the day at Mindy's Closet."

"You need the key."

"Yes."

"Once I find it, it's yours."

"I'm sorry, Dan." The words that Lindsay had had no intention of saying popped out before she could stop them. Not that she didn't mean them, she just wasn't sure now was the best time.

Not when his secretary could return any second.

He glanced up, fingers holding the key he'd located in the center desk drawer. Puzzlement blanketed his handsome face. "For what?"

"For putting you through everything last spring." When he opened his mouth, Lindsay continued without giving him a chance to speak. She'd started this, she would see it through. "I know we've spoken since our engagement ended, but I don't think I ever really said I'm sorry. And I am. I hurt you, and I embarrassed you by spending so much time with Owen while we were still engaged."

Dan shook his head. "Lindsay, this isn't necessary."

"Yes, it is." Her breath came in short puffs, and she tightened her grip on her purse. "At the time, all I could think about was consoling Owen. I told myself, and I still believe, that it was only out of friendship. But I didn't consider the position I put you in. I'm sorry and hope you can find it in your heart to forgive me."

"Of course, I forgive you." His warm smile, filled with such understanding, somehow made her feel worse.

"I had doubts about your feelings when I proposed. I put you on the spot that evening." Dan raked a hand through his hair. "I'm sorry, too."

Lindsay extended her hand. "Friends?"

"Friends." He took her hand briefly in his and gave it a shake.

For a moment, they just stood there, smiling at each other. Lindsay wondered why she hadn't taken this step months ago. Clearing the air could be so, so freeing.

"You were in love with Owen." Dan paused, then corrected, "You *are* in love with him."

What was the use in denying it? Especially to a minister during a conversation that revolved around honesty.

"I am." The admission came reluctantly.

"That's good to hear."

Lindsay whirled. Her heart slammed against her rib cage.

Owen stood in the doorway. Tousled by the wind, his hair stuck up on one side. His unzipped Carhartt jacket revealed her favorite plaid flannel shirt.

"Good morning, Owen." Lindsay forced a cheerfulness she didn't feel into her voice. "I'll leave you to speak with Dan. It's time for me to open up Mindy's Closet."

She was halfway down the hall that led to the part of the building where the store was located when she heard footsteps behind her.

Not until Lindsay was inside the store, with its racks of clothing and coats and displays of hats, gloves and scarves, did she face him. Holding up the key, she gestured with her head toward the door. "It's nearly time to open up."

"We have five minutes, and I'm going to need every second." His teasing tone fell flat.

Lindsay checked the impulse to ask him to leave. Her conversation with Dan had reminded her that putting off a necessary discussion accomplished nothing.

The desire to put some space between them became overwhelming. She moved behind the counter. "What is it you want to say, Owen?"

Instead of answering her question, he pulled a deck of cards from his coat pocket and placed it on the counter. "We never did do our questions."

"No." And now, she thought, it was too late. As of Saturday night, they were no longer in a relationship. The thought had her wanting to weep, but she somehow managed a smile. "We never did."

So many plans, so many dreams never to be realized.

"If you recall, we were each supposed to answer three."

Lindsay pulled her brows together, unsure where he was going with this.

"I'll go first." He took the top card from the deck and flipped it faceup on the counter. Though she could clearly see the question, he read it aloud. "What do you like about your partner?"

"This doesn't take any thought at all. Although full disclosure, I've spent a lot of time thinking about you the past couple of days. I like your kindness, your generosity, your sunny outlook on life. During those months after Mindy passed away, you were the bright light during the darkest period of my life. You, Lindsay Lohmeier, are an amazing woman. I can't think of anyone better."

Lindsay couldn't help it. A warm glow filled her at the sweet words.

He flipped over another card.

"What are the three most important things needed for a relationship to be successful?" Owen's face took on a thoughtful expression. "This one is more difficult, but I'll give it a stab. Learning to forgive without holding grudges. Trusting your partner and your instincts. And finally, being a shoulder your partner can lean on, no matter what."

"Lofty goals," Lindsay murmured.

The alarm on her phone buzzed before more could be said.

"I need to open up." She unlocked the door, then pushed it open to see if anyone was waiting.

Lightning cracked, and a thick curtain of water made seeing any distance impossible. She quickly shut the door and turned back to Owen. "It's raining."

Which meant it was unlikely they'd be disturbed. Lindsay didn't know whether to cry or cheer.

Owen selected another card. "Where do you see you and your partner ten years from now?"

Tears stung the backs of Lindsay's eyes. She'd been avoiding looking too far into the future. One day to the next was all she could manage.

He stepped close, and she caught the faint tangy scent of his cologne. "I love you, Lindsay. It's taken me a while to accept that fact. I was scared of having my heart broken again, but being with you, well, it's worth the risk. I can't imagine going through life without you by my side."

Lindsay had to steel herself against a nearly overwhelming urge to launch herself into his arms. "You're just saying that so we'll be together for the baby."

"Trust your partner and your instincts," he repeated, his voice a soft murmur. "You know me. Do you honestly think I'd lie to you about something this important?"

Lindsay wanted to believe him, but she also knew how much taking care of her and the baby meant to him.

When she didn't respond, he repeated, "I love you. In answer to where I see us in ten years, it's together, with our little girl and maybe a couple more kids. I think we'll have a dog. Maybe a cat.

Perhaps both. We'll be working hard but making family a priority."

The picture he painted stirred up a longing so intense her entire body quivered by the time he finished. But she'd let herself hope once, and those dreams had been dashed...

She needed to get him to admit his true feelings and his real priorities. Lindsay lifted her chin. "What about my career?"

"I support it a hundred and fifty percent."

"What if I discover I can't compete in Good Hope? What if I find next year, or the year after, that I need to move to grow my business?" Lindsay remembered him telling her that Tessa had been forced to commute to Milwaukee because he'd refused to sell his business and start over somewhere else.

Okay, so maybe she wasn't playing fair. Owen had spent years building the Greasy Wrench into the most successful automotive service center on the Door County peninsula. It was only natural his business would take priority over anything else.

"I love you," he repeated. "If moving is what you need to do for your business to thrive, I'll sell mine and we'll move."

Lindsay's heart pulled itself up from the floor. "Say it again, please."

A look of pain crossed his face. "If moving is what you want, I'll sell the business and we'll move."

"No, not that." She rounded the counter and stepped to him. "Tell me you love me."

"I do love you." His hand cupped her cheek. "So very, very much."

She thought he was going to kiss her. Wanted him to kiss her.

Instead, he dropped to one knee and pulled a jeweler's box from his coat pocket. The pear-shaped diamond flashed in the fluorescent lights. "Will you marry me, Lindsay? Will you be my partner for all of life's adventures? I promise no one will work harder to make you happy than I will. I know there will be challenges, but I also believe we can face anything as long as we're together."

The emotion clogging her throat made speech impossible, so in answer Lindsay held out her left hand, a sob of happiness escaping as he slipped the ring on her finger.

Then he was on his feet and her arms were around his neck. "I love you, too, Owen. I want to be your wife and the mother of your children."

"I'll move wherever you want," he whispered against her neck. "As long as I'm with you, I'll be happy."

She gave a little laugh and tilted her head back to look up at him. "I don't want to move. I want to build a life with you here in Good Hope, surrounded by our friends and family."

When his mouth closed over hers, Lindsay kissed him with all the love in her heart.

Lost in the moment, neither of them heard the door open. Neither of them saw Gladys peer inside, then step back, umbrella shielding her from the rain as she grinned and gave her two friends the thumbs-up.

∾

THANK you for coming along on Lindsay and Owen's journey. I think we can agree that if any two people deserved a happily ever after it was these two! The next book in the series, Reunited in Good Hope is one of my favorites...and one of the most difficult to write. When we first met Cassie in Christmas in Good Hope she wasn't very likeable. I believe that after you get to know her better, you'll fall in love with her strength and capacity to turn her life around. And I believe you'll also agree that her first love, Krew Slattery, is the perfect man for her.

Grab your copy of this wonderful book now Reunited in Good Hope (or keep reading for a sneak peek)

SNEAK PEEK OF REUNITED IN
GOOD HOPE

Chapter 1

When Cassie Lohmeier was fifteen, she never imagined she'd spend her thirty-fifth birthday dressed in a donkey costume schlepping drinks in the Good Hope town square.

Of course, back then, thirty-five had been so old, just visualizing herself at such an advanced age had been impossible. Coffee shops like the Daily Grind, where she currently worked, hadn't been in vogue. In fact, there hadn't been a single coffee shop in town. If you wanted a cup of joe, you made it in a percolator or grabbed a cup at Muddy Boots.

If shops like the Daily Grind *had* existed, she'd have likely considered working at such an establishment temporarily, or perhaps as a job to come back to during breaks from college. At fifteen, she had a dream. A dream that included graduating from high school and going on to the University of Wisconsin with the goal of getting a degree in finance. She'd wanted to eventually run her own business.

If Cassie had to describe herself back then, she could do it in three words. Serious. Stubborn. Naïve.

All three characteristics had contributed to her downfall. A slide into darkness that had started after a fight with her mother, when she decided to attend a party at the beach. When she'd—

"I wondered when our paths would cross."

Cassie whirled, and the blasted tail of her costume hit the front of the wooden booth. It knocked her just enough off balance that she stumbled. Or perhaps it wasn't the tail at all that had her fighting to right herself.

It was the boy from that long-ago beach party who'd played a starring role in the destruction of her hopes and dreams.

The benefit of being old—okay, so maybe thirty-five wasn't ancient, but these days she felt every year—was that she was in better control of her emotions.

She kept her face expressionless as she stared at Krew Slattery, NFL star and her crush from years back.

The years had been good to him. His body was lean and hard, honed from hours in the weight room and on the field. Though he had to be nearly thirty-eight, his wavy hair was still dark without a hint of gray.

That alone could cause her to despise him, as she'd found several wiry silver strands in her hair just that morning.

Though dressed casually, from the Italian loafers to his Oakley sunglasses looped around his neck, he breathed money.

When Cassie realized she was staring, she inclined her head and smiled politely. "What can I get you?"

"Coffee. Black."

Of course. No latte or cappuccino for Mr. NFL Superstar.

"Coming right up." Cassie knew Krew had returned to Good Hope for the first time in twenty years earlier this month for the retirement of his high school jersey.

She'd heard he'd been honored at halftime of the Homecoming game. Even with two boys in high school, there had been no reason to go. K.T. and Braxton weren't into sports, and she wasn't into setting eyes on Krew Slattery.

"How've you been?"

Cassie glanced around, coffee cup in hand, hoping Krew had directed the question at someone else.

No such luck. But then, luck had never been on her side.

Even though there had been a line at her booth all day, the traffic had disappeared. Probably because of the awards being given out.

The Daily Grind had set up a booth in the town square as part of the Howl-O-Ween celebration, where pets paraded through the business district and best-costume prizes were awarded.

"Great." To be wearing a donkey costume while he looked so... rich and happy was like a knife to her heart.

"I've been good, too," he said conversationally, though she hadn't asked. "Well, other than the injury."

A career-ending injury that had been talked about ad nauseum in Good Hope ever since it had occurred last month. When it had happened, Cassie had made no comments and contributed to no conversations for one simple reason. She couldn't care less about Krew Slattery.

"Momma." With arms open wide, three-year-old Axl—dressed in Spider-Man pajamas—flung himself at Cassie.

Trailing behind him, dressed as a gypsy, was her oldest child, Dakota.

"He insisted we come by to tell you about the weenie dog." Dakota cast a friendly smile at Krew, who still stood at the counter.

Cassie couldn't figure out why he hadn't left, then realized he was obviously waiting to pay.

After giving Axl a hug, she turned to Krew. "That'll be two dollars."

He handed her a five-dollar bill. "Keep the change."

She took the bill. Refusing the tip would only prolong the interaction. Still, she couldn't bring herself to thank him, so she settled for a forced smile and a nod before turning back to her children.

Cassie crouched before the little boy, not an easy task in a donkey costume. She wished for the thousandth time that she'd gone with the milk maid, the only other costume available. "Tell me about the weenie dog."

"He was wearing a hot dog bun. I touched it, and it was soft like a real bun." The boy had a slight lisp when he said his "s" sounds that she found adorable.

Actually, Cassie found everything about her youngest son adorable. Though he was high energy, Axl was kind and sweet. He was nothing like his father. Though the toddler had inherited the shape of his mouth from his father, Clint Gourley, thankfully all the boy's other features were from the Lohmeier side of the family.

"Did the weenie dog win a prize?"

Axl glanced up at his big sister.

Only when she shifted her gaze did Cassie realize Krew hadn't left. Her blood turned to ice when she realized the focus of his lazy gaze was no longer on her, but on Dakota.

At nineteen, Dakota was a dark-haired beauty with an unspoiled freshness. Her dark hair fell past her shoulders in loose waves, and her eyes were large and commanded attention.

"Frankie—that was the dachshund's name—did win a prize," Dakota confirmed, casting a hesitant glance in Krew's direction. "In the small-dog division."

Cassie rose and was ready to ask Krew to move along when the owner of the Daily Grind and her boss, Ryder Goodhue, strode up.

Dressed in his trademark black, Ryder had gone to school with Krew and considered him a friend. Of course, even if he hadn't played ball with Krew at Good Hope High, he'd have been just as friendly.

In Good Hope, strangers were considered friends you hadn't met.

"Nice to see you, man." Ryder clapped Krew on the shoulder even as he shook his hand. "I hope Cassie has been taking good care of you."

Cassie held her breath. She needed this job. Really needed this job. If Krew somehow screwed it up for her, she—

"Absolutely." Krew lifted his coffee cup in a salute in Cassie's direction. "I was just about to ask her for an introduction to this lovely young lady."

Krew's amber-colored eyes settled on the girl. "You've waited on me before at Muddy Boots, but I don't believe we've ever been introduced."

"I'm Dakota Lohmeier." Dakota extended her hand, fingers dripping with rings and wrists encased in bangles, all part of her gypsy costume. "Cassie's daughter."

Krew's gaze sharpened. He slanted a barely perceptible look in Cassie's direction before focusing his total attention on Dakota.

"It's a pleasure to meet you." Krew's voice oozed charm, and it took every ounce of Cassie's control not to give him a smack in the side with her tail.

Ryder's presence was all that held her back. That and not wanting to give Krew the satisfaction of knowing he mattered at all to her.

"I take it you live here in Good Hope?"

On the surface, the question appeared to be innocent. A polite inquiry that anyone would ask when meeting someone for the first time.

But Cassie didn't trust Krew. And she didn't like the way he was intently studying her child.

"I am for now," Dakota answered, apparently sensing nothing amiss in the question. "I was attending UWL—that's the University of Wisconsin branch over in La Crosse—but I ran out of money, so I'm waitressing and living with my grandmother until I earn enough to go back."

Krew nodded. "I know UWL, and I know how it is to be short of cash. Even if my family had wanted to help me back then, they could barely afford to keep a roof over our heads. If I hadn't gotten a football scholarship, I wouldn't have been able to go to school."

"That's how it is for me." Dakota appeared to regret her words the instant they left her mouth.

No apology was necessary. As the oldest in a family with four children and a single parent, Dakota had grown up knowing there would be no money for college.

"My mom still has three kids at home. My grandmother would like to help, but her money is tied up in her business. I don't mind. Earning my own way makes me take my classes seriously." As if determined to move on from the topic, Dakota shifted her attention to her mother. "I'd ask if you're having a nice birthday, but—"

Dakota gestured with one hand toward the booth.

"It has been a good day so far." Cassie spoke with a positivity that had been hard won. Several months earlier, she'd begun seeing a psychologist, and slowly but surely, she was pulling herself out of the dark hole that had been her home for what felt like forever. "The boys made me pancakes with chocolate chips for breakfast, and Axl drew me a lovely picture."

She tousled her son's straw-colored hair, then glanced up at Dakota. "Tonight, you and I will toast Lindsay and Owen."

Lindsay was Cassie's younger sister. This evening, Lindsay would marry Owen Vaughn in a small, intimate ceremony at Kyle and Eliza Kendrick's home. Cassie had no doubt the two would have a long and happy life together.

Despite having four children, Cassie had never walked down the aisle. Not once had she seen love shining in the eyes of any man she'd gone to bed with. She'd lived with Axl's father for a couple of years. Not having booted him out the door when he… well, not ridding herself of him sooner was her biggest regret.

"The wedding and reception will be a blast. I have a short shift today at the diner, so—" Dakota pulled her phone from her pocket and gave a little yelp. "I'm on duty in ten. You're off now, right?"

Dakota's gaze dropped to her little brother, who was running an ancient Hot Wheels car up the side of the booth.

"That's why I'm here." Ryder pulled his attention from his conversation with Krew. "I'm taking over now so your mother has time to get ready for the wedding."

Cassie didn't waste a second, pulling off the green apron in a single fluid movement. She hadn't realized it was so late. She had an appointment with hairstylist Marigold Rallis in fifteen minutes.

She was about to grab Axl's hand and bolt when she remembered her manners. "Thanks for letting me off early, Ryder. I really appreciate it."

"No worries." Her boss waved a dismissive hand. "I'm glad you agreed to take this shift. I know how busy you are today."

She only smiled and turned as she took her son's hand.

"Happy birthday, Cassie."

The deep rumble had her pausing for just a second. She should have known better than to think—to assume—that Krew would let her have the last word.

Unless she was prepared to dredge up dirty laundry—further sullying a reputation she'd only recently begun to rebuild—she needed to be civil. Besides, she was a mother, and it was up to her to set a good example for her children.

She took a second to turn back and smile with faux sweetness. "Thank you."

"Hey, maybe we can meet sometime to talk."

Cassie blinked. "Why?"

Krew slanted a glance at Dakota who, despite the need to get to her job, appeared to be listening intently to the conversation. "Old times."

"Thanks, but I'm pretty busy these days."

This time when she walked away from Krew, it was with her head held high.

∼

Cassie gazed into the salon's mirror and blinked, not recognizing herself in the reflection.

She and her sister were both dishwater blondes. Lindsay had been highlighting her hair since high school. Most months, Cassie could barely scrape up enough money to make rent, much less have extra for her hair. But doing the hair of the wedding party had been Marigold's gift to Lindsay. The varying shades of blond and deep conditioning had Cassie's hair shimmering in the light.

"I love it." She touched the soft wavy strands that had been accentuated with a crown of baby's breath.

Marigold studied her intently, then gave a satisfied nod. "You look fabulous."

"You're a miracle worker." Cassie breathed the words.

"Hey, give me a little credit for the transformation." Delphinium, known to friends as Fin, glanced over from where she was applying makeup to her sister Ami's face.

"I never guessed that mascara and a little color could make me look…so amazing." Cassie shot Fin a smile. "Thank you."

She shifted her gaze back to Marigold. "From the bottom of my heart, thank you."

"Our pleasure," Marigold said with a decisive nod.

"You've always been pretty, Cassie." Fin's gaze remained sharp and assessing. "You've just never let that light shine before."

Cassie shrugged and cast a glance at Axl, relieved the toys she'd brought along continued to keep his attention.

"It's going to be an amazing wedding." Ami obligingly closed her eyes as her sister applied a light primer to her lids.

The Bloom sisters—Ami, Delphinium, Primrose and Marigold —had been a part of Cassie's and her sister's lives for as far back as Cassie could remember. Their parents had been friends and had frequently socialized before Sarah Bloom died of leukemia and Richard Lohmeier was felled by a massive heart attack.

Cassie would be Lindsay's maid of honor, while Ami and another friend, Eliza Kendrick, would be bridesmaids. Cassie was under no illusions that Lindsay had chosen her because she was her closest friend. Though never spoken, Cassie knew she'd gotten the top spot because Lindsay couldn't choose between Ami and Eliza.

"Are we still meeting at Eliza's house at five?" Cassie didn't want to mess up.

She'd planned to confirm the time with Eliza, but Eliza had already had her hair done and left by the time Cassie arrived.

Unlike her and Ami, Eliza preferred to do her own makeup. There wasn't a single doubt in Cassie's mind that the results would be flawless, just like the woman herself. While many in town spoke of a softening in Eliza after her marriage and subsequent pregnancy, the business owner still intimidated the heck out of Cassie.

"That's the plan." Ami's lids remained shut as Fin worked her magic with a brush.

"I can't believe I'll be the only one standing in front of the minister who isn't pregnant." Cassie laughed. "For once, I'll be the skinny minny."

Ami, Eliza and Lindsay were all expecting babies this spring. Since Ami already had one child, her baby bump was a little more pronounced than her two friends. In fact, because of the cut of Lindsay's wedding dress, her sister didn't even look pregnant.

"I'd give anything not to be a skinny minny." Marigold heaved a sigh.

Cassie immediately regretted bringing up the pregnancies. She knew Marigold and her husband, Cade, the town sheriff, had been trying to get pregnant for more than a year without success.

She wasn't sure if Fin and her husband, Jeremy, were trying. But then, Fin had never been as open about her personal life as Marigold was.

"It will happen," Fin assured her youngest sister, her eyes as warm and supportive as her voice.

Marigold lifted one shoulder, let it drop. "What I can't understand is how some women, ones who can't even afford the ones they have, can just pop another one out, while Cade and I—"

Marigold shot Cassie an apologetic look, realizing a little too late that the type of woman she was describing fit Cassie to a T.

Cassie had become pregnant the first time she had sex. After five years, when she had sex again, she'd gotten pregnant despite using a condom. Two years later, birth control pills hadn't stopped her from becoming pregnant yet again. Then, four years ago, Axl had been conceived.

"It's okay, Marigold." Cassie waved a dismissive hand and forced an offhand tone. "You're right. It isn't fair. Then again, what in life is?"

Cassie tried to recapture the joy she'd initially felt when looking in the mirror. She reminded herself what Dr. Gallagher had told her when she'd called herself a failure who'd never amount to anything.

The psychologist urged her to remember that her past didn't determine her future. She was smart and young and healthy. There was no reason she couldn't move forward and build a better life for herself and her children. Unless she chose to stay mired in the past.

Cassie was still working on forgiving herself for past mistakes and was determined not to get off track. This time, she would not get involved with a man just because she was lonely.

She'd learned her lesson on that score.

She was on the road to a new, better life, and nothing—and no one—would get in her way.

Let this fabulous romance warm your heart today! Reunited in Good Hope

ALSO BY CINDY KIRK

Good Hope Series

The Good Hope series is a must-read for those who love stories that uplift and bring a smile to your face.

Check out the entire Good Hope series here

Hazel Green Series

Readers say "Much like the author's series of Good Hope books, the reader learns about a town, its people, places and stories that enrich the overall experience. It's a journey worth taking."

Check out the entire Hazel Green series here

Holly Pointe Series

Readers say "If you are looking for a festive, romantic read this Christmas, these are the books for you."

Check out the entire Holly Pointe series here

Jackson Hole Series

Heartwarming and uplifting stories set in beautiful Jackson Hole, Wyoming.

Check out the entire Jackson Hole series here

Silver Creek Series

Engaging and heartfelt romances centered around two powerful families whose fortunes were forged in the Colorado silver mines.

Check out the entire Silver Creek series here

Made in the USA
Middletown, DE
26 May 2024